THE MORETTI MEN

DEVIL'S
Thirst

JILL RAMSOWER

Devil's Thirst is a work of fiction. Names, characters, places, and incidents are the products of the author's imagination or are used fictitiously. Any resemblance to actual events, locales, or persons, living or dead, is entirely coincidental.

Copyright © 2024 Jill Ramsower

All rights reserved. In accordance with the U.S. Copyright Act of 1976, the scanning, uploading, and electronic sharing of any part of this book without the permission of the publisher is unlawful piracy and theft of the author's intellectual property. Thank you for your support of the author's rights.

NO AI TRAINING: Without in any way limiting the author's exclusive rights under copyright, any use of this publication to "train" generative artificial intelligence (AI) technologies to generate text is expressly prohibited.

Author's reassurance to readers: No artificial intelligence (AI) was used in the development/writing/editing/proofing/formatting/publication of this novel.

Edits by: Editing4Indies
Cover photographer: Michelle Lancaster
Cover Model: Chase

❦ Created with Vellum

Books by Jill Ramsower

The Moretti Men Series
Devil's Thirst

The Byrne Brothers Series
Silent Vows
Secret Sin (Novella)
Corrupted Union
Ruthless Salvation
Vicious Seduction
Craving Chaos

The Five Families Series
Forever Lies
Never Truth
Blood Always
Where Loyalties Lie
Impossible Odds
Absolute Silence
Perfect Enemies

The Savage Pride Duet
Savage Pride
Silent Prejudice

The Of Myth & Man Series
Curse & Craving
Venom & Vice
Blood & Breath
Siege & Seduction

PRONUNCIATION GUIDE

I've made this guide for those who are interested. Keep in mind that I'm not an expert in phonetic spellings and did the best I could.

Amelie "Mellie"— "ah-mel-ee 'mel-ee'"
Aria— "aa-ree-uh"
Conner Reid— "cah-nur reed"
Edoardo Genovese— "ed-war-do jen-oh-VEH-seh"
Freya— "fray-uh"
Gloria Ruiz— "gl-or-ee-uh Rewh-ees"
Hazel— "hay-zl"
Keir Byrne— "keer Burn"
Kennedy— "ken-uh-dee"
Lazaro Malgeri— "lah-sa-ro mael-jheh-ree"
Lina— "Lee-nuh"
Mia Genovese— "mee-ah Jen · oh · VEH · seh"
Moretti— "mor-eh-tee"
Noemi— "no-em-ee"
Officer Malone— "muh-lohn"

PRONUNCIATION GUIDE

Oran Byrne— "or-an"
Pyotr— "pyo-tur"
Pippa— "pi-puh"
Sante Mancini— "san-tay man-see-nee"
Shae— "shay"
Stormy— "stor-mee"
Tomasso— "toh-maa-soh"
Torin Byrne— "tor-in"
Umberto— "uhm-behr-tow"
Rowan— "row-uhn"
Renzo Donati— "ren-zoh doe-na-tee"

DEVIL'S THIRST

JILL RAMSOWER

This one's for all my ladies who simply want to be seen and desired the way only a stalker can achieve.
I got you.

1
Amelie

They watch me, completely entranced.

I feel their stares following me, unblinking with breathless anticipation of my every move. Devouring the subtle twists and turns of my body. They drink up the emotions pouring out of me as though I'm the fountain of youth, providing life everlasting.

The music ensnares me, but no matter how thoroughly I lose myself in the melody, a part of me is always aware of my audience. I have their full attention—hundreds of strangers all captivated by the story I'm telling with my body. Feeling exactly what I feel.

During that moment when I'm on stage, a connection

forms between my audience and me. An intimate exchange. They listen with their hearts, and I speak through movement.

I feel alive when I'm performing.

I feel seen.

I love it so much that I prefer to practice on stage, even when no one's watching. Most of my fellow cast members use the practice hall for independent practice time. I use it as well, but twice a week, I take the opportunity to stay after rehearsals to practice in the theater after everyone else has gone home. Alone on the stage.

Tonight is one of those nights.

Dancing under the lights isn't the same without an audience, but it's enjoyable in its own way. I wouldn't be where I am in my career if I didn't love dancing, regardless of who's watching. There's a peacefulness in dancing by myself. A solitude that I know all too well, which is how I can tell the second that bubble bursts and I'm no longer alone.

I feel it now. Someone else is in the theater.

They're watching me from the shadows.

The same thing has happened in the past two weeks at each of my private practices. The watcher hasn't shown themself or communicated in any way. They don't want to be seen, but I know they're there.

My love of dancing for an audience contorts to fear when that audience consists of a single unapologetic stare. Most people might assume it's a member of the janitorial crew who simply wants to enjoy a free show and skip out on a few minutes of work. I wish I could believe that. I've desperately tried to convince myself it's a harmless stranger, but with a past entangled in a grotesque secret society, I know better than to dismiss any unusual occurrences.

Not that knowing changes anything. If they want me, I could do little to stop them.

I don't want to believe they'd come after me after all these years, but I can't ignore the likelihood. I know how wretched people can be. After all, my parents were the ones who dragged me into the whole nightmare. They tried to sell my virginity to their secret society when I was only seventeen.

That sort of thing changes a person.

If you can't trust your parents, who can you trust? And then there was the random kidnapping incident that left me with amnesia for months. At this point, I'm suspicious of everyone, for good reason.

Ironically, my paranoia is also why I haven't reported the intruder to building security or called the cops. Bringing attention to myself could be just as dangerous as whoever is skulking in the shadows. I haven't said a word to anyone, though the frustration of remaining silent burns under my skin like an exposed wire. The fact that I should feel obligated to keep quiet out of fear for my safety when I've done nothing wrong is a stinging insult I'm sick of enduring.

I continue to move as though unaware of the onlooker while indignation and frustration consume my thoughts until I can't dance a second longer. I come to a sudden stop and face the darkened rows of red velvet theater seats, my eyes scanning deep in the shadows for signs of movement.

"If you're going to watch me, I'd prefer if you didn't hide," I call out with a confidence I didn't know I had.

My heart nearly implodes in my chest when the darkness moves.

Slowly, a figure glides into the light from beneath the dense shadows of the mezzanine. I can tell it's a man from his broad frame, though he's wearing a dark hooded sweatshirt to conceal himself and has stopped shy of allowing the light to touch his hooded face.

My arms cross over my chest reflexively.

The sliver of optimism I've kept alive over the years had more impact than I realized because despite knowing this moment was a real possibility, I'm still shocked that it's happening. I somehow managed to cling to the hope that the watcher was harmless—a curious onlooker and nothing more. I should have known better.

The energy emanating from the man is pure menace.

His unspoken threat is louder than the music could ever be when he brings a cigarette to his lips and lights it with a click. The cherry at the end blazes bright as he inhales, though not enough to unveil his face. It only sheds light on his cool indifference to the cloud of smoke billowing into the air.

Everything about him should instill fear and does to a degree, but even more so, I find myself brimming with outrage and injustice. How dare The Society send this man to invade my space and taunt me? I've done nothing to draw attention to myself. I've toed the line and minded my own business for years.

"You're not allowed to smoke inside the theater," I blurt defiantly.

I've lost my goddamn mind. I must have.

Why else would I risk engaging with someone who's clearly dangerous? I should run backstage and lock myself in the dressing room. I should do just about anything except stand here and confront this man. But that's exactly what I do, feet rooted to the stage.

Seconds tick by in silence before he raises the cigarette to his lips again, the cherry flaring back to life.

Defiance. He's defying me.

Two can play that game. He wants to watch me dance? Then no smoking.

I straighten my spine and glare. And glare. I make it

perfectly clear that I'm not moving a muscle until that damn thing is out. I dig my heels in so deep that I don't recognize myself.

Who the hell cares if this man smokes in the theater? It's not my damn theater. The only thing that should matter is my safety, but I'm sick of the fear and worry. Maybe the stage is to blame. It's the one place where I feel any sort of power in my world. Up here, no one can touch me. Theoretically. Reality is a different story, but my brain seems to have forgotten that fact.

He stands casually motionless for what feels like an eternity, then takes one more long puff before letting the butt drop to the floor. His body shifts as his boot snuffs out the embers.

An intoxicating thrill spikes my bloodstream.

It's almost as good as that first step onto the stage when the curtain goes up. I didn't think anything could compare to that feeling. I'm so stunned that my mind goes blank.

Left in a fog of uncertainty, I shift into autopilot and do what I do best. I dance.

I allow the music to sweep me away like a leaf in the wind. I give myself over to the melody, and when the song is over, I'm alone again. The shadows are empty.

Instead of being relieved, I feel deflated. Surely, it's a letdown from the adrenaline. That has to be it. No good could have come from him staying.

It's the truth. I know it. Yet there's an emptiness in my chest as absolute as the silence inside the cavernous theater.

The thought is depressing enough that my remaining energy drains from my body, leaving me weary and strangely hollow.

It's time to go home.

I realize I've stayed longer than normal when I find one of

the cleaning crew in our dressing room. I'm usually gone before they arrive. I smile at the older woman who is vacuuming, and she returns the gesture.

"Excuse me," I prompt, pleased when she removes her earbuds and turns off the vacuum. "I'm sorry to interrupt, but I was wondering about a man I saw earlier—if he was part of your cleaning crew." It would be the Olympic record for long shots, but I have to ask.

"No, not with us." Her dark brows knit with concentration. "We haven't had a man working nights with us for the past six months. Did he say he was a cleaner?" She props a hand on her hip.

"Oh, no. He didn't. I just thought I'd check. It's no big deal," I quickly assure her.

"If you think he's a problem, we could call security."

"He's gone now, and I really don't think it's a problem. But if I see him again, I'll call."

Placated, she nods. "I better get back to it, and you should get home. It's late. Your family will be worried."

I offer her a forced smile because I know she's being kind, but the truth is, no one will worry because no one is home waiting for me. And even when I did live with family, they didn't care.

Jeez, Mel. Pity party much?

My parents were duds, and sometimes that gets to me. I wasn't totally unloved growing up, but the problem is, nothing quite fills the void created by a parent's rejection. According to the therapist my sister made me see, the problem was on their end, not mine. It wasn't my job to earn their love. I get her point, but at the same time, I know I'm different from the people around me. I feel it down to my bones. It's enough to make me wonder whether I'm different because of my parents' treatment or if my parents couldn't love me because I'm different.

All I've ever wanted is to be normal. But if tonight has proven anything, it's that normal is simply out of my reach. That ship set sail, sank, and is supporting a small marine ecosystem by now.

After collecting my things, I give the woman one last smile, then make my way out front to hail a cab. I usually walk home from the theater, and my now mellow mood craves the cool evening air, but I'm not about to risk another encounter with the man in the shadows. I may be a mottled mess from my traumatic past, but I'm not reckless, and walking home tonight would be downright idiotic.

Better to be smart than normal.

My sulking inner voice has a point. My life experiences have shaped me into something unique, and I typically try to embrace that as a good thing. But sometimes normal is too bright and shiny to ignore.

The best thing I can do in response is shine even brighter until normal looks dull and dingy.

I look out the cab window at the brilliant lights splashing color across Manhattan and smile. Nothing about this city is normal, and that's what makes it epic. Maybe one day the fears will no longer haunt me, and I'll be epic, too.

2 Sante

SHE LOOKS PEACEFUL WHEN SHE SLEEPS. IT WOULD HARDLY TAKE any effort at all to hold a pillow over her face until she's resting in a permanent slumber.

I should do it.

She deserves it for planting herself in my memories like a weed that roots itself into the tiniest sidewalk crack. I could concrete over that damn crack every single day, and she'd still find a way to sprout new life.

Four fucking years. I've been completely remade from the inside out over the past four years, but the one tiny piece of my past self that I can't seem to eviscerate is the memory of *her*. Amelie Brooks. Cloying and incessant, she's clung to me like the ink beneath my skin.

She was the only reason I came back to New York. I wanted to prove that the image was a mirage—the same way a kid imagines Santa in all his kind-hearted glory when reality is closer to a haggard retiree who's overly fond of coaxing children to sit on his lap.

It's amazing what a good pair of rose-colored glasses can do.

Now that I've crushed those fucking glasses beneath the steel toe of my boot, I can see things more clearly. I planned to take one last look at Amelie, realize how wrong I'd been about her, then get my pathetic ass back home to Sicily and my new life.

That was two weeks ago.

Two weeks of watching and processing the fact that taking off the glasses didn't change a damn thing.

I've had to accept the unfortunate truth that I'm fucking obsessed with Amelie Brooks. Her proximity has only intensified my curiosity. My craving.

So, yeah. My plans are fucked.

I'll still be putting an end to the matter, but not in the way I'd hoped. That's fine. I can adapt. Better to be realistic than turn a blind eye to what's right in front of me. I will never be able to scrape this woman from my mind. Forgetting my past would be a whole lot easier without bringing a piece of it with me, but that's obviously not an option. The only way to move forward is to make her mine and end the torment. Once I have her, the rest will melt away.

It won't be easy, though.

She's not as pliant as I recalled her being that one and only time we met over four years ago. The forested depths of her evergreen eyes are as haunted today as they were back then. It's her defenses that have changed. She used smiles as camouflage when she was younger, whereas now, her outer layer is cool-tempered steel, able to deflect rather than simply hide.

I could sense when we met that she'd been hurt. The pain was impossible to miss when I saw the same thing in my reflection every time I looked in the mirror, no matter how much I hated to admit it. I was fascinated with the way she smiled through her heartbreak, but it was her irrepressible anguish that sank barbed hooks deep inside me and wouldn't let go.

When I came back two weeks ago and first saw her dance, I knew it hadn't been a fluke. She was just as beautifully broken today as she was back then, sealing her fate. My fascination with her grew exponentially in a handful of days until I couldn't deny my obsession.

Tonight is no different.

I nearly laughed out loud when she stood in that spotlight and tried to intimidate me into putting my cigarette out. I can't remember the last time someone tried to bully me, especially a woman. Amelie is an endless wellspring of mystery and surprises I can't wait to unearth.

I lean down and inhale a lungful of the floral scent surrounding her. "Get ready, tiny dancer, because I'm here to stay." A whispered promise I hope finds its way into her dreams. Maybe it'll make reality a bit easier to bear if she has a sense of what's coming. Life for Amelie Brooks is about to change.

I let myself out of her apartment, making sure to lock up —I can't be letting any old psychopath inside. Not that I'm overly worried. She lives in a nice place, making the next phase of my plan so much more palatable.

Once I've left the building, I call the only person who knows the truth about what the hell I'm doing back in Manhattan. Tommy's my cousin, but he's more like a brother, and he's the only person on this earth I'd trust with my life.

While it's the middle of the night here, I'm not worried about waking him because he's still back in Sicily. He'll be midway through his morning routine—first a thorough cleaning of his rifle, then an hour of methodically selected strength and cardio exercises, followed by a breakfast of six scrambled eggs, one slightly green banana, and a slice of sourdough toast with a conservative scraping of real butter. No juice or coffee. Just water. Three cubes of ice. Every day, no deviations.

Some people might see his need for routine and predictability as a flaw, but I appreciate his consistency. With him, no guesswork is required. It's so fucking refreshing in a world where everyone has ulterior motives.

"Time for you to come over," I say when he answers my call.

Silence.

"Is this move going to be permanent?" he finally asks.

"For me? Maybe, but I'm not ready to tell anyone yet." I haven't seen any of my New York family since leaving four years ago. We've been in communication, but it's a long time to go without seeing one another. I'm reluctant to suffer through the unavoidably dramatic reunion.

"When will you know?" The question would likely irritate someone unfamiliar with his style of communication. I know better. Tommy isn't trying to ask impossible questions; he's simply trying to plan. He likes to know what's ahead.

"Hard to say, but I'll keep you informed as best as I can."

"I'll be on a plane by tomorrow," he says tonelessly.

"Let me know your arrival time, and I'll pick you up."

"I'll have my larger suitcase. Better to bring everything if we might be staying."

My lips twist in the corners with amusement. No one prepares for contingencies like Tommy. "Sounds good. See you soon." The line clicks dead.

Unfortunately for Tommy, I don't think there's any way to predict what will unfold. I'm going to make Amelie mine, but I'll do it while staying true to myself. My father charmed my mother into marriage, then secretly beat the shit out of her on a regular basis. He was a pathetic coward in the worst ways possible.

And while I'm not as shitty as my father, I'm not a gentleman, either. Winning over Amelie would be a lot easier if I rode up on a horse like Prince Charming, but that won't happen.

I will *never* pretend to be anything other than what I am.

Amelie *will* see me for exactly who I am, and she *will* come to accept that she's meant for me. I'll prove to her that my brand of fucked up is what she needs. It may be a challenge, but that doesn't worry me. I can be relentless when it comes to getting what I want. And I don't just *want* Amelie Brooks; I'll go fucking insane without her.

3
Amelie

I'VE HEARD THAT JOY AND HEARTBREAK ARE TWO SIDES OF THE same coin but never understood it until the birth of my niece. Violet Ophelia Byrne is the most perfect, adorable little human on this earth, from her big blue eyes to her tiny, dimpled fingers. My profound love for her was instant and unshakable. I've never experienced anything like it.

I'll always be grateful to have known that sort of profound connection. However, it wasn't until then that I fully realized what I'd been denied as a child. Vi wasn't even my baby, yet I felt a glimpse of what a parents' love should look like. It shone a blinding spotlight on the grotesque disfunction that made my parents incapable of love and compassion.

My sister and I should have had the same love Violet will

grow up knowing. We deserved that as much as any child. And it came so easily to me where Vi was concerned. How could my mother not have felt a fraction of the love that should have come so naturally? How could my father be so indifferent to my mother's cruelty toward me?

Wounds that I thought had healed over were ripped wide open.

I began to question everything about myself. If a parent's love, biological or otherwise, is the foundation of a person's existence, how could a child ever grow into a functional adult without those key supports?

From the highest of highs after Violet's birth, I fell into a suffocating vat of despair, grappling with my own worth. I looked at my sister, Lina, who had the same mother, though different fathers, and she seemed utterly flawless while I was one glaring imperfection after another.

Her father had adored her before he died from a brain tumor. I wondered if that was why she was so strong. She knew love at one point from at least one parent. But where did that leave me? I questioned whether I was the root of the problem.

It took me weeks to sort through my emotions. My logical brain embraced my innocence for the most part. I never asked to be born. I was just as adorable and perfect as little Vi when I arrived on this earth, and if my parents couldn't bring themselves to love me, that was owed to their demons, not mine.

Where I still struggle at times is worrying about the damages done. I know the things I've experienced have marked me, and I pray that the scars won't keep me from finding my sliver of happiness in the world.

Oddly enough, the very thing that made me question myself most was the same thing that gave me the most reassurance that I'm not hopelessly broken. Violet. She's eighteen months old now and the most precious thing in this world to me because I know love. And if I'm capable of loving others, then I'm capable of being loved.

I am *not* my parents.

I will happily spend every day of the rest of my life devoted to my small family. My life means nothing without them.

"If you keep picking up her sippy cup, she'll never learn to stop throwing it on the floor." Lina glares at me, but there's no real bite behind her words.

"You're right. It could be rather awkward if she's still throwing her sippy cup on the floor in the high school cafeteria." I stare at my sister until we both burst into a fit of giggles at the mental image.

Vi shrieks with our laughter.

"Such a smart-ass," Lina mutters before taking a bite of her penne pasta.

I grab takeout for all of us on Wednesdays after practice. Today, I picked up Italian. Lina and I practically inhaled our food. Violet has eaten approximately two noodles and thrown the rest on the floor around her high chair.

Lina is beyond exasperated with her precious toddler, but I can't get enough. I think it's adorable. Every time her chubby hand sends a rejected piece of pasta to the stone floor, her bright blue eyes beam with accomplishment. How could I possibly begrudge her such happiness?

"I know. Sorry, but this won't last forever. She's learned a new trick, and look at her. She's so proud of herself."

Lina gazes at her baby girl with a reluctant smirk. "Yeah, she's pretty adorable."

"The *most* adorable thing on this planet, aren't you, sweetie Vi," I finish in a cooing voice directed at my niece.

"But seriously," Lina continues, "I could use your support

here. She's really testing her limits lately, and it's exhausting. *I'm* exhausted. I told Oran the same thing, but he isn't as fazed by it—like being a father is all fun and games." She rests her head in her hand, her elbow propped on the table. Wisps of her beautiful blond hair have pulled free in revolt against her attempt at a ponytail, and uncharacteristic circles darken the skin beneath her eyes. She's still gorgeous as always, but the strain is taking its toll.

"Sorry, Lina Bean." I place my hand over hers. "I'll be more help. I promise." My chest clenches tight to know my sister is struggling.

She nearly lost her own life trying to save me back when I first ran from my parents. As if their betrayal wasn't enough, I ended up with amnesia not long after and went missing for months. I wasn't in danger, but she didn't know that. She hunted day and night for me—faced the awful people of The Society even after her own horrible past with them—all for me.

I owe her everything, and I've been doing everything in my power to repay that debt and keep her safe. The Society will *never* hurt her again. Not if I can help it.

"No, I'm the one who's sorry." She shakes her head and leans back wearily in her chair. "I didn't mean to imply you're not doing enough. You help out so much. I've just been so tired lately. It's like no matter how much I climb, the mountain keeps getting taller. Then little things that ordinarily don't bother me suddenly seem like huge impositions."

I sit very still as I look at my sister—really look at her. "Are you *pregnant*?" I whisper. No one else is home, so I don't know why it comes out in a whisper except for the monumental implications of the question.

She stares back at me, speechless. "What? *No* … I … no. There's no way… Vi isn't even two yet."

My eyebrows sweep high on my forehead. "Not sure if you're aware, but her age doesn't have jack squat to do with your ability to conceive."

She glowers at me, head tilting to the side. "I *know* that. I just mean we haven't even talked about another baby. I'm on birth control, so I don't think that's it. Who knows, maybe I have a thyroid problem. I guess I could call my doctor and get checked."

"It wouldn't hurt, and then you'd know. And in the meantime, you call me if you need a break."

"I don't want to interrupt your practice schedule. Opening night is getting closer, and I know how important this production is to you."

I offer her a warm smile. "It is, but nothing comes before you guys. In fact, how about you go back and relax in the bath for a bit? I'll finish up dinner here with the chunky monkey."

"Oh, Mellie. That sounds incredible. Are you sure?"

"One hundred percent. You go."

The relief in her heartfelt smile fills my heart with warmth. "Okay. Oran will be home soon. He can take her off your hands then."

"Pshhh. No one's taking this cutie from me. Isn't that right, sweetie Vi?" I reach under her high chair tray and tickle her tummy, sending her into a fit of giggles.

Lina floats away, tossing one more thanks over her shoulder. With some concentrated effort, I'm able to get Violet to eat her supper over the next fifteen minutes, during which Oran makes it home. He gives me a hug and smothers his little girl with kisses. She coos "da-da" in response, her wide smile displaying adorable little baby teeth.

"I sent Lina back to take a bath. She was worn out," I explain.

Oran clicks on the television, then dives into his takeout. "I keep telling her to hire help, but she refuses. Maybe you can talk some sense into her. I think she has some kind of irrational fear that if she hires a nanny, she'll become her mother."

Huh. So maybe Lina wasn't as unscathed by our mother as she seems. I hate to think it's true, but it's also somewhat comforting.

My train of thought is derailed as newscasters drone on in the background. My shoulders tense as I glance at the big screen TV in the living room.

"Sorry, I know you hate the news, but an important press conference is about to start, and I need to listen."

I don't simply hate the news. I can't stand it. Literally. My anxiety goes through the roof—my hands sweat, and my heart ricochets erratically against the inside of my chest.

I force myself to focus on Violet. "Come on, love. Let's get you down." I wipe her face and hands with a wet rag, then lift her from her chair. She's off and running the second her feet hit the floor. Well, running might be an exaggeration. It's more like stumbling forward on the constant verge of falling over.

I'm in the middle of wiping down her chair when an authoritative, masculine voice filters out from the media system speakers. I don't look at the screen. I've heard the voice before and know exactly who it belongs to.

I freeze, but only for a second, then I'm in action, moving purely on instinct.

"I have to go. You're good with Vi, right?" I press a hurried kiss to Oran's cheek while he's in mid-chew, then race for the door before he even has a chance to answer. I probably look like a crazy woman, but I don't care. I can't stay a second longer. I'm already fighting back the need to vomit.

Thank God I live in the same building as Lina and Oran and can quickly escape to the safety of my apartment. While they live in a huge place that takes up the entire thirty-sixth floor, I have a much more reasonable one bedroom on the third floor—one of only a handful of single-bedroom units in the building. The first five floors consist of apartments that might seem small when compared to the upper floors but are huge compared to a standard place in the city. The materials and fixtures are top-notch, and security is fabulous. No one lives in this building without a sizable bankroll. I was incredibly fortunate Oran was able to snag this place for me.

The second I'm inside, some of the panic subsides. With my back pressed against the door, I take deep, even breaths—something I learned from the therapist to help calm my nerves. It helps surprisingly well for something so simple.

Once I've calmed myself enough that I no longer feel like passing out, I set my keys on the counter and head back to my bathroom for a shower. While the water warms, I put on music over the sound system that plays throughout my apartment. Something to drown out the voice now echoing in my head.

It's not until I'm fully immersed in my shower, scrubbing shampoo in my hair, that I remember I needed to buy conditioner. I'm horrible about going shopping for food and essentials. Between my long hours dancing and easy access to restaurants in the city, I spread out my shopping trips until I'm perilously low on supplies. I know things are bad when I start to ration cotton swabs and toilet paper.

It happens more than I care to admit.

Today, I'll employ the age-old technique of conditioner liquefication—a little water in the bottle with a few good shakes, and I can salvage what little product is left. That's my plan, except the bottle is full when I pick it up.

I stare at the floral-scented detangler as though it sprouted lips and spoke to me.

Did I pick up a new bottle and forget? Or was I misremembering needing more? It's the strangest thing, yet the same thing happened last week when I could have sworn I was out of Goldfish crackers that I like to snack on in the evenings. I checked my pantry, knowing I was out and expecting to stare pitifully into a barren cabinet, except a brand-new box was waiting inside.

I'd worry I'm suffering from some early-onset dementia if I didn't know from personal experience how easily memories can come and go. The brain is a mysterious place. There's no telling what's going on in there, but something is clearly misfiring because it's not like someone is sneaking into my place and stocking the cabinets. That would be strange, even for a girl who couldn't do normal if she tried.

More likely than not, I've been so worn out from rehearsals that I'm misremembering. I'll figure out tomorrow that I actually needed toothpaste or dish soap. That's the most plausible explanation.

I slather on the conditioner and finish my shower, acknowledging that I'm clearly in need of sleep. It's time for this day to be over.

4
Amelie

"You keeping me company tonight?" I ask Hazel with optimism. We first became friends three years ago when I joined the National Ballet Theater company. She's a costume designer extraordinaire—a creative through and through—so she rarely keeps the same schedule.

It'd be a relief to know she was sticking around since it's a Thursday, and I usually stay after practice. I've been debating all day about whether I should risk staying late after confronting the man who's been watching me. Opening night is only three weeks away. Aside from loving my time on the stage, I could use the practice. It's my first time in a principal role.

The more I thought about it, the more pissed I got that I

should feel threatened into hiding. I decided I'm not going to let anyone steal that from me. Dance is who I am—it's part of my soul. I've already had so much stolen from me that dancing is nonnegotiable.

"I'm just wrapping up, and I'll be out of here. Kennedy needed an adjustment to her hemline. I got her measured, and as soon as I get that pressed and stitched, I'm off to meet my brother for drinks. I haven't seen him in three weeks. Can you believe that?"

Hazel's family is super close, and they all live here in the city. I've been to a few family dinners with her, and I've never felt more like an alien in my whole life. Don't get me wrong. I adore every second of my time with them, but the way they interact is foreign to me. And there are a lot of them, so it can be a tad overwhelming. She has one brother, three sisters, and so many cousins I can't keep track.

"Hey, that's great! I'm glad you're getting to catch up with him."

"You should come! We're going to that chill Irish pub over on 46th Street."

She's super sweet to include me, and I know the invitation is genuine, but I need to practice. This is the first time I've been cast as a principal dancer. When I first heard the company planned to put on an innovative ballet production of *Moulin Rouge*, I put my heart and soul into earning a lead role. While I practice on stage because I enjoy the feeling, I also *need* the practice. Anything shy of perfection, and I risk losing this incredible opportunity.

"Maybe next time. I need to get a little more practice in."

The twist to her lips tells me she knows I'm obsessive about my dancing but wishes she could get me to relax a little. "Okay, but you know you're always welcome."

I give her a tight hug. "I know, and I really will take you

up on that soon. Promise."

"Okay, I have *got* to get this finished." She holds up a red can-can skirt adorned with yellow ribbons and bows. She's done an incredible job modifying the classic French motif for ballet. So far, all the costumes have been breathtaking.

I give her one more hug. "You and your brother have a great evening catching up. I'll see you tomorrow."

"Definitely. Don't stay too late!" She raises her perfectly sculpted brows at me.

"I won't," I assure her, meaning it this time more than any other. I want to get my practice in while a few company stragglers are still around. I want to practice and be smart at the same time.

I leave Hazel and head to the portable practice stereo kept backstage for rehearsals. A small group of dancers are still chatting as they pack up their things, and two set builders are staring up into the rafters discussing what seems to be an issue with curtain transitions. I lace up my pointe shoes, select the music track I want to work on, then take center stage.

When it comes to dancing, I'm an unapologetic addict. And when I love a production the way I adore this one, it's easy for me to lose track of time. Some people see therapists. Some meditate or journal. I dance. No matter what I'm working through, I always feel better after giving myself over to the music.

My plan for a quick thirty-minute session draws into an hour in a flash. I'm able to lose myself in part because the telltale weight of my watcher's stare never materializes—both a good and a bad thing. I'm glad he never showed, but it's no excuse to be so reckless. The set workers and dancers have all left the theater. I'm alone now, and it's time to quit pressing my luck and head home.

The evening dance session has left me feeling relieved and surprisingly peaceful. I smile to myself as I walk back to the dressing room. As expected, Hazel is gone, and all is quiet. I sit at the makeup vanity where I left my things and bend down to unlace my shoes. Once they're off, my gaze lifts to the mirror and locks on an unexpected black figure reflected across from me. I gasp and whirl around as I spring to my feet.

He's here.

The man in the shadows was here the whole time.

Shock and self-disdain wreak havoc on my ability to process. I feel like the worst sort of idiot for never even considering he might come backstage. I don't know how I could have been so stupid. Maybe I deserve whatever it is he has in store for me.

A surge of fear electrifies the blood in my veins like a bolt of white lightning.

Now that we're only a few paces from one another, I realize how huge he is compared to me. He rises well above my five-four frame and looks like he could snap my body in half with the flick of his wrist. Ballet keeps me lean, but that's only part of it. He's solid muscle. I can see the bulges through the hoodie he wears—the same hoodie he had on last time.

But most terrifying of all is what he's added to his costume. A black ski mask and gloves. Not a hint of skin is showing anywhere. Nothing to identify him.

If I still needed evidence of the malicious nature of his intentions, a balaclava fits the bill.

He wields his threat with practiced indifference, leaning against the wall as though listless with casual boredom. As though he's clueless to the terror seeping from my every pore.

"What do you want from me?" I hiss at him through clenched teeth. I don't understand why this is happening—

why The Society has decided to toy with me—and the helplessness spurs my anger.

His head angles to the side before he slowly peels himself off the wall.

I take a step back. "Stay over there. You have no reason to hurt me." My gaze darts back to the vanity beside me, where an unplugged curling iron rests. I grab it and wield it angrily at him in my tightly clenched fist. "I'll scream. The cleaning people will be here any minute."

Still, he doesn't say a word. Instead, his stare slowly sweeps the room as he takes a lazy step forward, followed by another.

"Goddammit, *stop*. I will fight you with everything I have. You hear me?" My voice takes on a savage edge as the reality of my situation sinks in. This man might not have been sent as a simple warning. He could be here to hurt me. Or silence me forever.

Well, he can fucking try, but I won't go down without one hell of a fight. I bare my teeth at him and steady my stance in preparation.

The man stills, his head listing to the side as though he's studying a circus attraction rather than a woman riddled with fear. *"Devi calmarti, piccola ballerina."*

My brain stutters for a second.

His indecipherable words catch me off guard. It never occurred to me he might be foreign. I have no idea what that means or how to interpret the new information or his words themselves. The only thing I can grasp hold of is the word ballerina.

If The Society wants to threaten me, wouldn't it make sense to use someone who speaks English? Or maybe he's been sent to teach me a lesson—one that doesn't involve words.

Or ... maybe he wasn't sent by anyone. Maybe he has his own agenda.

I clutch the curling iron and motion to the door. "Get out, or I swear to God, I'll poke my fingers right through your eyeballs like they were fucking grapes." I take one more small step back because, despite the fury of my words, I'm scared shitless.

"*Ho detto calmati,*" he clips back at me before continuing in a more placid tone. "*Mi piacerebbe marchiarti, ma non così.*" The melodic words spoken in his rugged baritone voice feel as intimate as a sensual caress. I get the sense he's trying to lull me into a false sense of security. As if I'm going to realize I'm overreacting and laugh off the whole thing. He's deranged. He has to be.

My heart threatens cardiac arrest, a vise clenching tight around my ribs.

He takes a determined step forward. "*Maledizione*, ti ho detto di smetterla."

The suddenly harsh edge to his voice commands me backward. My foot lifts as he lunges forward. I don't have time to scream before he grabs my wrist in his gloved hand and yanks me a foot to the side. He doesn't send me crashing to the ground or pull me against him. His hand isn't even clasped all that tightly around my wrist, though he still hasn't let go.

Confusion muddles my thoughts until my gaze follows his to where I'd been standing seconds before, next to the ironing board Hazel was using. The iron stands upright, light still blazing red. She left it plugged in, and I was inches from pressing my arm against its scalding surface.

The man had stopped me from burning myself.

My mouth opens and closes, words escaping me.

When the cuff of his strong hand falls away from my

wrist, I look up at him, my stare riddled with confusion. He stares back through impenetrable brown irises. It's the only piece of him I can see, though they reveal nothing. He's a study in impassivity.

We stand a foot away from one another, silence pressing in around us. I know I'm still not safe, but I'm not sure what else to think.

"Why are you here?" I whisper.

"Tu. Sono qui per te." He says the words without any hint of inflection before turning to leave. His commanding stride is effortless—the personification of predatory grace.

My eyes stay glued to the doorway minutes after he's disappeared. Not because I'm worried he'll return, though that would be a much better reason. I stare blankly because I'm so damn confused.

What the hell just happened?

His words are a blur except for the first one. Two or too. I know neither of those are right, but that's how it sounded. Maybe the word can help me figure out what language he spoke. It sounded like a romance language—something Latin-based—but I'm not sure beyond that.

I rush to my bag and take out my phone. If I were a normal girl, I'd call the police, but I'm so far from normal, it's laughable. Instead, I type in "what language is too," then I pause, delete too and retype tu. That seems more probable.

Tingles erupt from my scalp down my spine and out to my fingertips as the results flash on the screen. Three possible languages appear—French, Italian, and Spanish. But it doesn't matter which one he was speaking because the word means the same thing in all three. You.

When I asked the masked man why he was here, his answer was *you*.

5 Sante

Intrigue had me sneaking back into the theater tonight, but frustration spurred me to wait for Amelie in the dressing room. I couldn't believe she'd stay for one of her private dance sessions when she knew it was dangerous. Doesn't she have any sense of self-preservation? If she knew anyone off the street could come in after her, why would she risk dancing alone in the empty theater?

I was so damn pissed that I decided to show her how easy it would be for someone to corner her in a hopeless situation. It's not a pretty lesson, but one she needs to learn. Some seriously sick fucks exist in this world, and she'd make a perfect target.

She got a taste of the dangers out there, though she didn't

respond as I expected. I have to start expecting the unexpected where she's concerned, or I'll be constantly off-balance.

I was fully prepared to witness her cower and beg. Not my tiny dancer. She wielded a fucking curling iron and growled like she was half feral. Fuck if it didn't get me hard—something I would be ashamed to admit if I gave a fuck what anyone else thought.

Green eyes spitting fire. Lip snarling. Muscles coiled and ready for a fight.

So fucking majestic, I could hardly look away.

Ferocity was the last thing I expected from her. The response didn't align with the woman I'd come to know over the past two weeks. Of course, people can have odd reactions to fear. Hers wasn't out of the realm of reasonable possibilities, yet a niggling feeling in the back of my mind insists that something is off about the situation.

I don't ever ignore my intuition—not anymore—which means I'll be watching Amelie even more closely. See if I can read what's written between the lines.

I huff out a wry breath at the absurdity of my thoughts.

If I study Amelie any closer, I'll earn a fucking PhD. As if I needed another reason to justify my growing fixation. I can admit it. Hiding from the truth won't help anyone. I'm obsessed with Amelie Brooks, and I don't care who knows it.

I let the truth wash over me as I spot the woman herself leaving the theater. She's put on joggers and a jacket over her dance gear and heads straight for a car that stops at the curb. It's a paid ride. Not as safe as having a friend pick her up, but not as bad as walking home alone. I'll be following her either way, so I suppose her choice of driver is irrelevant. I'd do it myself if I thought she'd get in the car with me.

The only way I see that happening is if, by some chance,

she recognizes me. And even then, it would be a crapshoot. Better to let things play out the way I've planned. I'll stick to the shadows for now, but when I finally orchestrate our official reunion, I'm confident she'll believe she's meeting me for the first time.

I've envisioned the interaction over and over for days now. Years, if I'm honest.

Urgency claws under my skin to reach that anticipated moment, but I refuse to let it rush me. Amelie is enough of an unknown variable that I don't need to throw any others into the mix. I want this to unfold exactly to my specifications. I'm not leaving anything to chance if I can help it.

Aside from picking up Tommy at the airport yesterday, I made arrangements to secure the apartment next door to hers. That was a cornerstone of my plan and relied heavily on my persuasive abilities. Now that it's done, the rest will be a chess match—a matter of one calculated move after another.

With my plans for Amelie in play, my family is the next problem I have to tackle. If I'm sticking around, I need to let them know I've come home. The longer I wait, the more cumbersome the task feels, but I keep putting it off anyway. I've been telling myself that my stay here might be temporary, so telling them would be pointless.

The truth is, my visit would only be brief if I grew bored of Amelie. The chances of that happening are so minuscule that it's laughable. Will that kick me into action? Nope.

Right now, my focus is on Amelie, and I'm happy to keep it that way. My family has done fine without me over the past four years. A few more days will hardly make a difference.

6
Amelie

ALL I CAN THINK ABOUT FOR TWO DAYS STRAIGHT IS THE BIZARRE scene that played out with the masked man. I can't stop wondering what he wants from me. Surely, it can't be good if he had to make sure he was unidentifiable, but if he wanted to hurt me, why hasn't he done it already? He had the perfect opportunity in that dressing room. The one thing he did do—besides scare me to death and look bored out of his mind—was keep me from burning myself. What kind of criminal stalks a woman, puts on a mask, and hides in her dressing room, only to prevent her from accidentally hurting herself before disappearing?

I wouldn't believe it if I hadn't seen it with my own eyes. It sounds like pure fantasy.

And if I need more proof that I have more issues than brains, I find myself envisioning my masked watcher as some sort of hero like Zorro or Robin Hood.

What the hell is wrong with me? Just because he didn't rape me on the spot doesn't make him a good man. Decent human beings don't terrorize other people for no reason.

Maybe that's what gets him off.

Great. I'll add that to my list of fears to obsess over. Thanks for the support.

My eyes roll in a sweeping arc inside their sockets. I sometimes wonder if everyone argues with themselves as much as I do. I'd like to think so, but the more likely answer is that it's a manifestation of my inevitable spiral into insanity. That's what happens to people like me, right? All the good serial killer documentaries start with a detailed account of the killer's multitude of Mommy issues. I have those in abundance.

My internal dialogue has been so incessant that I've had to get out of my apartment and wander the city on my Saturday off just to escape myself. I did get a couple of errands run, including a trip to the grocery store. The distraction helped, but I'm barely off the elevator on my way home when the cyclone of thoughts swirls back into action.

I do my best to mentally put a lid on the subject while redistributing my packages to free up a hand. Between restocking my fridge and a few other stops, my arms are laden with heavy shopping bags. Just as I free my left hand, I round a corner and collide with someone. A very large someone who might as well have been a wall for all intents and purposes.

I yip with surprise as my body ricochets backward. My tailbone can practically feel the bruising impact of the floor already, but it never comes to pass because two strong hands clamp firmly around my arms and haul me back upright.

"Oh!" I gasp. "Thank you, I mean. I'm so sorry. I wasn't paying attention." Words tumble past my lips as I collect myself but die a quick death when I take in the man before me. He towers over me, but that's not what first seizes my attention. It takes a unique degree of confidence to tattoo your entire neck and presumably much more. That sort of statement demands attention.

The ink frames his angular jawline and gives the intensity of his stare a frightening edge. His eyes are deep set beneath a heavy brow such that his mahogany irises could pass for black. The man is imposing, to say the least, and I find myself totally captivated. The dichotomy of savage beauty is breathtaking.

Once I'm steady and begin to return to my senses, I realize he's yet to say a word—or release me.

I glance down at his hand on my arm and see that even his fingers and the backs of his hands are adorned with black ink.

"I'm good now. You can let go," I offer quietly before returning my gaze to his.

His grip slowly relents, but he doesn't step away. We're closer than is customary for two strangers. My proximity to him is dizzying, his spiced scent not helping matters.

"You need a hand?" he asks, helping to deflate the mounting tension but only marginally. His sultry tone is too heavy with undecipherable meaning to be fully reassuring. If this is his being chill, he probably sends women into full-blown seizures when he's trying. He'd have to be banned from clubs as a fire hazard when every pair of panties in the place spontaneously combusts.

Sweet Mother Mary, get ahold of yourself, Mel.

"No, I got it. I live right there." I motion to my door ten feet away.

"Then we're neighbors."

"I beg your pardon?" I peer wide-eyed at the open door behind me. "That's Mr. Sorrell's place."

"Not anymore, it's not."

"He moved? When? I never even heard him leave." Or anyone new move in. How had I completely missed this transition?

Good God, I *am* losing my mind.

"This week."

Okayyy, that explains very little.

He's not exactly a conversationalist, yet he's not making excuses to leave either. That puts us in an awkward in-between that I'm at a loss to define. He's somewhat blocking my path with no indication he's prepared to step aside, but his tone and demeanor drip with indifference. Maybe this is his best effort at being polite since we're neighbors now. For all I know, he could be a little neurospicy and be completely oblivious to the awkward tension quickly filling the air.

Whatever the case, it's time for my escape.

"Oh, okay. Well, it was good to meet you…" I wait for his answer to my implied question.

"Call me Isaac."

What an odd way to introduce himself.

Good grief, Mel. Stop overanalyzing every-freaking-thing.

Fine, but it's still weird.

"And you may call me Amelie," I say with a hint of mock formality.

You are so going to hell. What if this man is genuinely neurodivergent, and you're mocking him?

If I had a hand available, I'd clamp it over my mouth to keep me from saying anything more. I don't know what's come over me. Something about his unrelenting intensity makes me desperate to shatter his composure, and that's so not me. Not even close.

I spent seventeen years doing everything I could to earn the approval of everyone around me and the next four years trying to simply go unnoticed. I've never been difficult for the sake of being difficult until this very moment. It's strange and a little electrifying. And I don't feel quite so guilty when I note the tiniest twitch of his lips.

Was that amusement? It's hard to say because it's gone the second it registers, his mask of stoic indifference slipping back into place.

I give him a thin smile and start to squeeze around him. "Enjoy your evening," I mutter once I'm free.

"Amelie." My name on his lips is a lasso cinched tight around my waist, forcing my attention back to him. I stand, breathless as I watch him bend over and retrieve something off the floor, then lazily stalk toward me.

"You dropped this." In his hand is the zippered silicon pouch I keep in my purse filled with sewing supplies.

I try to take it from him, but he shifts, indicating he's not done examining its contents. "It's a sewing kit for my shoes."

"You sew your shoes?"

"Pointe shoes. I'm a ballet dancer." I don't necessarily want to tell him about myself, but I'll sound like a total weirdo if I don't explain. Women my age don't normally carry around sewing kits.

He slides the pouch back into my tote purse. "You really should have let me give you a hand," he continues in that devastatingly sultry tone of his.

"Why's that?" I ask dazedly.

"Because then I would have had a reason to come inside." The heat that flashes in his eyes and the implication of his words catches me by surprise. Is this man ... coming onto me? I'd questioned seconds ago whether he might be on the spectrum, but now, I'm starting to wonder if he's simply toying with me.

He's impossible to read—that alone should have me running in the opposite direction. I like attention as much as the next girl, but this man is one giant red flag.

"That's not going to happen," I say softly, hoping I don't anger him. I've known him all of two seconds and have no idea what rejection might do to him. I discreetly punch in the code to my door and turn the handle.

He leans his broad shoulder against the doorframe. "And why's that?" he asks in a soft murmur that matches my own words. The words feather across my skin, clearly meant to seduce. "Is someone waiting inside for you?"

His question winds me like a punch to the gut.

He has no idea that he's struck at my most exposed nerve, and I don't care to share that with him, so I douse my sparking anger with a cauldron of icy water.

I consider lying to him for a split second as I stare motionless at my door. It's only the briefest whisp of a thought brought on by shame that I refuse to give power to.

The fact that I am alone is not a reflection of who I am or my worth.

I say the words in my head with fierce conviction, yet the backs of my eyes still burn from the unintended reminder.

"*No*, there's not," I say before boldly meeting his stare. Who cares if he can see the glassy tinge to my eyes?

I don't offer any further explanation. I don't have to. I owe this man nothing. Instead, I let myself inside and close the door behind me.

7
Sante

WHAT I CALL PROTECTIVE, SOME MIGHT CALL POSSESSIVE. I DON'T give a shit how you label it. I will *never* willingly allow someone else to lay a finger on the people I care about. I own my actions because I know my intent aligns with my values. I've never questioned whether those instincts bordered on excessive.

Until now.

When the mere suggestion of Amelie being in a relationship that I know damn well doesn't exist still manages to spark a jealous rage inside me, I have to question whether I'm losing my goddamn mind. I can see the explosive nature of my emotions toward her. I recognize how they cloud my judgment, but I can't find a way to rein them in. And the more I'm around her, the worse it gets.

Even a day later, my blood pressure pulses in my ears when I think about the possibility of Amelie with another man. The whole damn situation with her is mind-boggling—that I could lose myself so completely in the need to possess another person. I don't understand it. I only know that this itch beneath my skin won't stop until she's naked beneath me. Maybe then I can finally cleanse her from my system.

In the meantime, my dick refuses to even look at another woman, especially after the way Amelie responded to me. Eyes dilated. Lips parted. Pulse thundering at the base of her neck. Nipples so goddamn hard they were two perfect pebbles straining against the fabric of her shirt.

Her body told me all I needed to know.

The pull I feel toward her isn't a one-way street. She's still affected by me, even if she has no idea who I am. She didn't recognize me, but I hadn't expected her to. More than that, I'm glad she didn't. I don't want her to see the old me in the man I am now because we are *nothing* alike.

All that matters is that she wanted me. Beneath the layers of societal conditioning and innate caution, her body practically begged for my touch.

Everything about our first interaction went exactly as I'd hoped until I asked whether anyone was waiting for her. In an instant, the delicately woven spell connecting us dissipated like dust in the wind.

What was it about my question that upset her?

I mulled over the possibilities all night and got nowhere. It made me feel helpless, which is not something I've experienced since I first moved to Sicily, back when I was at my lowest. Drawing me back to that time period has me feeling like I'm wearing a suit two sizes too small. I want to flex and rip the uncomfortable fabric from my body, only there's no suit to blame. Therefore, I'm doing the only other thing I can think of to relieve the irritation because I have to do *something*. I refuse to wallow in helplessness.

I swore to myself that Amelie would grow to accept me exactly as I am, and I am *not* the kind of man who puts effort into charming a woman. At least, I never used to be, but damn if I'm not about to knock on her door with a steaming cup of Starbucks.

Cazzo.

It doesn't take her long to answer. She's tentative when she does, only allowing the door to open enough for her to warily check me out. "Hey, did you need something?"

I extend the cup toward her. "Coffee."

"For me?"

"For you."

Her eyes dance from the cup to my face, then back to the cup before she fully opens the door and accepts the offering. She sniffs at the hole in the lid as her brows knit together.

"Is this a caramel macchiato?" she asks with surprise.

"It is."

"Mmm... my favorite."

And fuck if I'm not hard again.

"Lucky guess." My voice has gone ragged with the strain of regaining control of my dick.

Her eyes peer up at me through dark lashes as she takes a sip. And when her eyelids drift shut in satisfaction, I let slip an audible grunt. She's the sexiest fucking thing I've ever seen, and she's not even trying. Hell, she's wearing an oversized Led Zeppelin T-shirt and sweatpants so baggy that I have no idea how they're staying up.

Her eyes pop open as if realizing her effect on me,

drawing her attention to the writing on the paper cup. The corners of my lips quirk upward at her huff of amusement.

Never say never.

It's my response to her insistence that I won't be joining her at her place.

"Is this a friendly gesture or an attempt to get in my pants?" she asks in a casually curious tone.

"Is there a difference?"

"One is much more self-serving than the other."

I snag the bottom of her shirt with a crooked finger and draw her closer, then lean in so that my lips are close to her ear. I feel her quick intake of air all the way to the bottom of my balls.

"Judging by the goose bumps dotting your skin, I'm serving more than myself."

"Maybe you're just scaring me," she whispers shakily.

I pull back enough to peer down at her chest. As expected, her nipples are seconds from slicing their way through her shirt. I slowly step backward, my smile positively dripping with masculine satisfaction.

When she follows my gaze and realizes the situation, she gasps and crosses her arms over her chest to hide the evidence of her obvious arousal.

"I'll see you around," I promise seductively.

"Not if I see you first," she pops back at me.

I toss a smirk over my shoulder and fuck if she isn't fighting back a smile before she slams her door shut. The tension eases from my neck and shoulders as I head back to the elevator. This was definitely the right move. And while I may have brought her coffee, I stayed true to myself. I'm not at risk of being confused for a gentleman anytime soon.

Onto the next matter of business—burying the dead.

"You know I hate hotels." It's damn near the first words Tommy's said since we met up at the storage facility. I'm glad he's finally spitting it out. I knew something had to be bothering him.

"It's not forever, Tom."

"Might as well be until you give me some other timeframe."

I shoot him a withering look as we approach my unit. "I know you like specifics, but I don't have any. You're a smart guy. Trick your brain into believing I told you it's going to be a month. Even better? Go buy a damn place of your own. You have the money."

"Why would I do that if I'm not gonna live here?"

"Maybe you keep it and stay there when you visit? No one's saying you can't come back." I pull out my phone and look for the email Noemi sent a couple of years ago telling me the entry code to the storage unit she rented for me.

"I guess that's true," he says pensively. "Remind me what we're doing here."

I punch in the code on the panel, which releases the bars holding the garage-style door in place. It lifts a few inches on its own. I have to help it the rest of the way, the movement triggering a motion detector light inside the unit.

Tommy and I stare at the fuck-ton of shit piled in a space much larger than I expected it to be.

"Jesus." My hands rest on my hips in disbelief.

"All this stuff is yours?"

"I guess it is now, but not originally."

Our childhood home sold while I was away. When Noemi asked what I wanted to keep, I told her to get rid of it all. She refused. Weeks later, I got the email telling me my stuff had been put in storage. I guess she considered "my stuff" to be anything she thought I might want, whether it was mine or other random shit from the house.

I wander inside and take a cursory look at a few of the storage bins. Some things are easy to identify like my old manga collection, a box of Yankees memorabilia, and she's even got a tub full of my old shoes. When I peek into a tub with Dad's ancient archery awards, I toss it aside with a sneer. I get why she kept it. I used to love looking at those things in his office when I was a kid, but they mean nothing to me now.

"Hey, this looks like it might be stuff from your desk." Tommy's sifting through a small box. "Might be worth going through." A sly smile tugs at his lips as his hand appears with a set of brass knuckles on it. "I don't remember you having these when you moved in with us. Holding out on me?"

I huff wryly. "If I'd been the kind of kid who had a set of those, I never would have had to move into your place." I take the scuffed metal from him and look at it more closely. "It was Umberto's. My father's thug sidekick." When they took me into the fold, I used to think of us as a team. Turned out they were a team; I was just a tool.

Tommy rubs his palm along the side of his jaw. "Makes me think of those Russians—you remember that?"

I grin. "Of course, I do. Best joyride I ever took." How was I supposed to know the yellow Lamborghini belonged to the head of the Russian mob?

"Those assholes nearly broke my jaw." He's staring off as if remembering that day. We were shipped off to Sicily not long after. Pure mischief sparks in Tommy's eyes. "The ride was pretty incredible, though."

"So worth it."

We both chuckle at the memory, which is only possible

because his brother Renzo sorted the matter for us. If it weren't for him, the Russians probably would have tossed us into the river. In pieces.

I take off the brass and toss it into the bin.

"Whatever happened to him? He go down when Conner shot your father?" Tommy motions to all that's left of Umberto. I'm sure he was told the basics of what went down with my father, but he and I never talked about it. I never talked about any of it with anyone.

"Yeah. I killed him." I stare at my cousin as I say the words devoid of emotion.

Tommy stares at me, then gives a single nod of approval. "We done here?"

"Yeah. This is garbage. As far as I'm concerned, it can all burn."

"Kind of harsh," he mutters. "What'd those manga comics ever do to you?"

And just like that, the mounting tension melts away. Tommy has his quirks, but he can also be fucking hilarious. No one jokes with a straight face the way Tommy can.

"You want 'em? Take 'em," I tease.

"What I want is to be out of that damn hotel."

"*Jesus*, again with the hotel," I groan as I lead us out of the storage unit.

"Wouldn't be an issue if you weren't chasing a piece of ass all over the city."

I freeze and cut him with a menacing glare. "I know sometimes you misread things, so I'll give you this freebie. Call her a piece of ass again, and I'll dig out those brass knuckles to finish what the Russians started."

Tommy stiffens. He gets agitated with himself when he missteps. "Understood." He's come a long way both in understanding himself and others, but it still frustrates him when he fails to read cues properly.

I nod, then pull down the metal door. "Think you can take care of this shit for me?"

"I'll sort something out."

"Good. Let's get outta here. We need to find an apartment for you."

"About fucking time."

8
Amelie

DO THE PROTECTIVE POWERS OF THE EVIL EYE CHARM HAVE AN expiration date?

They must. I've been wearing the same evil eye bracelet for years and carried on my merry way with no problem, but now I swear I've been jinxed. Most people don't buy into that sort of thing. I don't blame them. It sounds like something only kids believe in, but when you've got luck like mine, you'd be willing to buy into it, too. Anything that might help is worth a try.

I got my first evil eye jewelry from a street vendor not long after recovering from my episode of amnesia. The wrinkled old woman who sold me the ring convinced me of its powers more than the ring itself. Something about her was old-world—a sage glint in her hooded eyes. She looked like she could have wandered off a movie set, perfectly cast as the wizened old hag. It was almost comical, but I was way too scared of her to laugh.

She was convincing, but more than anything, I liked the idea of believing in a protective power. I still do. And since starting to wear the charms, the horrible luck from my past seemed to fade away. I've been flying under the radar for years without any major catastrophe. Then, all of a sudden, danger has closed in around me from every direction.

I spent my evening debating whether the masked man or my calculating new neighbor was the worse threat. My stalker is unquestionably dangerous—who knows what he has planned. On the other hand, Isaac has made his plans crystal clear, and they could be equally devastating. Maybe not to my body, but to my heart. Both men have the potential to shatter me.

It's definitely time to upgrade talismans. Maybe buy some sage and a little holy water.

It wouldn't hurt.

Good grief. Why me? I might as well be a danger magnet.

In a strange way, Isaac has me the most on edge. The stalker, I get. His plan is to terrorize me, either of his own will or because he was sent to do so. Easy enough. But what is Isaac's deal? I don't seem remotely his type. Maybe that's the thrill—bad boy looking to defile the good girl. Maybe he's not interested unless there's a chase.

Maybe he and my stalker have more in common than I realized. They should grab lunch together.

Thoughts like that right there are why you'll never be normal.

Never was and never will be.

Unfortunately, those abnormalities in me are drawn to Isaac. Something about him calls to me. Something dark and seductive.

I told myself not to give him the time of day after our first encounter. Yet I had to open the door when I saw him through the peephole yesterday morning. I had to know what he would say.

I have a horrible feeling that this incessant curiosity about him will continue to get in the way of logic. Isaac isn't the sort of man I should be interested in. He's the epitome of everything I've tried to avoid for years—risk and danger and heartbreak.

Surely, I'm not dumb enough to ignore the dangers simply because of a pretty face.

You mean epically gorgeous?

I am so screwed.

One can only hope...

I smack my palm against my forehead like an absolute lunatic. Nothing to see here. Just a touch of crazy having a conversation with herself on her way home from work.

The universe must be enjoying the show because when my hand falls away, my gaze locks on Isaac sitting outside our apartment building entrance staring right at me.

Well played, Universe. Well played.

He's smoking a cigarette—add that to the list of red flags that have me questioning whether I'm color-blind. I need to nod politely and keep walking. I steel myself to stay strong and chant in my head to keep going.

It's no use.

His gravitational pull is too intense, slowing each of my steps until I stop beside him.

"Smoking's a nasty habit." It's not at all what I would

have said to anyone else. The comment is way too confrontational, but my frustration at his effect on me unleashes a boldness I didn't know I had.

What's worse? I like the Amelie he brings out. She's confident and doesn't take shit from anyone. She's the me I've been too afraid to be.

Isaac inhales and holds my stare. I raise a challenging eyebrow, daring him to respond. He does, but not in the way I expect. He blows a long stream of smoke past full lips, then extinguishes the butt on the sidewalk beneath his booted foot.

I'm struck with a sense of déjà vu at the similarity to my odd exchange with the watcher at the theater. Before I can examine the thought more closely, Isaac responds in a gravelly, smoke-worn voice that captures my every sense. Rugged and raw, just like him.

"You have an admirer?" His gaze drifts behind me down the sidewalk.

I glance back and immediately hone in on a man in a dark sweatshirt with the hood up leaning against the building next door. He's not super close—probably fifty feet away. He's looking away, so even if it wasn't dark, I still wouldn't be able to see his face, but I don't need to. It's the man from the theater. His clothes are the same, and he's got the same build. The same casual menace about him.

My blood plummets to my feet so quickly that my head spins.

He followed me home.

Has he done it before? Does he show up at every practice in addition to solo sessions?

Tonight was a regular full-cast rehearsal. I didn't stay late. Had he been inside while the others were there, or had he waited for me on the street? I never sensed him in the slightest.

That, more than anything, terrifies me.

If The Society wanted to threaten me, they'd make themselves heard. I'd been so confident that was why the man was watching me. Following me. He was sent as a warning. From the minute he stepped out of the shadows, I assumed that was his purpose. But the longer this goes on, the more my thoughts cloud with uncertainty.

I was already unsure why The Society would hound me now when I've done nothing wrong. When he showed up in the dressing room, I wondered if he might not have been sent by anyone.

The Society is vile, but at least its intentions have always been clear. If this man is acting on his own, he's a complete unknown.

The question I first asked him resounds in my head. *What do you want from me?*

You. Maybe his answer was more literal than I thought.

I turn back to Isaac but have trouble meeting his perceptive stare. "Was that man following me?" I finally ask, trying to sound less rattled than I feel. I know the answer but don't want to explain to Isaac that I may have a stalker—I just met the guy, after all. And even more importantly, an admission like that would stir up questions I'm not going to answer.

"I'd say so by the way he pulled up short when you stopped."

I nod. "Probably harmless. The city's full of weirdos."

Isaac stares up at me. His assessing eyes feel like they strip me wide open, exposing every last one of my ugly secrets. I have to wrap my arms around my chest to keep from feeling utterly naked. I don't know how he does it or why, but I'm about to make a hasty retreat inside when he stands and tells me, "Wait here."

I swivel in place and watch in stunned surprise as he

starts walking straight toward my watcher. Lightning fast, he's suddenly moving at a dead sprint. The man in the hood catches on but not soon enough. He only makes it a few steps before Isaac snags the back of his sweatshirt. I gasp, my hand pressed to my mouth as Isaac clamps his arm around the man's neck, easily overtaking him.

Isaac's back is to me, his body between me and the other man, so I can't fully see what's happening. The two seem to have words. They stand in place but struggle against one another. I'm sure it's only a matter of seconds, but it feels like time slows to a crawl. Then, in a burst of movement, Isaac releases the man only to pull back and punch him squarely in the face. The hoodie guy reels backward. I try to see his face, but the two are close to an alley entrance ensconced in shadows. I never get a clear look. And then it's over as quickly as it began—my stalker fleeing into the night while Isaac strolls casually back to me.

I can hardly believe what I've witnessed. I'm still standing with my jaw hinged open when Isaac approaches. He shakes his fist a time or two, then runs the other hand through his hair.

"That should take care of it," he says as if he'd sprayed for bugs to help with an ant problem rather than chased down and beat up a stalker.

Who is this guy?

Not everyone covered in tattoos is dangerous, but men like Isaac are the reason the stereotype exists. I get the sense he doesn't suffer from the burden of fear like a normal person. He truly is half wild.

I re-examine him with new eyes, though it's pointless. I still have no idea what to think about my new neighbor or my growing attraction to him.

"Did you seriously beat up some stranger?"

"You busting my balls for helping you out?"

"What? No. I mean, we don't even know if he was actually following me."

"Yeah, which is why he only got a warning," he says in a chilly tone. "Not a fan of men who prey on women."

Holy crap, that's so freaking hot and terrifying at the same time.

"You're bleeding," I say dazedly. "If you come to my place, I have bandages."

He inches closer, a smirk teasing at his lips. "Changed your tune already, have you? That was quick." If it weren't for the tiny creases in the corners of his eyes, I might feel the urge to slug him in the stomach.

"To clean up your bodily fluids, not exchange them," I jab back at him. "Now come on. There's no telling what kind of germs are getting in that cut as we speak."

I walk to the glass doors and reach for the handle. His arm snakes around behind me and grabs it before I can. A waft of his spiced scent finds me through the lingering smoke remnants, and the heady combination leaves me breathless for more.

I don't know what's come over me. I've always hated smoking, yet it seems to add to his appeal. How is that even possible? What is it about his unapologetic lifestyle that draws me in and makes me forget who I am? It wasn't ten minutes ago I was contemplating how dangerous he is, and suddenly, I'm asking him up to my place.

He did risk his own safety to protect you.

True. It would be rude of me to ignore such a selfless action.

Some antiseptic and a thank-you is the least you can do.

Am I rationalizing a way to spend more time with him? Probably.

Do I care? Not until the elevator doors close behind us, sealing us inside.

9
Amelie

WE STAND ON OPPOSITE SIDES OF THE ELEVATOR FACING ONE another. His unrelenting stare roots me in place while his indomitable presence fills the space between us so thoroughly that my lungs struggle for air.

I'm as helpless as a butterfly trapped in a jar. If the jar was in his hands, would he release me or pluck off my wings as a souvenir? Release doesn't seem an option for a man like him.

"You going to call the cops?" His casual question brings me crashing back to reality.

Here I was, letting romantic delusions distract me from who I am and the realities of my life. I absolutely cannot call the police. Calling attention to myself like that would be too dangerous, but he won't understand. Not when I can't offer an explanation.

"On you?" I ask with a perfect sprinkle of confusion in my voice.

Isaac's chin dips a fraction as his gaze prods me to get serious. He's not letting me off the hook.

It was worth a try.

"Oh, you mean about that man. I'm not sure what good it'll do. It's not like I have any information to offer about who he is, and he didn't actually do anything to hurt me."

The elevator doors open. He places a hand out to keep them from closing while I walk through. As we start down the hall, he walks beside me close enough for our arms to touch. Closer than two acquaintances would generally walk. Heat blazes across my skin with each gentle sweep of his inked arm.

"Still doesn't hurt to file a report. That way, you have it on record."

Each word is a scrutinizing prod. I appreciate his concern —for anyone else, it would be the right thing to say—but I need him to let it go.

I face him when I reach my apartment door and smile. "You know, you're right. As soon as we're done, I'll give them a call."

Isaac leans against the doorframe, his large body looming over mine. Wavy strands of his hair have broken free of their gelled confinement and hang down over his forehead, perfecting his bad-boy look. He even has a hoop nose ring in one nostril. He's the spitting image of what the Devil would look like, should he choose to walk the Earth—an irresistible mix of rebellion and angelic perfection.

"Anyone ever told you you're shit at lying?" he asks in a low rumble.

"No, they haven't. Maybe you're just a skeptic." I press a finger into his chest, summoning every ounce of confidence I can manifest.

"Oh, I'm definitely a skeptic. Doesn't change the fact that you're a liar." His eyes grow hooded as they drift lazily down to my lips. "You were scared to death when I told you someone was following you. Why the sudden indifference?"

"Because," I start, my voice husky. "I have a protector." I lift my wrist and display my evil eye bracelet. "This little guy keeps the monsters away."

My aim is for a playful distraction, but I miss my mark, judging by the way his entire body stiffens. Even the seductive warmth of his gaze chills to an icy glare.

I'm baffled by his reaction. Had he thought I was going to name him my protector? Or was the opposite true? Did he resent the insinuation that I might rely on him for protection?

I'm at a total loss and desperately wish I could evaporate into thin air.

My hand slowly falls away from him until his fingers circle my forearm, stopping my progress. I have to hold my breath to keep from trembling at the feel of his scalding touch on my skin. Considering his sudden change in demeanor, I should pull away, but I can't. I'm hopelessly captivated by his every movement, desperate to know what he'll do next.

He angles my arm so that the inside of my wrist and forearm are horizontal in front of him. I hear a click before his other hand appears with a pen. He uses his thumb to slowly slide my bracelet back to my wrist. The touch is infinitely more intimate than it needs to be, causing my lungs to lose function. I have to force the silly organs to suck in a small supply of much-needed air as he takes the pen to my skin and begins to write.

I watch raptly as his tattooed fingers, strong and steady,

mark me with ink of my own. The location is achingly sensitive, and I feel each meticulously penned number as though he were spelling out his phone number with his tongue on my clit rather than a pen on my wrist.

If I wasn't already planning to shower, I'd have to change clothes anyway after this because he's drenching my panties.

To top off his sensual assault, he uses his thumb to take one last leisurely caress across my skin. When he finally releases me, I am nothing but a puddle of desire pooled on the hallway floor.

"Trouble finds you again, you call me," he murmurs, then turns toward his place.

"What about your cut?" I blurt dumbly, all rational thoughts escaping me.

A flash of warmth returns to the gaze he tosses over his shoulder. "I think I'll survive."

Then he's gone, taking my sanity with him.

10

Sante

WHEN TOMMY AND I FIRST ARRIVED IN SICILY, WE WERE FORCED to sleep in my uncle's barn for an entire month. If you're picturing a cozy hay loft inside a sturdy red building used to store tractors and equipment, try again. This time, think rotting wood, dirt floor, and six huge pigs for roommates.

Uncle Lazaro owns an enormous estate—technically, he's a distant cousin, but I use the term uncle out of respect. And I do respect him despite what he put us through. He could have welcomed us into his home from day one, but no matter how bitter and furious I was at the time about our accommodations, I needed that month in the barn and everything that came after to shift my perspective. I respect Uncle Lazaro *because* of what he put us through. I wouldn't be who I am now without his unorthodox teachings.

According to Lazaro, you can't truly appreciate what you have unless you know what it's like to have nothing. He was right.

I'd been dealt a shit hand when it came to my father, but that was only one facet of my life. It was also in the past. At the time, I was too busy wallowing in self-pity to see anything besides what I'd lost and the ways I'd failed. I was stuck in a negative feedback loop. But when I lay awake at night on the cold ground, I found myself wishing for the creature comforts of home, which morphed into imagining how I wanted my life to look. I thought about the ways I'd be different from my father and the things I wanted to change about myself. I started to get excited about the opportunity to redeem myself. About the future. I realized that I wasn't a passenger in my life. I was the fucking pilot. If I wanted things to be different, I had to get off my ass and make it happen.

From that point on, I honed my ability to get what I wanted out of life. I refused to ever feel as inept and clueless as I felt when I learned my father had killed my mother and tried to do the same to my sister, all right under my nose.

My growth was a process. I had setbacks, and the Sicilian way of life wasn't forgiving, but it made me stronger. One of the most important lessons I learned was to listen to my intuition. Uncle Lazaro's zero-tolerance governing style gave me a wealth of opportunities to practice—identifying, interpreting, and honing my ability to read a situation so that I could anticipate potential consequences of my actions. Once I figured out that intuition was life's little cheat sheet, I made that skill my top priority.

At twenty-two, I'd say my ability to pick up on the subtle

nuances in people's demeanor is exceptional for someone my age. My radar is always on.

Therefore, when something strikes me as odd, such as Amelie not calling the cops, I pay attention.

My alarm sounding doesn't necessarily mean there's a problem. The reason behind her unexpected reaction could be totally benign—her brother-in-law is Irish mafia, after all. Maybe they've told her to steer clear of the cops. But until I sort out why, I can't know if the ping on my intuition radar is relevant or not. That makes it a new priority.

I take out my phone and press the first name on my favorites list. There are only three names on the list. Tommy, Uncle Lazaro, and the third is a number I haven't dialed in ages but can't seem to remove. The instant Amelie reaches out, and I know she will, hers will be the fourth.

"I thought you said tonight was for show," Tommy barks at me in lieu of a greeting.

"It was."

"Then there was no need to put your full strength in that punch. You could have broken my jaw, asshole."

I bite back a grin, glad we're not having this conversation face-to-face. "I had to make it convincing. And besides, you can take a hit better than anyone I know."

"Just because I can doesn't mean I should have to." His tone is even, but I hear it for the pout that it is and I smirk.

"Told you I'd owe you."

A heavy sigh crosses the line. "I don't understand why any of it's needed in the first place. Why all the smoke and mirrors? She's just a woman like any of the others who fall at your feet."

Tommy's lucky I have more patience for him than anyone else in this world. Implying Amelie is anything less than exceptional has my muscles coiling in outrage.

"Amelie is different." My tone is clipped, but that means little to him. Tommy doesn't pick up on inflection and nuance like most people do. His intuition never fully matured, so I have to have enough for us both. The flip side of that coin means that no one will ever be as honest and loyal as my cousin Tommy. Those qualities are worth their weight in gold.

"Different how?" he asks.

"She's *mine*." Or she will be soon enough.

I give him a minute to process.

"We aren't going back, are we?"

"You're free to do what you want, Tommy. Always have been." Which is why it was so fascinating to me that he chose to follow me to Sicily in the first place. I'd been sent away, but he didn't have to go. He valued our friendship enough that he'd rather suffer with me than let me go it alone.

How many people do you know would do that sort of thing for you? Not fucking many.

Tommy wasn't big on the idea of coming back to the city. To be honest, I wasn't either. I liked the new life I'd forged for myself. I liked that the only version of myself anyone in Sicily knew was the new version. Everyone except Uncle Lazaro, but he was the one behind my transformation, so he doesn't count.

I'd rather not upend Tommy's life again for me, but Amelie isn't up for debate. That means I'm staying in Manhattan for the foreseeable future, which means so is Tommy.

"You know that's bullshit, right? That I'm not going to abandon ship after all we've been through."

"Yeah, I know," I say with a grin. "I love you for it, if it's any consolation."

"Fuck you," he grumbles.

I fight back a laugh, not wanting to truly piss him off.

"Give me the latest rundown on the Irish relationship with the cops. They have a falling out?" I asked Tommy to do some recon on the local crime climate when I decided to come back. We had a basic idea of the atmosphere from Lazaro, who always keeps up with the goings-on in New York even though it's an ocean away. In his words, trouble can come from anywhere. But if we were going to be on these streets, I wanted details.

"The Irish and the cops are as strong as ever. Aside from being related to half the force, the Irish handpicked the current commissioner years ago."

Interesting. So Amelie probably wasn't steering clear of the cops for that reason. I cross it off my mental list of possibilities.

"Why do you ask?"

"Amelie was pretty adamant against filing a report with the cops, and I was trying to suss out why."

"Why the hell would you try to get her to report me?"

"I wasn't trying so much as curious why she didn't. Not like it would have mattered if she did. She has zero information to give them."

"That could be the answer to your question, then. Or it could have something to do with the botched investigation when she went missing. Maybe she simply doesn't trust them."

"What do you know about that?"

"Renzo told me back when they found her that the hospital filed an assault report for a Jane Doe amnesiac, but it was never cross-checked with missing persons. Amelie's sister had to do the legwork to hunt down Amelie herself."

"Just because she had a shit investigator then doesn't mean it'll happen again." I don't like decisions based on fear or other emotions. I find it beyond frustrating to watch people rationalize bad decisions because it makes them *feel* better. That shit comes back to bite you every time.

"You're arguing your point to the wrong person," Tommy says flatly.

"You're right." I sigh. "Thanks for the info. Let me know if you think of anything else."

"You do realize that's a broad fucking statement, considering who you're talking to."

I huff out a laugh. "Good. I'd hate for you to get bored."

Tommy grunts before the line goes dead. I toss my phone on the kitchen counter and open a bottle of Masseto Merlot. That was another thing I learned from Uncle Lazaro—appreciation for a fine wine. He'd have a few choice words if he saw that I wasn't using a proper decanter or aerating. The mental image of his tirade brings a small smile to my lips as I take that first sip. This is exactly what I need after executing today's production.

Looks like Amelie isn't the only one interested in theater.

I sit on the sofa facing the TV, but I don't watch the TV. I watch the wall because that's the wall this apartment shares with Amelie's. As I stare at the cream-colored wall texture, I envision her place and what she might be doing. Did she wash my writing off her arm yet? Or is she reluctant to see it fade along with the memory of my skin touching hers?

She was so entranced watching my every movement that I'm not sure she realized her entire body shivered from my touch. So fucking responsive. And when she was giving me attitude, pressing her haughty finger into my chest, a simple touch from me instantly melted her hard edges. I've never felt such overwhelming satisfaction over something so simple.

A full gambit of emotions pummeled me during those few short minutes, especially when I thought she'd recognized me for a split second. I was certain I hadn't wanted her to remember me, yet when I realized what I took for recognition was a misunderstanding, I couldn't deny the stabbing disappointment.

Even now, I want to go next door and show her exactly who I am and how she's owned me since the minute we met. Four years of frustration and longing—clambering to the surface, threatening a total loss of control. The urge is maddening, seething under my skin.

That was why I had to walk away.

If I had followed her into that apartment, I wasn't sure what I'd have done or might have said. That sort of emotional instability is unacceptable. It leads to unintended consequences, and this campaign I'm conducting is nothing if not calculated. I will *not* fuck it up by losing my cool.

My phone vibrates with a call on the kitchen counter. It's Lazaro. I answer in Italian because that's the only language we use between us. He speaks English, but made it clear from the beginning that I was responsible for learning his language if I wanted to survive in his territory.

It's amazing how quickly someone can learn a language when properly motivated.

"Sante, it's been weeks, and I've heard nothing from you. You forget your uncle Lazaro so quickly?"

"Forgive me, Uncle. I meant no disrespect. I simply had no news to share," I assure him. He's not genuinely hurt—his comment is more of a reminder. We share blood relations, but our family businesses are not one and the same. I'm straddling the line between two worlds. He's granted me the permission to do so for now, but that won't last forever.

"Nothing? You can't tell me you haven't at least paid respects to your cousin Donati—he'll be your boss if you stay there."

"I didn't see any point in announcing myself if there was a chance I wasn't sticking around."

Lazaro makes a tsking sound. "I taught you better than to lie to yourself. You can't stop others from lying to you, but if you lie to yourself—"

"I'm the only one to blame," I finish for him. It's a sentiment I've heard him make time and time again. I absolutely believe it, but catching the lie can be tricky.

"You think I've avoided Donati for other reasons." Even as I say the words, I feel their truth.

"You're avoiding your family. Call it what it is."

I lean my elbows on the granite counter, my body deflating. He's absolutely right.

Fucking hell.

"I hear you." The words are heavy beneath the weight of my conscience.

"Good, good. For Americans, they're not such bad family," he admits. It's as glowing a compliment coming from him and brings a weary smile to my lips.

"You're right, and I appreciate the role they've played in my life."

"That's a good boy. Always good to appreciate what you have. I'd hate to see you back with the pigs." His light tone makes me smile even broader because we both know it's not entirely a joke. If he thinks I've lost perspective, he'd have my ass back in that barn in a heartbeat. Sure, I'm a grown man now, but that's how things work in the old country. If Uncle Lazaro orders you to the barn, you take your ass to the barn.

"Glad you called, Uncle. I'll do better to keep in touch."

"Eh, you're busy. I understand." He brushes off my comment, but only because he knows the message has been received.

"Talk to you soon. Give my love to Aunt Giulia."

"Ciao, Sante."

What a fucking day. I swirl the tart wine in my glass before taking a long drink. I'm past the point of savoring and ready to feel the potent liquid soothe my racing mind.

Once a pinkish residue is all that's left in the glass, I grab my keys and head out. I'm not sure where I'm going except away from temptation. I take a drive, expecting to use the time to cool off, but find myself parked outside a familiar building. A place I haven't been since the day I watched my father die and learned the extent of his treachery. Some thirty floors up, my sister Noemi and her husband live with their three kids—all born after I left the country.

In four years, she hasn't failed to inform me via email of their every milestone, even in recent months after the birth of her twin boys. She has to be exhausted keeping up with them, yet she never quits writing. I've refused her offers to visit. I've been slow to respond when I write. I've generally failed her in every way possible.

She is the one person I've struggled most to face.

Renzo isn't an issue. The problem is, if I talk to him, I'll have to talk to her, too. I've told myself every story under the sun about why there's no need to rush into it. Most prominently, I've relied on my desire for anonymity where Amelie is concerned. She can't get to know me without bias once our families are involved.

It's an excuse like all the others.

I could accomplish my goals with Amelie if she knew the truth about who I am. I simply don't want to. I don't want to mess with any of it, so I haven't.

It's been four years of avoidance, dickhead. Time to grow a pair.
I will.

I'm not a coward like my father. I *will* face the things I've done ... just not today. But soon.

11
Amelie

LINA AND I MAKE IT A PRIORITY TO MEET UP FOR LUNCH ABOUT once a week with our former nanny, Gloria. She was our de facto mom growing up and gave us the love our parents never did. I hate to think what a disaster our lives would be if we hadn't had her.

While Lina and I can see each other anytime since we live in the same building, Gloria still lives in the small apartment she's always lived in some twenty minutes away. Life gets busy. We want to make sure we set aside time to see her, thus, girls' lunch.

Today, we meet at a cute sandwich shop and have the pleasure of little Violet's company as well. Gloria and I both love when she tags along, but it makes lunch noticeably more harried for Lina. She assured me on our way over that she's feeling better since I saw her last. I'm glad, but I'll do my best to help with the little cutie and give Lina a break.

Once we've given Gloria hugs and are settled at our table, Lina gives Violet a cracker to gnaw on.

"She's getting so big," Gloria says with love creasing the corners of her eyes. "Reminds me so much of you girls when you were little."

Vi dangles the cracker over the floor and shoots a sly look at her mother. Lina gives her a warning rumble from the back of her throat.

Hearing my signal, I snatch the cracker and send Violet into a fit of giggles.

"You see her, Mama G. Surely we weren't that sassy as babies," Lina says with exasperation.

Gloria's head tips back as laughter bubbles up from deep in her chest. "Oh, mija. That's not sassy. That's just being a baby."

Violet slaps her hands on the table with a squeal of joy, then goes still, her face turning red with strain. No guesswork is needed to know she's making a mess of her diaper. Now I'm laughing hysterically with Gloria, and Lina's shaking her head but can't stop a smile from spreading across her face.

"Yup, just a baby," Gloria confirms.

"I don't mind changing her," I offer honestly.

"No, it's okay. Really. Won't take me but two minutes." Lina stands and collects her squirming bundle of joy, who is now proudly announcing "poo poo" to everyone in the restaurant.

"I wish I could be more help," I tell Gloria once Lina has disappeared to the back of the shop. "She has so much on her plate."

"Me, too, mija. If my sciatica didn't give me such trouble, I'd watch the little one more often for her."

"You do plenty, Mama G."

"At least you girls have one another. It's the one decent thing your mother did for you." Gloria knew our mother lacked maternal instinct but didn't know the true depths of her depravity until Mom took Gloria hostage to manipulate Lina. That was the day both my parents were killed. It needed to happen, but I'm glad I wasn't there to witness it like Lina and Gloria. I can't imagine how awful that would have been.

"I hadn't thought about it like that, but I suppose you're right." I can feel Gloria studying me, prompting me to look over at her. "What?"

"Are you taking care of yourself, Mellie girl? I think maybe you're practicing too much and not eating enough." Worry is etched in the furrowed creases of her forehead.

I smile reassuringly and squeeze her hand. "I promise I'm doing fine. We're practicing a lot, but that's because the show starts in less than three weeks."

"Yes! I'm so excited for you. Lina already got us tickets for opening night."

"I told you guys I could get you tickets."

She shrugs. "You know your sister. She wanted to do it herself."

I'm suddenly overwhelmed with love for my tiny family. Being surrounded by a thriving family tree of relations who offer a sense of belonging sounds very appealing, but what my family lacks in size, it makes up for in quality. I need to remember to be more grateful for my blessings rather than focus on what I lack. Like my ability to keep them safe and make them happy. Sometimes I forget that my choices aren't a burden but an honor.

If I can keep The Society at bay, I'll do it. Whatever the cost.

⟡

"Go home, goober. You've practiced enough," Hazel chides me as she packs up her sewing bag.

"I'm not staying long, promise." I raise my right hand with my pledge.

According to the director, the lighting crew will be working in the rafters for hours. I'll have people around, and the choreographer changed up a sequence of mine, so I'd feel better if I could get in a few repetitions while it's fresh in my mind.

"Good. No reason to wear yourself out before the show even starts."

"Thirty minutes max, Scout's honor."

She flicks a thumbs-up, then heads for the door. "Text me."

"Will do!"

I keep my word and stick to a short session focused on the new steps. While on stage, I feel the presence of someone watching, but several techs are moving around behind the scenes. It's hard to know where the sensation is coming from.

When I call it a night, I pause, letting my gaze scour the shadows at the back of the theater.

"Is someone there?" I call out, giving in to my need to know.

My question is met with silence until a voice with a heavy New York accent slices through the air from above. "You talkin' to me?"

It's so unexpected that my heart launches itself into my throat.

"Oh! No, sorry," I yell back, hand over the pounding in my chest.

I don't like this.

People are around me, but I can't see them. I can't tell who is supposed to be here and who may be a dangerous stalker. I need to leave, but I realize how poorly I've thought through this now that it's time to get my things and go outside. I was so concentrated on not being alone in the building that I hadn't put thought into how I'd get *out* of the building. I can call a cab, but that would still require me to walk outside alone. I've done that plenty of times before, but not since knowing the stalker followed me home.

Could he be waiting for me outside?

I stop near the thick velvet curtain and peer into the shadows toward the dressing room. What if he's waiting for me again? The lighting crew is around, but could they hear me from the dressing room if I yelled? How well soundproofed is it back there?

I can't do it.

Sticking around was a bad decision, and while I won't repeat the mistake, I need to find a way to safely get home, and not just a ride. I need someone to come into the theater and escort me out.

I give myself props for at least being smart enough to keep my phone with me. I move closer to the safety of the stage lights and call my sister.

"Guess I know what that diaper explosion was about earlier today," Lina says after our hellos. "Little Miss is running a fever. I think she has an ear infection."

It's hard to hear her over the wailing baby. My heart hurts for them both.

"Oh no! Poor thing."

"Yeah, and Oran is in Jersey on business for the night. I

got the family doctor on the phone, and she's going to come by sometime in the next hour. Hopefully, she has antibiotics with her, or it'll be a long, miserable night for both of us." The *family* doctor is the pediatrician the Byrnes pay to be on-call for house visits.

"I bet she gets you all taken care of," I assure her, striking Lina off my list of possible rides.

"Did you need something, or were you just calling to check in?"

"Just checking in. I'll let you go. Give my sweetie Vi lots of kisses."

"Will do. Wish me luck," she says with a sigh.

"You got this."

We end the call, and I consider who to turn to next. I could call one of Lina's sisters-in-law, but most of them have little ones, too. I'm probably closest to Stormy, but she's been having wicked morning sickness. With two other little ones to deal with, I hate to bother her or her husband.

I shoot a quick text to Hazel and confirm that she's already on a train out of the city. While I'm lucky enough to afford a spacious one-bedroom apartment in the center of Manhattan, most of the people I work with live very different lifestyles than me. It's yet another of the many differences that single me out from the people around me.

My disheartened gaze drifts to the faint remnants of numbers still inked on my inner wrist. I put Isaac's number in my phone already but couldn't bring myself to scrub away the evidence of one of the most erotic moments of my life.

Could I ask him for a ride? Wasn't that the whole reason he gave me his number? He said to call if I felt unsafe. Does this count, or would he think I'm being silly?

This is your safety. Who cares what he thinks?

Yeah, but texting him so soon after he gave me his number will send the wrong message.

What message is that? That you appreciate his help?

I was more worried about him thinking I'm desperate and alone.

My inner debate partner goes silent.

Okay, that's rude.

The truth hurts sometimes.

I scowl and send a text before I chicken out.

Me: Hey Isaac, it's Amelie. Any chance you could come get me at the theater?

Isaac: What's the address?

A breath I didn't know I was holding whooshes past my lips.

Me: I'm at the Metropolitan Opera House

Me: Thank you. I'm sorry to bother you.

Isaac: Wouldn't have given you my number if I didn't want you to use it.

Isaac: Your stalker show up?

I type out a phony explanation before erasing all but one word and hitting send.

Me: No

Isaac: Lie to me again, and I'll bend you over my knee.

I'm so stunned by his reply and embarrassingly turned on that it takes me a solid minute to respond.

Me: I'll find someone else to give me a ride.

Isaac: You ride anyone else, and you'll get worse than a spanking.

If my eyes rounded any wider, they'd fall right out of their sockets. It's the most presumptive, domineering thing a man has ever said to me, and I've never heard anything hotter. I shouldn't like it. I will never admit to him how his words have affected me, but I can't lie to myself. My core is so swollen with need that I can hardly keep from squirming.

The longer you wait to reply, he'll know what you're thinking.

I shake off my disbelief and text back my reply.

Me: THAT IS NOT WHAT I MEANT AND YOU KNOW IT

Isaac: Still applies. Be there in ten.

Holy freaking crap. What have I gotten myself into?

12
Sante

I was confident Amelie would use my number at some point, but I hadn't expected it quite so quickly. I'm relieved she's finally starting to take her safety seriously. One of these days, though, we'll have words about why she didn't report a stalker the very instant she suspected someone was watching her. I haven't pushed the issue, but I haven't forgotten, either.

I take a slow walk around the block to disguise the fact that my ass was already sitting in the theater when she texted. I wish I'd been able to see her face when she read my texts. I bet her expression was priceless. I like knowing I can rile her. She sure as fuck has the power to get under my skin more than she should.

When I round to the front of the building, she comes out to greet me before I have a chance to go inside.

"Let's talk," I say coarsely as I take her hand and move us to the brick wall beside the door. I make sure to position us so that I'm caging her in against the wall. She needs to know I'm not playing.

"When I ask you a question, I expect you to give me the truth."

"I wasn't exactly lying."

I level her with a withering stare.

"I didn't *see* anyone," she says in an attempt to weasel out of a reprimand. "And that man following me could have been a random creep off the street—that doesn't make him a stalker. I just realized I need to be a little more careful. You said to reach out, so I did." She widens her eyes in her best Bambi impression.

Fuck if it doesn't work.

She's still lying to me, but I can't be too upset. She did reach out and text, after all, and she hardly knows me. But she's hiding the fact that she has a stalker. I saw her sense my presence. She knew she was being watched, so why hide that fact? Why not admit to me someone's been watching her for weeks? It makes no sense.

Then it hits me.

Could this be a normal occurrence for her? Being on stage could draw all kinds of lunatics to fantasize about her. My fingers curl into tight, angry fists.

Better not be the fucking case because I'll carve out the eyes of anyone who steps a toe out of line.

"That sort of thing happen often?" I ask gruffly.

"Someone following me? No. Not at all."

I let a steadying breath out through my nose and place my hands on either side of her head. I let my body list forward until there's nothing but a breath of air between us. "Would you tell me if it did?"

"Probably not," she says on a hushed breath. "For all I know, you could be the biggest bad. You didn't even bat an eye about going after that man."

"I'm not afraid of a creep like that."

"Most people would be."

I bring my lips closer to her ear. "I'm not most people." I let the words draw out slowly. Seductively.

Her shuddering inhale of air presses her chest against mine. I have to pretend my palms are glued to the brick to keep from pulling her body flush with mine.

"So I've gathered. Who are you, Isaac? I don't even know your last name."

I pull back so that I'm gazing into her forested stare again. "My name won't tell you anything about the man I am."

"That punch told me plenty." She arches a perfectly sculpted brow. "You know how to fight."

"Lucky for you, since you have a stalker problem." A smug grin teases at my lips.

"I *don't* have a stalker problem," she repeats, this time more forcefully. "And even if I did, it wouldn't be any concern of yours." Her attempt to be firm with me is precious.

I lift my hand away from the wall and trail my knuckles gently down the side of her neck, around her shoulder, and down her arm until I reach her wrist. At my touch, her pulse point flits like a drunken butterfly. My hand encircles her wrist, so delicate and breakable, and lifts it between us so that the ink still marking her skin is visible. I use my other hand to trail my fingers over her porcelain skin.

"The second you chose me, you made it my concern," I explain in a voice ravaged with emotion.

"I chose you?" she asks, baffled.

I nod. "You did. You reached out to me when you could have called literally *anyone* else in the world."

"I tried others, but they were busy," she cuts in defensively, but the jab lacks strength. She knows it's an excuse as much as I do.

I lift her wrist to my lips and press three claiming kisses slowly along her flushed skin. "You chose me, Amelie. And that's a decision that can never be undone."

Her lips part in disbelief. She wants to argue, but I don't give her the opportunity. I twine my fingers in hers and guide us down the sidewalk toward my car. "Now that we have that settled, I'm taking you home."

I'M SITTING IN THE PASSENGER SEAT OF ISAAC'S GUNMETAL GRAY Mercedes before I collect myself to the point of formulating coherent thoughts.

I *chose* him? Can never be undone?

What did he mean by that? If Hazel had spoken those same words, I would have laughed and agreed that we were friends forever. I'm certain Isaac's intent wasn't remotely as lighthearted ... or platonic.

A cascade of tingles like twinkling starlight trickles from the top of my spine down my extremities. I wish I could say it's fear, but I know the thrill of excitement when I feel it. Isaac is trying to stake some sort of claim on me, and I'm not repulsed like I should be.

We hardly know one another.

He chased down a man on the sidewalk and probably broke the guy's face. He's covered in tattoos and gives new meaning to the word domineering. I should be *petrified*, but there was no mistaking the cloying need I felt when his lips left a trail of scalding kisses along my wrist. The heat from his touch was so intense, I'm surprised the skin didn't blister. My body's response to him isn't normal. I know I shouldn't feel this way, but I don't know how to stop it.

My fingers trace the impeccable stitching of the leather seat in an attempt to ground myself. It's a gorgeous car. Expensive. So's the apartment he lives in. His finances are the last thing I should focus on, yet that's what I do because everything else is so damn overwhelming.

"The car's brand new, isn't it?" I ask, taking in the exquisite high-end features. This thing cost a small fortune. Maybe even a large fortune.

"Got it last week."

My eyes finally cut over to him. He's devastatingly handsome behind the wheel—commanding in a casual way that oozes confidence.

"What do you do?" How does he make this sort of money? I'm pretty sure investment bankers don't show up to shareholder meetings with bloody knuckles and ink rising up past their collars and into their hairlines.

"I'm sort of between jobs right now. Trying to decide what path I want to take."

"You're lucky to have that sort of freedom." So maybe family money. I come from a similar situation, so I can't fault him for that.

We arrive at our apartment building quickly since it's not far from the theater. He stops out front and gives the keys to the valet service, who seem to know him well. I don't wait for him to open my door. This isn't a date. I don't know what it is, but I intend to find out soon enough.

Tension builds on our way through the lobby, thickening exponentially in the bright lights of the elevator. Once the escape route of my apartment door is within view, I force myself to say what needs to be said.

"Isaac, I know I reached out to you for a ride, but you can't read more into it than that."

His eyes light with what looks to be amusement. "Why not?"

"Because you can't assume what I'm thinking when you don't even know me." *You'll be in for a world of disappointment if you do.*

"I know you feel safe with me. You wouldn't have asked for a ride if you didn't." His tattooed fingers reach out to guide a strand of wayward hair back behind my ear. "And every time I touch you, your eyes dilate, and your entire body quivers with desire. That tells me plenty."

I want to stomp my foot because he sort of has a point. "But I'm more complicated than that. And maybe you feel like you know me, but you don't know everything, and I know *nothing* about you."

The glint in his eyes sharpens with ardent intensity. "Then give me a chance to show you."

"You haven't even told me your last name."

"That's meaningless. I said give me a chance to *show* you who I am. I'm not like any other man you've met before. I'm not easy to label or categorize. The only way to know me is to set aside your fears and expectations and see me as I am."

I'm at a total loss.

How do I argue with that? I feel crammed tightly between a rock and a hard place because I desperately want to tell him yes, but I don't see how I possibly can. He's the sort who will ferret out every last one of my secrets. He'll leave no stone unturned.

I can't allow that to happen, which means I have to find a way to keep him at bay.

"I have to think about it," I force past the rapidly swelling ball of emotions clogging my throat. "I need to go now." If I don't hurry, he'll see me cry, and I absolutely cannot let this man see me cry. "Thank you for the ride. I really do appreciate it." I punch in the code to my door and give him a quick smile over my shoulder before escaping inside, taking with me the snapshot memory of his face carved in determination.

I COME FULLY awake in the night, eyes open and senses alert, though I have no idea why until I detect that familiar sensation of being watched. At first, I wonder if I've had a hyper-realistic dream about my stalker. I'd been dwelling on my situation for hours when I finally gave in to sleep, so the feeling of fear could have stuck with me when I woke.

I lie perfectly motionless, straining to keep my breathing slow and steady while I get my bearings, but it doesn't take long to rule out the dream theory. I can feel his presence in my bedroom like the touch of a heavy fog coming off the bay. I have no idea how I know, but I'm certain I'm not alone.

Oh God. What do I do? Would it be best to pretend to sleep?

That might make me look like an easier target. Maybe showing him I'm awake will scare him away.

Or trigger an unwanted confrontation. Maybe he prefers a challenge.

Adrenaline spikes my heart rate and coats my skin in a sheen of sweat. I'm not sure what the right choice is, but I don't think I can lie here a second longer, regardless. I have to see. I have to face what's coming.

Heart pounding against the inside of my chest, I swiftly sit up with the covers pulled tightly against me. My gaze instantly locks on the dense shadow that doesn't belong. He's leaning against the wall by my bedroom door, unmoving.

He watches me, and I watch him.

I don't scream or panic like I know I should. I should be scavenging for a weapon or doing *something*. Anything besides serving myself up on a platter. But my body and mind are locked down in shock. The feeling is familiar, and I hate it.

Fight or flight—at least those show a person is trying to avoid harm.

Then there's the freeze instinct.

It's a totally normal reaction, though rarely talked about. And I think I know why. Because it feels pathetic. My body may think it's protecting me, but it's not. Freezing feels like the most worthless response possible. I'm not a deer hiding in a grassy fucking meadow, and I wish to God my brain would get that memo.

I can't force myself to move, so I scour the shadows for his face as though identifying my tormentor will somehow make him disappear.

It's no use, of course. He's as much a mystery now as before.

My lips part as though I might actually gain the wherewithal to do something. The man doesn't give me the chance. He peels himself away from the wall and slips soundlessly from the room. Proving myself as worthless as ever, I sit like a fucking bump on a log and listen to the quiet click of the front door closing.

What the *hell* is wrong with me?

A man was here in my bedroom while I was *sleeping*, and I did *nothing*.

My hands curl into furious fists. What little nails I have dig into my palms before I repeatedly pummel the mattress beneath me, tears blurring my vision.

What's it going to take for you to learn to defend yourself?

If I'm going to be so goddamn worthless, maybe I deserve what happens to me.

I have to clamp my hand over my mouth when a wave of nausea sends my stomach heaving.

I can't do this anymore. I can't.

My entire body begins to shake as I reach for my phone.

I have to report this. I have to. I can't continue to do nothing, especially now that I'm doubting The Society's involvement. My stalker is growing more and more brazen, and involving the police could make things worse, but at least I'll know I tried. I'll know that I did what I could to fight back.

I take a deep breath and dial 911.

Twenty minutes later, a fist pounds on my apartment door, followed by a deep voice announcing the arrival of the police. I grab a fleece blanket off the floor to wrap around myself and cover my thin tank top and panties before flipping on the lights and hurrying to open the door. I was confident the man was gone but couldn't force myself to leave my bed until reinforcements arrived.

"Ma'am, we got a report of an intruder." Two uniformed officers stand in the hallway. The one in the lead is young and decently attractive, while his partner looks close to retirement and likely coasting until his pension kicks in. He rocks back on his heels while his eyes drift down the hall.

"Yes, that's right. Please, come in."

"Are you alone here?" The officer's warm brown eyes scour the inside of my apartment.

I step aside to allow them in. "Yeah, it's just me."

He dips his chin. "How about we have a seat at the table, and you tell us what happened?"

I do as he suggests, a dizzying cocktail of relief and worry filling my veins. These guys seem genuine. I desperately want to believe they wear badges for the right reasons and that my decision to call them won't backfire in my face.

I give a basic rundown of what happened—waking up and seeing the man in my room. How we stared at one another, and then he left. Retelling the events makes me realize it sounds a little absurd.

The anxious pit in my stomach grows thorny barbs.

"So he didn't run when you woke up? He just stood there, then walked out, locking the door behind him somehow?"

I stare at the young officer blankly, realizing I did have to unlock the deadbolt to let them in. If the stalker could unlock the door, he could lock it when he left, but why would he? Once he was seen, wouldn't he make a getaway as quickly as he could?

"I dance on Broadway," I try to explain. "Lately, I've felt like someone's been watching me."

What if the stalker really was sent by The Society? What if they think you're calling attention to them?

A new wave of nausea roils through my stomach.

Unaware of my panic, the officer continues. "Can you tell me what they look like?"

"No, it's more of a feeling than anything." A lie because I'm not sure I should have said anything. I don't want this guy to think I'm crazy, but I don't want to stir up trouble either.

"And you think the person watching you was here in your apartment?"

"I think so. I don't know who else it'd be." I sound like a

paranoid lunatic, and I know they must be thinking the same when the two cops exchange a glance.

The older man, who has yet to say anything, finally speaks up. "Is there any chance the worry about this person watching you from the theater gave you a bad dream that felt real?"

I open my mouth to refute him, but nothing comes out.

It was real, wasn't it? Wouldn't I know the difference between reality and a dream?

I think about the conditioner and my crackers—the odd slips in my memory. Then I think back to the agonizing months when I had amnesia nearly five years ago. My brain had hidden my entire identity away from me, and I was helpless to access my own memories—emotions and thoughts and everything that makes me who I am—they were all gone. That experience taught me to never underestimate the power of the brain.

"I don't think so, but I understand what you're saying," I finally concede.

Hell, maybe it's best to lean into that theory, no matter what I think. Aside from questioning myself, I can't help but wonder if the older cop's suggestion that I was mistaken is actually a message. Could he be involved? Is he warning me to keep my mouth shut?

It's official. I'm completely losing my mind.

The handsome cop places a kind hand on mine, sensing my uncertainty. "Hey, it's much better to be safe than sorry. Don't worry about any of that, and just tell me a little more about this feeling of being watched."

I nod and then jump when three sharp knocks sound on my front door.

"Amelie?" Isaac's voice reverberates through the door.

I want to drop my head on the table and wish it all away. It's too much.

Isaac will insist on knowing what happened. I can't lie to him with the cops in the room. Once he learns the stalker was here, he'll be that much more persistent. I'll never be able to put distance between us.

But there's little to be done about it now.

I've tipped over that first domino. All I can do is wait and see how they fall.

14

Sante

I MUST HAVE WALKED BACK AND FORTH TO MY DOOR AT LEAST A dozen times before finally deciding to go next door. Making an appearance with cops present could make a mess of everything and is 100 percent an emotional decision. I know why they've come. I don't necessarily *need* to check on Amelie, except that I do. The urge to be in there with her while some asshole cop questions her is so overpowering that my muscles literally twitch from the strain of holding myself back.

That whole be-careful-what-you-ask-for bullshit is true. I've been concerned about her reluctance to call the cops when she's in danger. I'm glad she did it, and if I wasn't so fucking obsessed with her, a visit by some overweight donut pusher wouldn't be an issue. But I'm too far gone to let her deal with this alone. I need to be there.

When the door finally opens, a uniformed officer stands on the other side. He's young but confident, immediately engaging me in a stare down. The manufactured bravado most cops flaunt usually flickers with insecurity when they face me, but this guy is steady and cool. His brand of unruffled self-control is the sort that can cause real problems.

"Can I help you?" he finally asks.

"I'm Amelie's neighbor. I heard you guys knocking and wanted to make sure she was okay."

The guy has the balls to narrow his eyes. Suspicion. If only he knew how right his instincts are.

"It's fine, you can let him in," Amelie calls from somewhere behind him.

That's right. Back off, fucker.

The sentiment flashes in my eyes, and he reads it loud and clear but is still slow to step aside.

I cross to where Amelie sits at her dining table and cup her chin to bring her eyes to mine. "You okay?" The contact eases the tension in my chest.

"Yeah, I think I just got confused. Bad dream felt too real."

Her eyes flee from mine, prompting me to release my hold on her. That dissipated tension cinches back into a tight knot. What the hell does she mean a bad dream? I know she doesn't believe that because she's avoiding eye contact—amateur lying tell number one.

The cops probably think she's embarrassed, but I know better. She was wide-awake when I left her bedroom and knows damn well there was an intruder. That's why these pencil pushers are here. So why the change of heart? Why claim the incident was a dream when it wasn't?

I certainly can't challenge her and reveal my part in this. The hotshot cop seems to be taking his role very seriously, though I'd say that has a lot more to do with Amelie's big green eyes than his concern about an intruder. The only one of us in the room with any sort of transparency is the overweight asshole eyeing a bag of cookies on the kitchen counter.

"Seems Ms. Brooks might have had an intruder while she was sleeping. You didn't happen to hear anything or see anyone suspicious recently?" Hotshot asks, eyes boring into me.

"Not until I heard you banging on her door. There was someone in here?" I turn my question to Amelie, who stands and fidgets with the blanket wrapped around her.

"No, I was about to explain to Officer Malone that I'm more and more convinced it was a false alarm. I've been spending too much time working lately, and the fatigue got to me."

Why is she backing out? Who or what is she scared of? Was she already having doubts before I came over, or has my appearance played a role in her change of attitude?

The whole time she gives her rushed explanation, Officer Hotshot's eyes bore into me. He didn't like me swooping in, and all I can surmise is that he had designs on what's mine. He has no reason to suspect me as the intruder. If not that, then why the open animosity?

He wants to play the hero, but as far as I'm concerned, he might as well be a mosquito flattened beneath my palm.

"If you truly believe that's the case," he says, "we'll let you get back to your night. But I'd like to have a private word before we go." He motions to the front door.

"Of course," Amelie readily agrees and joins him at the door. Fuck if Officer Hotshot doesn't guide her out with a hand pressed to the small of her back, and to top it off, he glares over his shoulder at me.

I draw deep from my reserves to keep control of myself because I've never wanted to kill a man more.

That's not true.

One man will always hold that dubious honor for me. No one could ever top the murderous rage I felt for my father when I learned the truth about him. This guy's gunning for a close second.

Tweedledum follows his partner into the hallway, leaving me alone in the apartment.

329 seconds.

That's how long I stare daggers at the door until it finally reopens. Amelie offers repeated thanks to the officers coupled with an apology and a final goodbye. Once the door is shut, she leans against it and sighs heavily.

"He warn you away from me?" I know the answer, but I'm curious to hear what she says.

"No, he was just being cautious." She pulls away from the door and wanders into the kitchen. "Want some hot chocolate? I think it's a hot chocolate kind of night," she murmurs in a weary voice.

I slowly amble after her, enjoying the view as the blanket she's draped around her relaxes lower. "Man didn't need to have his hands on you to ask you a few questions. I'd say he was overstepping his bounds."

She gets a packet of cocoa from a box and shoots me a look on her way to get milk from the fridge. "He's a cop trying to do his job."

"And you're naive if you think that's all he was trying to do."

"Even if he was, it's none of your business. It's not like

we're in a relationship." Her words take on an edge, energized by her frustration.

She's not the only one riding that train. This is the second time she's tried to put up walls between us in less than a day. I fucking hate it. I'm glad her body responds to mine, but I want the whole package. I want Amelie Brooks to feel as helpless without me as I feel without her.

It's time she understands where I'm coming from.

I close the distance between us as she reaches up into a cabinet for a mug on the top shelf. She stills as my body aligns with hers. I use the momentary distraction to reach above her and retrieve a mug, relishing the feel of her small frame pressed against me. I want to wrench the blanket out from between us, but the tease of what's beneath will have to suffice for now. I'm still able to feel her body shiver when I bring the mug down to the counter. With my arms curved around her, I remove the lid from the milk and pour some into the mug.

"Sorry to burst your bubble, but that's not how this works. You chose me. I chose you. We haven't fucked, but that's only because I want you to get to know me first. We can skip ahead, though, if it means you start to understand that you're *mine*."

15
Amelie

I WHIRL AROUND TO FACE HIM, TOO STUNNED TO CONSIDER HOW close we'll be. If I wasn't already off-balance, falling into his stare has me disoriented.

My thoughts struggle to catch up from intruders to questions from cops, now Isaac claiming we're … what? Boyfriend and girlfriend? It sounds absurd.

"We haven't even gone on a date."

I could have said a million different things to contradict Isaac's assertion that I'm his, and somehow *that* is what I lead with. Thank God I'm not a courtroom lawyer. My clients would be royally screwed. But it's not entirely my fault. Isaac's lips are so dang close, I can't stop staring at them, imagining what it would be like to feel them pressed against mine.

This is one thousand percent not how a healthy relationship begins. I may not have had great role models in that arena, but I've spent a lot of time daydreaming about my happily ever after, and not once did it unfold like this. I want healthy and nurturing—something based on friendship and not merely physical desire. But the girl in me who only ever wanted her family to want her is completely drunk on the idea that this man is desperate to have me.

Would it be so bad to test the waters?

Maybe! He could be dangerous!

The entire freaking world is dangerous for me, and so far, he's the one person who's tried to help.

"We'll get there, but in the meantime, I can't be worrying about whether you're letting another man touch you." His hand cups the back of my neck, bringing his lips just shy of touching my own. He's so close I can smell the mint on his breath. "There are only two things I'll ask of you—loyalty and honesty—because that lays a foundation of trust. Everything else is negotiable. Set aside whatever worries you have and answer this. While we sort this out, can you be loyal and honest?"

His request is so earnest—so honorable—how can I say no?

My lungs have quit working what feels like ages ago. All I can do is command myself not to overthink this and nod.

"Now, I'm going to ask you one more question. I expect the truth, Amelie. Why didn't you tell the cop you have a stalker?"

The question is so unexpected that my eyes widen and my mind blanks.

"Who says I didn't?"

His hand at the back of my neck tightens a smidge in warning. "The *truth*, Amelie. You give me the truth, or I call them back and tell them everything."

Crap! How is this man so freaking observant?

He's worse than a dog with a bone—repeatedly poking in the one area I need him to ignore. There's no time to fabricate an explanation. Besides, I've barely slept, and his proximity has scrambled what little brain power I might have at this late hour.

Who knows, maybe the truth is exactly what I need. Hearing how screwed up my life has been would scare off most anyone. I keep that stuff to myself for more than one reason. Primarily because I prefer not to dwell on the past. But a close second is my fear of people's reactions. In this case, however, giving Isaac a reason to reconsider his interest in me would be a good thing. If I give him a peek at what's behind the curtain, and he decides to retreat, then I can strike him off my worry list.

And if he doesn't run?

I'm not sure, but I think ... I think I might like to find out.

I nod again, this time to myself, then take the first big risk I've taken in four years.

"I know it sounds crazy, but there was a secret group here in the city called The Society," I begin in nearly a whisper. "They were the very worst sort of people you could imagine—power and wealth and horrible depravity. My parents were involved in the group. They were members before they died. Since then, the group has been dismantled, but I prefer to stay off the radar, just in case." Dismantled but not gone. I know of at least one man who still carries their torch.

"And you think talking with the police could bring you to their attention?" He doesn't even question the veracity of my seemingly outlandish claim, which, in a deplorable show of hypocrisy, leaves me wondering about his sanity.

"They don't even exist anymore. It's a precaution more than anything." My attempt to gloss over the situation goes unnoticed.

"Why would you even ping their radar? What interest would they have in you?" His hands clamp around my upper arms while his penetrating stare attempts to dissect me piece by piece.

In response, I press my hands against his chest to give myself some breathing room, but he refuses to budge.

"I'm paranoid, okay? Is that what you want to hear?"

"I want to hear the *truth*, goddammit."

"That *is* the truth, and it's more than I've told anyone else. You say you chose me, but you don't even know what that means." Frustration swells into anger, sharpening my words. "Everything about me is complicated, so if you don't like that, then great, you can leave. Better for you to figure it out now."

Better now than after I've fallen for you.

I leave that part unspoken because it feels too vulnerable. I can't tell him more than I already have—it's too dangerous. And my duty to keep my family safe is far more important than appeasing his sense of curiosity.

When he remains silent, I slowly return my gaze to his, silently pleading for him not to give up on me. Pleading for him to be the man I need him to be.

His eyes glint like shards of black onyx. "You have no idea how committed I am. If you did, you'd be the one running."

It sounds like a warning, but I can't see how being committed to someone could be a bad thing. The thought of having someone at my back, no matter how rough the seas—

someone who regards me above all others—sounds like a dream, not a nightmare.

"I'm not going anywhere so long as you don't give me a reason to," I whisper.

His hands cup my face as his body once again presses against mine. "Tell me you won't let another man touch you." His words are raw with desperation. "So long as I don't give you a reason to leave, I need to know that this—" His thumb tugs lights at my bottom lip before his knuckles trail gently down my throat and chest until his hand cups my breast. "And this—"

I gasp when his thumb intentionally swipes across my straining nipple, only now realizing I must have dropped my blanket somewhere along the line. I'm so lost in the feel of his touch that I'm practically panting when his palm cups my sex over my panties.

"And every delicious inch of this ... is *mine*." His forehead comes to rest against mine, his eyes pressing tightly shut. "Jesus, you're wet for me already."

I watch in fascination as his eyes pop back open with an intensity that borders on madness. "Tell me, Amelie. I need to hear you say it."

I've fantasized about how it would feel for someone to look at me with the same degree of unguarded desire as I see in Isaac's stare. Like I am the center of his entire universe. Surely, no greater feeling exists.

I would give him everything in my possession if it meant I could bask in this glow for a moment longer. The promise of monogamy is hardly any price at all.

"I won't let anyone else touch me. Only you." The words tumble from my lips as though they've been perched there for days, waiting for their cue.

Isaac's lips crash against mine.

It's so unexpected that I gasp and stiffen before melting into his arms.

This man only knows the tip of the iceberg in regard to my crazy life, but he didn't run, and I'm overwhelmed with dizzying relief. The heady taste of his tongue swiping against mine has my eyes rolling back in my head. I have to cling to him to keep myself upright.

Isaac doesn't kiss. He devours.

The ravenous intensity of his lips moving against mine makes me feel like the greatest treasure in the world. Like there is no world without me in it.

I'm instantly addicted.

When he pulls away, I have to fight back a swell of panic in my chest.

"I know I said I'd only ask those two things of you, but I have one more to add."

My defenses are too intoxicated from his kiss to raise an alarm. I peer up at him with a lopsided smile. "What's that?"

"Swear to me that you'll tell me if this Society contacts you? If you feel in danger in any way."

"Okay," I breathe, in awe that he took me at my word about The Society. As though my safety is of more importance to him than validating my claims of a threat.

If that's not devotion, I don't know what is.

"You know," he continues, his voice dropping an octave. "There are other ways to handle issues like that. Ways that don't involve the police." He makes the comment casually, like tossing a bit of bread onto the surface of a lake to see if it floats.

I know what he's implying, but I'm stunned that he'd offer such a suggestion when we've spent so little time together. My sister's husband is Irish mob. I know a whole subset of people who live outside the law. Could he be one of them? Or is he simply taking inspiration from movies without any real knowledge of how these things work? I didn't want to make assumptions about his menacing appearance, but having a criminal association would track, and it would explain why he wouldn't scrutinize the existence of The Society.

Maybe he's the answer I've prayed for.

Even my inner voice whispers the thought, afraid to hope.

I've been burned so many times by life that I can't jump blindly. I can give him a chance to prove himself, but that's the best I can offer, no matter how tempting it may be to finally not feel so alone.

"Who are you, Isaac?" I ask quietly. His answer threatens to bring me to my knees.

"I'm the man who's going to keep you safe."

16
Sante

I'M NOT SURE WHAT WAS BETTER—THE FEEL OF HER WETNESS soaking her panties or the words "only you" on her perfect pink lips. And her taste. *Jesus Christ*, the honey taste of her kiss had me starved for more.

I can't fathom how no one else has locked down this woman and claimed her. That's simply more evidence that she was made for me. I've never been more certain of anything in my life.

The trick will be convincing her of the same.

While the walls between us have thinned, they started out thicker than the Great Wall of China. What I'd like to do is toss a stick of C-4 at the damn thing. It's tempting, but it'd make a holy mess of everything. I have to earn her trust. At least now, I have someplace to start.

I've heard of The Society. Amelie's brother-in-law infiltrated their organization before I left for Sicily. I heard after I left that members were picked off one at a time until nothing was left, but I'll have to get more specific details. At the time, it wasn't relevant. I wish I'd paid more attention. I want to know every goddamn thing there is to know about the group and why Amelie is so terrified of them when they're supposed to be nonexistent.

She's blaming paranoia, but I don't buy it.

I watched her every movement for two whole weeks. She didn't show a single sign of delusional paranoia. Whatever has her running in fear is very real, and if I can't get her to trust me with the truth, I can't keep her safe.

Gaining her physical surrender won't be an issue. Her body is already attuned to mine and primed for submission. But that's not enough. I need every part of her. If I'm going to lose my fucking mind over a woman, I'm not settling for scraps. I will own all her hopes and fears—her secrets will be *my* secrets—and she will be my purpose on this earth. That's where this madness has taken me. Nothing else seems to exist beyond my need for Amelie.

How ironic that she expects me to run scared.

She couldn't get rid of me if she wanted to. Granted, I plan to ensure it never comes to that. I'll lure her in slowly, convincing her to rely on me until she can't find her way without me. And I won't feel a lick of guilt because she'll know the devil at her side when she finally relinquishes her soul.

Until then, however, I have to stick to the plan. That included ending our kiss in a way that left us both wanting. I need her to be fixated on what might come next, unable to focus on anything else.

Maybe then she'll have a tiny idea of what it's like to be me.

17
Amelie

Officer Malone reached out midmorning to ask if I could come to the station. He didn't give a reason for his request except to make sure I didn't forget anything in the heat of the moment. I'd rather break both my big toes than go down to the police station, but I don't want to draw any more attention to myself than I already have.

I force a banana into my queasy stomach and trudge to the station. Each step is more cumbersome than the last, and when I finally arrive, I'm certain I've made a horrible mistake. However, before I can chicken out and escape, a young officer escorts me through a station packed with cops.

My brain knows none of them are paying me any attention. My fears claw at my heels and hiss in my ears that they're all watching me. Keeping tabs. I have to train my eyes on the floor in front of me to keep from bolting back out the front door.

"Ms. Brooks, I'm so glad you were able to come by. Please, have a seat." Officer Malone smiles broadly beside a desk and motions to an empty chair. He's even more handsome in the light of day. His sandy-brown hair is neatly styled to the side, and his perfectly pressed uniform gives the impression that he takes his job seriously. He seems wholesome and genuine.

I don't like it, and I don't even know why.

Hello, paranoia, my old friend.

"Please, call me Amelie." I return his greeting with a warm smile. I need to convince him that I'm not in any danger and the whole incident was a silly mistake.

"I hope you were able to get some rest last night."

"I did. If anything, I felt embarrassed for getting worked up over nothing."

"Not at all." He holds up a hand to stop me. "That's what we're here for. I'd much rather make sure you're okay than sit around this stuffy station bored all night."

My cheeks flush with heat. "That's very kind of you to say."

"It's the truth. Though, I'll admit I had more than one reason to ask for this visit today." He shifts forward, resting his arms on the desk and leaning toward me as though preparing to say something confidential.

A whirlpool of nerves swirls in my stomach. Is he about to hit on me? Was Isaac right about ulterior motives? Or maybe Malone looked into my past. Could The Society have gotten to him?

A frenzy of questions buzzes through my head as I try not to let my smile falter.

"Oh, and what would that be?"

"I looked up your neighbor on the Department of Finance's property assessments website last night. You said his name was Isaac, but are you aware that apartment is owned by a Mr. Gentry Sorrell, who has been claiming that address as his homestead for the past four years?"

"Sort of. Mr. Sorrell used to live there, but he sold it to Isaac, who moved in last week."

He does a slow nod as if in understanding, but his eyes narrow in a contradicting gesture. "I'm afraid I didn't get Isaac's last name while I was there."

Why is he so fixated on Isaac? When we stepped into the hallway before the officers left last night, Malone asked whether I felt safe around Isaac. I could tell he was suspicious and did my best to reassure him that my neighbor wasn't a threat. Apparently, I wasn't convincing enough.

"I actually don't know his last name," I admit.

"He sure acted like he knew you well. How is it you don't know his full name?"

"Like I said, he's only lived there a week. We've only spoken a few times."

"So you don't actually know him at all. Generally, home invasions are often perpetrated by people known to the homeowner. Is there any chance he could be behind it?"

I can't suppress a frustrated sigh. This whole thing would be so much easier if I could simply explain about my stalker and how Isaac punched the guy, which would make it awfully hard for them to be one and the same. But that would force me to tell Officer Malone more than I'm comfortable sharing. If The Society wasn't already watching my every move, they certainly would be after a report is filed about me being followed. Reporting a random break-in is one thing. I'm not pushing my luck by making an even bigger deal out of it.

"I totally get why you'd be worried about that, but I promise you, Isaac did *not* break into my place." This time, I can speak with absolute sincerity, and he must hear the conviction in my tone because he visibly relaxes.

"Alright, then. I just have one other matter I'd like to ask about. You rent your apartment?"

Not what I'm expecting, I stare dumbly for a second before answering. "Ah, no. It's not a rental."

His lips tug down into a frown. "You don't own the place either, though, do you?"

"No, I believe it's in the name of my brother-in-law."

"Oran Byrne's your brother-in-law?" he asks warily.

Every hair on the back of my neck stands on end.

"Yes, he's married to my sister, Lina."

Mark that in the books as a win for paranoia.

Here, I'd scolded myself for being skeptical about the intentions of a genuinely nice guy when he had ulterior motives the whole time. In the span of a few minutes, a friendly visit shifted into an interrogation. I'm suddenly intensely aware that we're not in a private office, allowing our conversation to be overheard by anyone passing by.

Again, Officer Malone leans forward, this time speaking in a whisper. "You know what that Byrne family is into?"

My spine stiffens as every protective instinct I have goes on high alert. "What I know is that I love my sister, and if you have concerns about her husband, you should talk to him directly. Now, if we've covered everything, I need to get going." I stand and nod, not waiting for his dismissal before making my exit.

I don't mean to make a scene, but my claws come out where Lina's concerned. I power through the station entrance with enough adrenaline in my veins to get me through a marathon. I'm so hyped up, in fact, that I don't notice I have company until a hand takes hold of my arm.

"What the—?" I yank free and honest-to-God put my hands up like I'm going to karate chop whoever touched me.

"Amelie, it's me," Isaac says smoothly. "No need to pull out the big guns."

My wide eyes drop from his smirking smile to my Kung Fu hands. I instantly drop them to my sides and scowl at him. "Jerk, you scared the crap out of me."

"Hey, if anyone has a right to be annoyed, it's me."

"*What?*" Disbelief has my voice hitting an all-new high. "Why? What did *I* do?"

He holds out his hand for me. When I don't immediately take it, he waits with an arched brow until I cave, then leads me to an alcove between buildings. We aren't entirely out of sight, but it's better than having a private discussion smack in the middle of the sidewalk.

Hands on my hips, I signal for him to explain.

He moseys closer, forcing me back against the stone wall behind me. "Thought we agreed if there was a problem, you'd call me."

"Yes, and that's still the plan."

"If there wasn't a problem, why've you been chatting up Officer Hotshot in the station for the past half an hour?"

I start to answer, then clamp my jaw shut, my gaze cutting toward the police station, then back to Isaac. "Wait, did you know I was *here?*"

"I know all kinds of things. What I don't understand is *why* you're here." He brings his lips to my face and places one agonizingly slow kiss after another along my jaw. "If there aren't any problems, then I have to wonder—" He places two more kisses down my neck. "If you had other reasons."

I'm trying to listen and hold on to my outrage, but the feel of his lips on my skin and the scent of his spiced cologne spiked with a hint of mint have my thoughts disappearing in a hazy fog.

"He called me ... asked me to come in," I manage, my voice low and breathy.

"He try to hit on you?" he murmurs against my skin where my neck meets my shoulder.

"No, he asked questions about you ... and my family."

Isaac pulls back, his gaze meeting mine. "This body is mine—you haven't forgotten, right?"

I've told him the police were asking questions about him, yet the only thing he can think about is me. I know that's probably not healthy. My heart doesn't care in the slightest. It's doing backflips in my chest that this gorgeous man isn't worried about anything but making me his. It's an amazing feeling, but I have to be smart. What I say and do now sets an expectation for things to come.

"I haven't forgotten, Isaac," I say softly. "But you can't be following me. It's not right, and it makes it hard for me to trust you."

"How can I keep you safe if I don't know where you are?"

I bite back my reply that it's not his job to keep me safe because I know that won't go over well. "What if I'm more transparent about where I'm at? Send a text before I'm out and about?"

"You going to text to let me know if you're being assaulted or abducted?"

Uncertainty draws my lips to a frown. "No, but there's not much we can do if that happens. You can't follow me around twenty-four seven."

"True, but one thing would ease my mind. I wouldn't worry so much if you shared your GPS location with me. That way, I know I can find you if something does go wrong."

To anyone else, the suggestion would probably seem like a massive invasion of privacy, especially considering we've only recently met. But this is me—the girl who was kidnapped and ended up lost with amnesia. The idea of being tethered to someone sounds reassuring instead of stifling.

"Okay," I say quietly.

"Really?" he asks with a touch of wariness. I get the sense he prepared for an argument.

"Yeah. I'm not going anywhere I shouldn't be," I tease, "so if it eases your mind and keeps me safe, then you can track my location." I get out my phone and scroll to my contacts. When I find Isaac, I choose to share my location. "There. All done."

"I appreciate that, but I had something better in mind." He raises his hand, a gold chain dangling from his fingers. It's small—a bracelet—and it has a beautiful evil eye engraved on a round medallion in the middle. "Real protection from the monsters," he says in a low, seductive tone that has warmth pooling deep in my belly.

I'm stunned—at the gesture and at the fact that he remembered my words.

"It's beautiful. I don't know what to say." I watch his fingers deftly unclasp my old bracelet and replace it with the new one.

"You don't have to say anything. Just hand me your purse."

I do as he says, too dumbfounded to ask questions. He drops the old bracelet inside, then digs down to the bottom. Embarrassment flushes my cheeks. I'm about to fuss at him to stop when his hand resurfaces with a silver disk.

"Purses can be left behind. The bracelet is a much safer bet."

"Is that ... were you already tracking me?" I gape at him incredulously.

"You told me you were fine with it."

"Starting *now*. I didn't know you were already tracking me."

"Why would yesterday be any different from today?" he asks as though he genuinely sees no difference.

"It's different because I've only known you for a week. Each day makes a big difference. I'm allowed to be a little freaked out." I thought I was being incredibly understanding, but he's even pushing my limits.

His eyes narrow a fraction. "Not gonna apologize for keeping you safe."

"Locking me in a tower would keep me safe, but it would also make you the villain," I say with exasperation.

Isaac stares at me intently, his hand lifting to trace warm knuckles along my jaw in a featherlight touch. "This feel like something a villain would do?"

"No." I have to swallow before I can get the word out. "But it sounds like something a villain would say."

The corners of his lips twitch. "You're learning."

"What does that mean?"

"It means plenty of people would label me their enemy, but you'll never be one of them." Something so archaic and absolute flashes in his eyes that the air leaves my lungs in a whoosh. He carries on, however, as if some sort of wordless blood oath didn't just pass between us. "That cop of yours—why was he asking about your family?"

"What? Oh ... just general questions." I'm going to end up with whiplash if he keeps changing subjects like he does. He's got me more off-balance than I was when I got my first pair of pointe shoes.

"You said your family was part of this secret society. I

gather from what you've learned that you're worried the group has ties to the police. Is there any chance this guy could be one of them?" Suddenly, we're venturing into deep waters. I need to steer us back to dry land.

"No." I shake my head adamantly. "And besides, that's not the family he was asking about."

"Who was he asking about?"

I realize my mistake too late. "Please, don't worry about it. You want me to trust you—" I hold up my wrist to show him the bracelet. "I have. I'm wearing your tracker, aren't I? The least you can do is trust me in return. I'm telling you to leave it alone." Our locked stares go to battle.

"Fuck, you're stubborn," he grumbles.

"Like looking in a mirror, isn't it?"

He shakes his head as though exasperated, but I can see the humor glinting in his eyes. Seeing his amusement makes me feel like I can fly. Like a wall of stormy clouds has parted so that sunshine can paint a miraculous rainbow across the sky.

I never knew it was possible for two people to affect one another on such a molecular level. I've dated before. Nothing overly serious, but I've yet to reach leper status. This thing between me and Isaac is different. It has a life of its own.

I suppose that's why I don't fault him for moving so quickly. I feel the pull as strongly as he does. It's a raging river sweeping us along in its powerful current. I want to believe it will lead us to tropical new shores more beautiful than I can imagine, but it's equally as likely to drown us both in its treacherous depths. One thing's for certain—there's no going back.

18
Amelie

"You have plans for Mother's Day?" The female voice penetrates the thick velvet curtain beside me. I've decided to stretch before heading home, so I'm sitting out of sight to be out of the way. Practice is essentially over for me since I'm not in the scene they're working on, but I'm in no particular rush to get home and deal with my Isaac situation.

"Just going to relax," another voice responds. "My parents are in Seattle, so we'll have to settle for a video chat. What about you?"

"Mom's coming in from Providence. We're gonna do brunch. It'll be good, but a day on the sofa would have been divine."

"Same. I don't know how Amelie does it. That girl is up here practicing *all* the time."

I was only half listening at first. Now, the two women have my full attention.

"She doesn't have a life, that's how. Bet I know what her Mother's Day plans are," the voice adds snidely.

"Yeah, doubt she can stay away from this place. She practically lives here. I could have gotten the lead too if I was psycho-obsessed."

They're jealous. That's what this is about. I got a principal role, and they didn't. I know that's at the root of the catty comments, yet I still feel the knife's blade wedged in my back. The part that stings the most is that they're right. I don't have a life. Not really.

Dance is my world. It doesn't ask questions or look at me strangely when I can't stand the TV on. Dance doesn't judge or ask anything of me. Dancing is happiness—is that so wrong?

Done listening to the criticism, I go back to the dressing room, where I find Hazel sitting on the floor in front of a mound of scraps.

"Whatcha doing?" I ask, joining her on the floor.

"Trying to organize this mess." She glares at the beautiful glittering heap as if expecting it to move on its own.

"You planning on using the Force?"

She barks out a laugh, her eyes brightening as they find mine. "I wish. I don't even know where to begin."

"I'll help. How about we pull out all the ribbon to start?"

"Sounds good. Any trim can go in that pile, too." She holds up a length of delicate pink lace, then continues sifting. "You going to see Gloria this weekend for Mother's Day?"

"I'm not sure. I've been invited to a lady's brunch with

Lina and her crew. If I have time after, I may run by to see her."

"Who is Lina's crew?"

"The Byrne ladies."

Hazel looks at me quizzically. "That's your family, right?"

"It's *her* family. I'm not sure I'd call it mine."

"You guys are so close, though…" Her voice lifts as though asking a question.

"We're closer than we were, but an eleven-year age difference and living apart most of our lives always made her feel more like a cousin than a sister. Don't get me wrong—I love her more than anyone in this world. Except for little Violet, of course … but don't tell Lina I said that." I tease with a mischievous grin, hoping to keep things light.

It's hard to explain my relationship with my sister. I trust her implicitly, yet I tell her very little. In part because I spent the first seventeen years of my life keeping things to myself, but also because of the guilt. I've already put her through so much that I hate to burden her with more worries. And now that she is maxed out with Violet, I'd feel horrible to pile more on her shoulders. She'd be absolutely decimated if she knew the secrets I've kept.

"I forget that you were sort of an only child. It seems so foreign to me not to grow up with your siblings. We practically lived on top of one another." A smile peeks like a ray of sun from behind her stormy words, diminishing their effect.

"I was definitely on my own, and to this day, I'm not very good at opening up. I don't know if I genuinely prefer to be on my own, or if I'm just really bad at meeting people."

"You made friends with me!" she offers as evidence otherwise.

"No, *you* made friends with *me*," I correct her playfully.

"And I adore you for it. If there weren't people like you to pick up strays like me, we'd never find friends."

"Psh, you would, too. It just might take a bit of effort. Fortunately, there *are* people like me out there to make it easier." A giddy grin splits her face. "You know, I could always set you up with my brother."

"Actually," I start hesitantly, "I've sort of started talking to someone. My new neighbor."

Her jaw drops. "I. Need. Deets. Like yesterday."

I laugh, my cheeks heating. "There's not much to tell, I promise. It's still new."

"Girl, you best not be holding out on me."

"I swear—"

Our conversation is interrupted when one of the dancers bounds through the door and nearly trips over us in her rush to get where she's going.

"Crap, didn't see you. Sorry!" Kennedy, a girl with noticeably more cleavage than your average ballerina, stops at the closest mirror and checks her makeup. "The most gorgeous man I've ever seen is out front watching rehearsal. Pete's talking to him now, but if he's still there when I go back out, I'm so getting a piece." She tugs at her boobs to make sure they're amply displayed at the top of her corseted tutu, then runs back out of the room.

Hazel and I exchange a wide-eyed stare, then burst into laughter.

"What was that all about?" I ask, not expecting an answer.

"Maybe a producer?"

I shrug. "Not sure, but I have to admit, she's got me curious."

"Same, girl. Let's get these piles in separate bags, then go have a look."

A few minutes later, we've cleaned up the scraps and are

making our way toward the stage. When we peer out from behind the curtain, I see Isaac standing in the aisle talking to our director. And they're not alone. Kennedy has joined them and is laughing flirtatiously with her hand resting on Isaac's arm. He's smiling down at her. I've never seen him smile like that—so devilish yet charming.

I feel a chaotic impulse to do something. To scream or run and hide, maybe both. Anything to stop the cavernous ache from prying my chest wide open.

God, I *hate* this.

I hate that she's everything I'm not—bubbly and outgoing and inviting. I hate how jealous I feel. I hate that I can't simply be her. That I couldn't have had normal parents with normal hobbies who didn't make life hell for me, even after their deaths.

"Okay, she wasn't wrong. That man is scrumptious," Hazel says under her breath, eyes still glued to Isaac.

And I am nobody.

No life. No purpose beyond dancing.

Here I was, worrying about keeping Isaac at a distance as though there's any real threat of him sticking around. How delusional am I? A man as enigmatic as him will get bored of me in no time. He won't want my hot mess express, and I certainly shouldn't want him for a myriad of reasons.

That's quite the shift from wanting to keep him at arm's length.

It's the truth, though. I don't know what I've been thinking entertaining the possibility of a relationship with him. It was never going to happen.

A hailstorm of shame, regret, frustration, and pain pummels my insides. I want to lash out to keep the horrible feelings at bay even though this is for the best. Let him flirt. Let him find someone else who's much more likely to satisfy his needs. He's bound to be disappointed in me eventually—

ending things now will save us both the trouble of an awkward breakup.

In fact, I'll get the ball rolling. Why delay the inevitable?

I fight the tears burning the backs of my eyes and cross the stage to where Andrey is talking to another cast member. He's a highly celebrated dancer from Russia, though he's been in the States long enough that he only has the hint of an accent. His technique is flawless. I've been incredibly lucky to work with him as my co-lead in this production. But right now, I only have one use for him.

"Andrey, sorry to interrupt," I say with an apologetic smile.

"No problem, we're pretty much done here." He nods at the other male dancer, who says his goodbyes and heads back to the men's dressing room.

"I can't shake the feeling that my angel lift timing is off in the diamond scene. Do you have a minute to run through it with me before we go?"

"Of course. Do you need the music?"

"No. I think it would be helpful without."

He nods, then pulls me close. "We take it from the cabriole."

Ballet sculpts the body in muscle like no other pursuit. Andrey feels like he could be carved from stone, yet I've never felt any sexual awareness around him until now. Until our bodies connect within view of a man whose scalding stare sears my back. I don't have to see Isaac to sense his fury.

Nerves electrify my skin as we start to move.

I know what he's seeing. I've specifically chosen the most intimate dance Andrey and I perform in the entire production —the pinnacle moment when two ill-fated lovers embrace the emotions felt for one another. The choreography is breathtaking—exquisitely beautiful yet tragic.

Except my own emotions are getting in the way.

This doesn't feel like I'd hoped. I don't feel relieved.

I feel regret.

I feel dirty.

My spiraling thoughts and Isaac's incessant stare keep me from focusing on the moves. I didn't plan to actually mess up, but my head is in too many places at once. I make a half-second error, prompting Andrey to stop.

"I didn't notice any issues with this dance earlier," he notes curiously.

Embarrassment blazes across my cheeks, sparked for a half dozen different reasons. I can hardly meet his gaze, nor can I summon the courage to peek at my surly neighbor fuming in the aisle.

"I think it's just a mental hiccup. I'm probably more tired than I realized."

Andrey cups my cheeks and brings my gaze to his. "These things are normal, Amelie. Do not let it get to your head."

I nod, emotions constricting around my throat as commanding footsteps march up the wood stairs at the side of the stage.

Andrey releases me, his brow furrowed. "I am busy this weekend but have time Monday evening. You should come to my home studio, and we can do a few passes so it doesn't create a block. Will that work?"

"Okay, yeah." At this point, I'll do anything to find a way off this horrible stage. I need to disappear.

"Amelie, we're going to be late if we don't get going." Isaac's voice, flat yet unyielding, slaps at my back. To anyone else, he probably sounds like a bored boyfriend not wanting to miss a dinner reservation.

I know better.

We're not late for anything, and Isaac is furious.

I'm lost in my own swell of emotions, but I'll be damned if I put on a show for my fellow dancers. I turn and smile broadly as if his appearance is an unexpected delight.

"Oh! Hey, babe. Sorry about that. I'll grab my things." I shoot a catty glance at the dancer who'd been flirting with him because I'm human, after all, then stride quickly back to the dressing room. I switch to my sneakers and grab my things. I'm about to run back out front when Hazel snags me by the arm.

"Not much to tell—girl, is that *him*?"

Hell, I'm in trouble.

"Yes, and I know. I'm sorry, but it's complicated!" I toss over my shoulder the second she releases me. There'll be no escaping her questions the next time I see her.

The second I close in on Isaac, he wordlessly turns and leads us up the sloped aisle to the lobby. I scurry behind him like a chastened child. I hate that I can't simply be mad at him. That's how this whole thing started, but I'm too conditioned to appease. Acting out in any way makes me feel ill. I'm literally sick to my stomach.

Isaac is silent on the short drive to our building. I force myself to use the time to think rather than blurt whatever I can to ease the tension. I need to be intentional to work toward my ultimate goal instead of bumbling out of control.

I wait until the car is parked in the garage before vocalizing my thoughts.

"I'm sorry," I say quietly. "I was lashing out, and I shouldn't have."

Isaac stills but doesn't respond before exiting the car. I do the same, wondering if he will say anything at all when he finally speaks.

"I give you a reason to lash out?" he asks quietly.

My instinct is to deny and take the blame, but I remind

myself I'm making a go at honest communication. No matter where this strange relationship goes from here, I want to be proud of how I've handled myself. I already carry enough shame. I don't need to shoulder any more.

"That girl was touching you, and you were smiling at her."

"Feels pretty shitty, doesn't it," he murmurs, jabbing about my stunt with Andrey.

"Yeah, but dancing with a partner is different. I can't *not* touch my dance partner," I point out, choosing to sidestep the fact that I'd used the dance in a malicious fashion. "You didn't have to look so happy with her flirting."

"You're right. I didn't have to, but I also didn't want to make a scene in front of all the people you work with. I tried to be polite for your sake. And I know what dancing entails. That wasn't what pissed me off." Isaac presses the elevator call button and turns to me. "What I don't like is the fact that you did it intentionally to upset me *and* agreed to go to his place for a private *practice* session." He says the word with disgust, raising my defenses.

"Opening night is just over two weeks away." My voice wavers. I want to defend myself, but I hadn't even considered that he was trying to be respectful of my workplace. I realize I may have been wrong on that count. Practices with my co-lead, however, are a must.

"Doesn't mean you need to be at his place, *alone* with him. You have no idea what he might try."

"I'm alone with you, and I've known him a lot longer than you," I point out, dumbfounded. It never even entered my mind to think of Andrey as a threat. "Hell, I even know his last name."

"You're really fucking hung up on names, you know that?"

"No, Isaac. I'm hung up on not getting involved in a toxic relationship. You and me? We make each other crazy. It's too intense." I look at him pleadingly, begging him to understand. To see the insanity and not to make this any harder than it already is. "This isn't going to work."

His jaw muscles flex and strain. "It isn't going to work, or you're too scared to try? Because the only issue I see is a scared little girl who's looking for every excuse she can find to run from the one person putting her first."

His words sting more than a vicious slap across the face.

The shock winds me so thoroughly that I have no rebuttal. I'm speechless.

When the elevator doors open behind me, I walk blankly inside and press the button for the third floor. Isaac makes no move to follow me. I'm relieved. I'm devastated. I feel everything and nothing at once, and like opposite sound waves canceling each other out, an eerie numbness descends.

I meet Isaac's piercing stare as the elevator doors close between us.

His eyes say *you're running again.*

I know mine are blank, but a tiny voice cries from down deep in my soul.

Please, don't give up on me.

The elevator deposits me on the third floor. I walk to my apartment in a daze. Once inside, I drop into a chair at my dining table and let my eyes lose focus as they stare out the window at the horizon.

Isaac's parting words slowly filter back into my mind.

Scared little girl.

I am scared, but is that so wrong? I have good reason to be.

But what if he's right? What if I'm letting my fear keep me from ever finding happiness?

You have dancing to bring you happiness, remember?

Yeah, but dance doesn't keep me from being lonely. And I'm so incredibly tired of feeling alone.

My fingers absently wipe at the tear trickling down my cheek. I drop my gaze to my hands and notice a folded piece of paper in the middle of the table.

I don't remember leaving anything there.

Curious, I reach for the paper and see it's a small notecard the size of a thank-you note, but the front is blank. Two sentences are handwritten on the inside in all caps. When I read them, my stomach plummets to the floor, and the sobs threatening to consume me finally gain the upper hand. I lay my head in my hands, and I cry. And cry.

I know you spoke to the police.
Do you need another lesson?

I WALK THROUGH THE NEXT FOUR DAYS ON AUTOPILOT. NO WORD from Isaac. After days and days of near-constant run-ins, it's like he's fallen off the face of the earth. Gone.

I should be relieved. His absence means I can focus on bigger problems like the note left on my table. Except I can't seem to summon the appropriate fear to manufacture a response.

All I feel is hollow. Gutted and empty.

For weeks, I've tried to make smart choices and keep my focus on what's most important—protecting my family. So long as my family is healthy and happy, I've been able to be sufficiently happy, but it's not working anymore. Every choice I make seems to drag me further into this wretched pit.

Now that I sit at the bottom, I can't see a way to claw myself out.

If I can't trust my ability to know what's right, where does that leave me?

Frozen, that's where.

Four days of going through the motions of life without actually being present. But today is different. It's Mother's Day, and I have to summon enough energy to pass as human, or my sister will know something's wrong.

Fortunately, the spotlight is on Noemi today—she's married to Oran's cousin Conner—and this is her first big outing after having twin boys a few months earlier. Eight women, half of which are pregnant. The estrogen in the room is overwhelming, as are the hugs and teary greetings.

They're all so busy catching up and wrangling their hormones that my minimal effort is passable. I'm surprised to admit that being around them feels good. It could be the distraction alone that helps, but no matter the reason, I'll take it.

"Noemi, how are you holding up? How are the boys?" asks Shae once we've all taken our seats. She's Oran's sister, so I've seen her around more than some of the others, but we're about as opposite as you get. She's also the only one actually born into the Byrne family rather than wed into the mix.

Out of all the women, I'd say I'm closest to Stormy since I've known her the longest. I've also spent a little time with Rowan because she's a fellow dancer. I should try to spend more time with them. I think about Hazel's comments and wonder what's truly holding me back.

"They're doing amazing, and I think we're finally settling into a routine. It changes almost daily, but it's still sort of a routine. Sort of."

The group reassures her with a chorus of encouragement and laughter.

"It would be exhausting if it weren't for Conner and all of you," Noemi continues. "The meals. Taking Luna out and giving her loads of love and attention. It's all been so incredibly helpful." Aside from twin boys, she also has a daughter. Knowing what a handful Violet can be, I can't imagine juggling twins as well.

"That's what we're here for," Lina offers. "You reach out anytime you need us."

"Hear, hear. I'll drink to that." The toast rings out, prompting everyone to raise their drinks. Mimosas for those of us who aren't pregnant or breastfeeding, which is only three out of eight women because the family has been reproducing like rabbits lately.

"Sweet baby Jesus," the girl next to me says under her breath. Pippa's sister—I believe her name is Aria—is the closest to my age, and like myself, she's a fringe member of the group. Younger and not a Byrne by blood or marriage. "Do not look all at once, but there is one *fine*-looking man at the bar."

The group's attempt at discretion would be comical if I wasn't too busy reeling over what I see. *Who* I see. Laughter and giddy whispers fill the air around me, but all I hear is the thundering of my heart pounding in my ears.

Isaac is here.

Why now? It can't be a coincidence. Did he merely want to see what I was up to, or is he planning to finally talk to me? Do I want to talk to him?

Yes. Undoubtedly. I feel like I can breathe for the first time in four days.

"Amelie, you okay?"

The sound of my name draws my attention. I frantically try to pull myself together.

"Yeah." I smile at Shae, who studies me more critically than I'd prefer. "Just a little tired."

"*Y'all, he's staring right at us,*" Stormy cries softly in her Southern twang. "And he *is* beautiful but a little scary, too."

Like everyone else at the table, I look at the devastatingly handsome man at the bar. Our eyes lock as he lifts a glass of amber liquid to his lips. The burn of his drink heats my insides as though I were the one holding the glass. His unrelenting stare strips me bare, scalding my skin and claiming me.

Not only has he not given up but he's also doubling down on his efforts. I see it in the determined set of his jaw.

What does it mean? What does he plan to do?

"Holy shit." The whispered curse echoes my thoughts but didn't come from me.

I look across the table to Noemi who looks like she's seen a ghost.

"Right?" Pippa says without looking at her cousin. "He looks like the best kind of trouble."

"Pip, do you seriously not recognize him?" Noemi hisses back at her.

Recognize him? Confusion has my already chaotic thoughts stuttering. Does Noemi know Isaac?

Time and space seem to draw out like a piece of caramel stretched into a thin whisp of a string. When Noemi finally explains, she sweeps the floor right out from beneath me.

"That's my brother. Sante's finally come home." Her heartbreaking relief is the last thing I hear before my ears begin to ring.

Isaac is Sante?

Noemi's brother is my neighbor, Isaac?

My vision blurs, making me realize I've quit breathing. I coax a shaky breath in my aching lungs.

He knew.

He knew all along who I was and that we'd met once before, albeit years ago.

Why not say something? Why did he keep it a secret? Was I some kind of joke to him? Did he think it was funny that I didn't recognize him? Surely, he can't blame me. He's changed so much that his own family didn't recognize him.

My stomach roils like a small boat stuck in a summer storm at sea.

Half of our table jump from their chairs and cross the restaurant to the bar where they swarm around Isa—not Isaac. Sante.

I can't do this. Not in front of everyone.

I refuse to be the butt of his cruel joke.

While he and the Byrne women are occupied with one another, I slip away and escape outside. I'll text Lina later and explain that I was feeling sick. All that matters right now is getting far away from here. I look left, then right to get my bearings, then start my retreat back home to lick my wounds.

"Amelie, *stop*." Sante's sharp command bites at my heels, spurring me faster. A few grumbled curses later, feet pound the pavement behind me. I can't outrun him. I don't even try, but I'm not following orders either.

His strong arms clamp tight around me with relative ease, pinning my back against his front. "You asked for this," Sante says in a winded growl.

"Are you *insane*? I never asked for any of this."

"You wanted to know who I am. Now you know."

I try to bend and twist against his hold, fighting back the truth. In a way, he's right, but I never would have needed the information if he'd been honest from the beginning.

"Why did you lie? Was this some kind of twisted *joke*?" I can't keep the pain from my words.

Sante stiffens, then spins me around, keeping his hands clamped around my upper arms to prevent me from fleeing. The savage intensity blazing in his eyes steals my breath, answering my question. Humor played no part in whatever motivated him. It's a small concession but not enough to assuage the hurt.

"I *never* lied to you. My name is Sante Isaaco Mancini. I didn't correct your belief that we'd never met because I'm not that person anymore. The past is irrelevant."

I open my mouth to argue, but words fail me.

He's technically correct—he didn't lie. Not exactly. But that doesn't mean what he did was right. He misled me and made me feel like a fool. And for what purpose?

"Why?" I finally ask, bemused. "Why are you doing this?"

"Because you need to understand that I'm not playing. No more excuses. No more running. You know exactly who I am now and that I'm not going anywhere."

"Know exactly who you are?" I ask incredulously. "We spent a half an hour together four *years* ago. That doesn't mean I know you."

"You know my background, my family, my occupation—add what you've learned about me over the past week, and only a handful of people know me better."

He's deadly serious.

It occurs to me that this man may open up to people even less than I do. His family was shocked to see him—he's not even close to them. Yet he's set his sights on me. Why?

The fight drains from my body, leaving me confused and exhausted.

"What I know is that you lied and manipulated me," I try to explain calmly. "That's not a foundation for a relationship."

He lowers his hands from my arms. "Is that what you'd say about Oran and your sister? Because from what I understand, their start was no different."

Again, he turns my words against me, leaving me speechless. He's exactly right. Oran and Lina met one another while both weaving a web of lies. Lina was trying to find me by infiltrating The Society. Oran had his own agenda. The two never planned to fall in love, but fate interceded. Despite the crazy odds against them, they ended up married, and I've never seen my sister happier.

It's so unsettling that this man I thought was a stranger suddenly knows so much. Too much.

Oh God.

I told him about The Society and my fears. He knows about my stalker. And for all I know, he may have an entire dossier on my past.

Sensing my rising panic, he clasps my face and guides my gaze to his.

"I told you from the beginning not to get hung up on names and labels. You *know* me. I'm the one who'll keep you safe. I'm the one who makes your pussy drip with need. None of that has changed. I get that you're upset, so I'll give you a little time to wrap your head around it all. But Mellie," he continues, his voice pitching even lower, "don't be mistaken. You can't escape me."

He lowers his hands before slowly backing away, eyes still boring holes deep into my soul.

I'm at a complete loss, blindsided by all that's unfolded. I don't know what to think. I only know that I need space. I need room to breathe and figure out what to do next.

I turn away and take one unseeing step at a time toward home.

You can't escape me.

He's right.

I can't report him to the police. I can't ask my family for help because they're more his family than mine, and telling them anything will only dredge up more questions.

There truly is no escaping Sante Mancini.

I think back to that night so many years ago—the night of Lina and Oran's wedding—and the boy I met with torment in his eyes.

20 Amelie

Past

It's been four months since I got my memories back.

Seven months since I was drugged and kidnapped.

Ten months since my mother arranged to sell my virginity, forcing me to run away from home.

I don't have my GED yet. I haven't managed to snag any dance jobs since my role in *Chicago*, which only happened because half the cast came down with the flu. I work so hard every day to focus on the positives, but the only thing that seems to change is this expanding emptiness that fills my chest.

Sometimes, I wish my memories had never come back. It

would have been easier, in a way. During those confusing days, I would spend hours daydreaming about the family who was probably worried sick about me. Judging by the jewelry I wore when I was found, I was certain I'd had money. Money meant family. Family meant home and belonging. I knew everything would be okay if I could only remember.

Then Lina found me, and as the memories flooded back, I had to relive the horrifying lessons from the past, proving that family can also mean heartbreak. Coming to terms with the past year of my life has been more of a struggle than I could force myself to unload on my sister. She's done so much for me already, and on top of it all, she's been planning her wedding. I couldn't burden her. She deserves a world of happiness. I want her to enjoy this time in her life and not have to deal with my drama.

Lina spent years trying to protect me from our mother. This is my chance to return the favor. Some days are harder than others, like today. I should be over the moon to see Lina so incandescently happy on her wedding day. We're surrounded by her new family, all of whom are ecstatic to take her into the fold.

They're welcoming toward me as well, but it's not the same. I'm not one of them. I don't seem to belong anywhere anymore. No parents. No friends. I'm adrift in the world.

If I were as strong as Lina, it wouldn't be a problem. She left home at the same age as me, grateful to never look back. She's independent and self-assured. She doesn't need anyone, whereas I feel like a sailboat whose sail has been ripped away by the wind.

The root of my issue is more complex than overcoming my parents' deaths. The war I wage is against the painful loneliness of knowing they never wanted me in the first place.

I've convinced myself that my presence will burden other people's lives. An intrusion. Unless I can think of some concrete value I have to offer, my default is to isolate. I hate being alone, yet I bring it upon myself. The vicious cycle has held me captive for months.

Even here, surrounded by a tent full of people, I'm desperately lonely.

Every chance I get, I slip out to the parking lot and try to fill the gaping chasm in my chest with the bottle of vodka I snagged from the bar. A sip here and there since I don't want anyone to catch on. Drinking is so out of character for me that it would draw unwanted attention. I sip just enough to shave down the thorns of my self-loathing.

On my way back inside from my latest excursion, I see a guy leaning against a car, looking about as sullen as I feel. Maybe it's the alcohol—I'm normally not outgoing—but I decide on a whim to join him. The wedding is being held in a private garden. Anyone out here has come for the wedding, so I don't feel too worried that I don't know him. Again, it's probably the vodka.

"Are you part of the Byrne family?" I ask once I'm standing across from him. He looks about my age—skinny but pretty in a haunted way. His hair is dark and held stiffly in place by a healthy supply of gel. He's made an effort to look presentable, but not enough to cut the shaggy length from the sides and back. If I had to guess, I'd say he's here because he has to be and not by choice.

"Not me, but my sister is. Noemi," he says curtly. He's not interested in talking to me, that's clear. Unfortunately for him, the fact that I've found someone who might be as miserable as me is the best thing that's happened to me all day.

"Then you must be Sante. I've met your sister; she's really sweet."

His face flinches with a scowl. "Yeah, she's pretty great," he mutters.

What an odd reaction, except I can totally relate. I consider telling him about my sister Lina but don't get the chance. He steps away from the car and reaches inside his inner jacket pocket.

"Look, unless you've got something to refill this"—he holds up a black pocket flask—"then I'm not really in the mood to chat."

He turns to walk away. My hand snags his wrist before I have a chance to think about what I'm doing. He cocks a brow at me that draws out the first genuine grin I've smiled all day.

"I think I can help with that." I release his wrist and motion for him to follow me.

"Aren't you full of surprises," he says when I show him my secret bottle stashed by a tree.

I unscrew the lid and take a sip. He takes the bottle when I hand it to him and downs two healthy gulps.

"Fuck, I needed that." He shakes his head, then looks at me, eyes assessing me for the first time. "Who did you say you are?"

"Amelie. I'm the bride's sister."

"No shit?"

I flash a full-on grin. I love that I've shocked him. I don't even know why, but the spark of life I've brought to his eyes makes me want to run through a field of wildflowers.

"Yup, which means I probably need to get back inside."

"You shouldn't have been out here alone to begin with— no telling what monsters you might run into." He begins to fill his flask, his gaze briefly drifting to mine.

I want to giggle, and it occurs to me that I might be feeling the alcohol a bit more than I realized. "Trust me, I know all about the monsters. That's why I wear this." I hold up my finger, showing him my evil eye ring. "Keeps the monsters away."

He huffs. "Wish it were that easy."

"Can't hurt." I shrug.

He puts the lid on his flask, then caps the vodka bottle before handing it back to me. "You're a lifesaver."

I swallow hard, fighting back a swell of emotions. This is the best time I've had in months. I refuse to let my stupid thoughts bring me down.

"Come on, let's get back inside."

It's easy enough to slip back in unnoticed. I go to the dance floor and find a groove with some of the ladies, though I don't stay long because I can sense Sante watching me and am drawn back to him like a moth to the flame. I wind my way to the refreshment table and snag a cup of punch, then zigzag casually to where he's standing. I do my best to look like I'm meandering with no real purpose. Not that I need to hide what I'm doing, but it feels sort of … fun. I like feeling fun.

Once I'm close enough, I set my drink down on the table by him and dance in place. After a moment, I see him catch on and discreetly deposit a small amount of the vodka from his flask into my cup. As though oblivious, I flit back to the dance floor with my spiked drink and give myself over to the music.

21
Sante

Past

I CAN'T TAKE MY EYES OFF HER. WHILE SHE DANCES, I WONDER what she's trying to escape in that bottle and how she's doing it with such joy on her face. Like whatever is bothering her is inconsequential compared to the strength of her spirit.

If that wasn't enough to mesmerize me, her body does the job. She moves like a fucking goddess. Never seen anything more beautiful. Even the tiniest sway of her hips and flick of her wrist is seductively graceful.

I have to force myself not to stare.

We meet again at the refreshment table sometime later. She's playing this silly game as though we're sneaking booze when my family knows damn well I'm drinking, and I doubt hers would care if they knew she was. She's about my age, and we're at a wedding. All Irish and Italian. Drinking's in our blood. But this game she's playing—it feels carefree. Like I'm not the biggest fuckup I know, and my father didn't just try to kill me and my sister. It's the first time I've felt like there's hope that things won't always be utter shit. Like maybe the tides are turning.

A hint of a smile ghosts across my lips as I hold her vibrant green gaze.

"Excuse me, I think this one is done for the night." The bride strips the drink from Amelie's hand, then glares daggers at me.

"What? Lina Bean, what are you talking about?" Amelie cries.

It pisses me off that this woman is upsetting her. "It's all good. She's fine." I try to reach for Amelie, hoping to defuse the situation, but Amelie's sister refuses to let me near her.

"*You* stay out of it. You've done enough." She points an angry finger at me.

Then Renzo is behind me, his voice a threatening rumble of thunder. "Everything okay here?"

"This one's been spiking my sister's punch," says the bride, motioning to me.

Out of the corner of my eye, I see Amelie open her mouth to argue. I shoot her a glare and give one sharp shake of my head.

She stills immediately at my command.

I raise my hands and give a lopsided grin. "It's just a tiny bit of vodka. No need to make a big deal."

"Can't fuckin' take you anywhere," Renzo growls behind me, ready to believe the very worst in me. He's been in a shit mood all day, begging for a fight. I'm happy to oblige if it means I take the heat off Amelie. Judging by her sister's reaction, I was wrong about their tolerance of her drinking.

I turn to face him and sneer. "You mean you don't ever want me to have any fun." I'm not helping matters. I know that. But A, the alcohol is running its course, and two, this whole scene is pissing me off.

Before I can blink, Renzo has me by the throat, my feet almost entirely off the ground. Jesus, it hurts. And I can't fucking breathe. What the hell is wrong with him?

"What have I told you about disrespecting me?" he hisses through clenched teeth.

"Just ... a little ... fun," I manage to wheeze while clinging to his wrist.

"No, you're embarrassing our entire family, and now we're leaving." He drops me, adding a little shove for good measure. "Lina, Oran, I'll make sure this is handled appropriately. You have my apologies."

"We're glad you could make it," says the groom, now part of the circle of onlookers to our little show. The two shake hands before Renzo directs me to the exit.

I take a single step when a delicate hand snags mine. Amelie. She deposits something in my palm, her eyes glassy and grief-stricken. I clench my fist tightly shut and try to look as unaffected as possible to keep her from worrying. This isn't the first time my cousin and I have clashed, and it won't be the last.

So much for the tides turning.

I follow Renzo to the car and get in the back seat rather than the front. He doesn't say a word, and neither do I. We both need the distance from one another. I also wanted a bit of privacy because I want to see what Amelie's given me.

When I open my palm, I see the silver ring she'd flashed earlier. The one with the evil eye.

Keeps the monsters away.

She was trying to protect me the only way she knew how.

I rub at the strange twinge in my chest as I stare at the ring. She couldn't have known how much it would mean to me, yet here it sits in my hand.

I close my fist and feel the metal imprint in my palm, suspecting little Amelie may have done the same to my heart.

22
Sante

Present

WHEN I HEARD ABOUT THE BRUNCH GATHERING, I DECIDED IT would be an efficient way to announce my return and clear the air with Amelie. Two birds, one stone, no more secrets.

The public setting kept drama to a minimum, as I'd hoped, and I can guarantee the entire Moretti organization will hear word of my return within the hour. The ladies are probably all inside the restaurant now texting everyone they know. I need to go back inside and deal with the chaos I've stirred up, but my feet have bolted themselves to the concrete sidewalk so long as Amelie is still in view.

I hate letting her walk off into the city alone. It takes everything in me not to follow her, but I can't. Not until I've spoken to Noemi.

She's the only one who recognized me—the one person I've let down most in this world.

At least I've learned from my mistakes and won't repeat them where Amelie is concerned. I'll keep my tiny dancer safe no matter the cost, whether she likes my methods or not. That's been our theme since the beginning, and now she knows it.

She may not have recognized me, but she *remembered* me. I saw the memories play out in her wide green eyes the second Noemi said my name. She remembers that night as vividly as I do.

I'd told myself it didn't matter whether she remembered —it was a tiny hiccup in time, after all—but I was wrong. It means more than I care to admit that our interaction impacted her. That despite the alcohol and the brevity of our exchange, she remembered.

The knowledge is empowering. It confirms that I'm on the right path.

"I went by Mom's grave this morning," Noemi says softly as she joins me on the sidewalk. "There were pink peonies already there—her favorite. I wondered who ... but I suppose now I know."

I steel myself before meeting her loving gaze. It's fucked up, but a part of me wishes she'd be angry with me. Avoiding her would be so much easier if she wasn't so damn understanding.

"It's good to see you," I say stiffly, giving her a hug.

When she pulls back, she looks me over with perceptive eyes. "How've you been?"

"I'm good. A lot better than I was."

"I can see that," she says with the hint of a smile.

"Oh yeah? What can you see?" I'm not entirely sure what she means, and my need to know is too overwhelming not to ask.

"I see a man who's confident and sure of himself. A man who's taken ownership of his life. Maturity suits you."

Fuck, I can't breathe.

I don't want to do this. I don't deserve her kindness, and I don't know how to explain myself without sounding like a fucking asshole.

"Had no choice but to grow up," I say with a grimace.

Noemi rests her hand on my arm. "Were they hard on you? I worried about you constantly."

"That's not what I meant," I bite back with more venom than I intend. "I had no option because I was a fucking waste of space. I had to get a clue or let someone put me out of my misery."

"You were a kid, Sante."

"Look, I don't have time for this." I pull away from her touch. "I need to handle some things." My eyes cut inadvertently in the direction of Amelie's departure.

"You have feelings for her?" Noemi asks gently.

It's so much more complicated than that, but I don't want to discuss it right now. "Something like that," I say under my breath. I turn back to my sister and force a degree of warmth into my voice. "I know we need to catch up, and I definitely want to see your little ones, so I'll come by your place soon. I have some things I need to do first."

She grins broadly. "Hey, I'm your little big, remember? I'll be here whenever you're ready."

The nickname I gave her reminds me of the naive kid that

I was and grates on my already fraying nerves. "I'm not that person anymore, Em."

"You may have changed, but you'll always be my Sante."

That's it. I'm out.

I place a kiss on her cheek and walk away without another word. I don't want to stay and say something I'll regret. I already have enough regrets to last a lifetime.

"Someone knows how to make an entrance. My phone hasn't blown up like that since my father passed away." Renzo stands at his front door, having opened it before I finished walking up the steps to his brownstone home.

Renzo is my cousin and the boss of the Moretti crime family. All the men in my family have been part of the organization, and if I stay in the city, I'll need his acceptance to return to the fold. He'd be entirely in his right to refuse me for a number of reasons, most prominently being concerns about my loyalty. I've spent four years as part of another organization. The fact that Renzo is the one who sent me there is irrelevant. I stayed longer than expected. He has good reason to be wary.

"Word got around," I say in an even tone. "Sounds like the method was effective."

"Effective, if not a tad dramatic."

Tension coils in my shoulders. Renzo is a master at cloaking his emotions, and I've been gone long enough that reading his tells is a challenge.

"Wasn't my intent. I'm not the same kid I was when I left." I decide to cut to the chase, not sure if he's giving me a hard time or genuinely concerned I'm still trouble.

"I can see that. Didn't mean to imply you were." He takes

a step backward out of the doorway. "Why don't you come in? I figure we have plenty to catch up on."

Not an outright rejection.

I take it as a good sign and follow him inside, scanning the unusual style of the front entry. He bought the place right before I left, so I never got a chance to see it. It's not what I expected from him, but it's not terrible. A little rustic for my taste.

Renzo takes me back to his office and pours us each a drink.

"Would it be a safe bet to assume with you back in town that my brother is here, too?" He hands me a glass, his steely gaze monitoring my every minute movement. His vigilance is unnecessary. I have nothing to hide. When I decided to announce my return, I spoke to Tommy first so that I'd know how he wanted his own homecoming to unfold. I knew this exact situation was unavoidable.

"He's here. I asked him to lay low until I had a chance to come by. He should be reaching out later today."

His shoulders relax a fraction when he exhales—a movement that's hardly noticeable to the naked eye but a surprising show of relief coming from him.

"I started to doubt you two were ever coming home. You planning to stick around, or is this a temporary visit?"

"I suppose that depends on a number of things."

"One of those being me?"

I nod. "Obviously, you have the ultimate say on whether I'm welcome here."

"You were never unwelcome, Sante. Hope you know that I didn't want to send you away. I didn't know what else to do."

"You don't have to explain anything. I get it. I needed a fresh start, and you had a lot on your plate. I'm not sitting on some kind of childish grudge. I told you, I'm not that person anymore." Finally saying those words to him is a brick off my chest. I mean every bit of it, though that wasn't always the case.

My cousin studies me, and I hate that I'm tempted to fidget. It's amazing how we regress to former behaviors when around people present in our youth.

"Alright, then," he finally responds. "If we don't need to talk about why you left, how about you tell me what brought you back. I assume there's a reason you've returned after four years away."

"I'm back for Amelie Brooks." A simple statement for a simple fact.

I note the tiniest twitch under his right eye. I've managed to surprise him.

"Lina Byrne's little sister?" he asks in a curious tone.

"That's right."

"Did you two stay in contact while you were away?"

"No." I don't offer more of an explanation. I'll give it if he asks, but I'm not one to spill my guts for no reason.

He nods slowly. "How's she feel about you being back?"

"It's ... complicated."

He takes a drink, his lips forming a thin line as he swallows. "I remember complicated. It fucking sucked, but it was worth it."

"This is really fucking complicated," I say into my glass before taking a healthy gulp.

He doesn't attempt to hide the amusement in his eyes. He wants to know more but refrains from asking. "Anything I can do to help?"

Fuck, that's what I was hoping he'd say.

"Yeah, actually." I swirl my drink and measure my words carefully. "I know her family was mixed up in this thing called The Society, but I don't know much about it. I'd like to learn more so I can understand her past better."

He rubs his hand over the stubble on his jaw and lifts his gaze to the ceiling. "That was some pretty messed-up shit."

I set down my drink and lean forward. "I want to know. Tell me everything."

23
Amelie

YOU KNOW WHEN LITTLE KIDS CLOSE THEIR EYES TO HIDE AND think that if they can't see anyone else, no one can see them? That's me. I'm that kid as I sit in my apartment, curtains drawn shut, lights low, hiding from my problems. They're still out there. Hiding doesn't change a thing, but it feels necessary because I don't know what else to do.

You can't escape me.

I hear his words whispering on repeat in the back of my mind. What bothers me the most is the relief I feel. I'm also scared and worried and embarrassed—a whole cocktail of decidedly negative emotions—all somehow offset by a heavy blanket of relief.

I've held such a tight grip on my reins for so long that the threat of losing control has been terrifying. The uncertainty of the unknown loomed as dark as any storm cloud. I had no idea that once that control was stripped from me, I might experience ... freedom. The consequences may not be ideal, but if events are entirely out of my hands, I can't do anything about it.

The allure of that sort of release of responsibility is incredibly tempting.

But I have to ask myself, what kind of horrible person would ever give up fighting if it meant bringing horrible pain to their loved ones? How do I know if circumstances are out of my control or if I simply quit trying? I'm petrified of making a mistake I'll regret for the rest of my life.

Which brings me back to hiding in my apartment.

Lina called not long after I got home. I wasn't up for talking but was glad I answered because she was dead set on skipping the rest of brunch to come over, worried about why I'd run off. I told her a version of the truth—that I met Sante recently, and he intentionally concealed his identity. I explained that I was upset and simply needed a little time to cool down. Assured that I wasn't on the verge of emotional collapse, she agreed to give me space, though I could tell she was itching to know more.

I'm sure they all are after my disappearing act. Everyone will know something is going on between Sante and me. And what's better than emotional turmoil? Having that trauma put on display for the whole world to see.

Did I mention I may never leave my apartment?

The credits begin to scroll up the screen, signaling the end of *The Princess Bride*. I pause it and select start from the beginning—for the second time. I could watch this movie all day long, and that's my current plan until I hear a knock on my door.

I don't have to look through the peephole to know who it is, but I do anyway, just in case.

"Go away, Sante. I'm not ready to talk yet," I call through the door.

"I'll break it down, Amelie." He doesn't yell or sound angry. He doesn't have to for me to know he's serious. His crazy ass will do it.

I heave a dramatic sigh, then open the door, one hand on the knob, the other propped on my hip.

"What?" I ask in a clipped tone, though he's still in the suit he was wearing earlier, and the sight winds me for a second. Something about the dichotomy of tattoos with silk ties is mesmerizing.

On the other hand, I am wearing flannel pajama pants with little sheep on them and an oversized sweatshirt with a faded image of Winnie the Pooh and Piglet holding hands.

His eyes take a sweeping survey of me from top to bottom. "You're fucking adorable."

I cross my arms over my chest. "That is so not fair."

Sante prowls forward, not waiting for an invitation. I backtrack, doing my best to look disapproving. He kicks the door shut behind him and continues toward me.

"Told you I'd be honest. Never said I'd be fair."

"After the stunt you pulled, you don't think you owe me just a little?"

The only word that adequately describes his answering grin is diabolical.

"You're absolutely right. I do owe you." His guttural words tease my inner ear and send tingles down my spine.

Before I can argue, he backs me up against the dining table, then seats me atop it with his body pressed between my thighs.

"Sante," I warn. "That's not what I meant, and you know it."

His teeth rake over his bottom lip. "What I know is that I've been denying this craving for you for too damn long, and now that everything's out in the open, I'm not waiting a minute longer."

He trails his nose along the length of my neck on a deep inhale while his hands, around my waist, pull my center against the enormous bulge in his pants.

The sensual assault short-circuits my brain.

My head falls to the side, making room for him. He nips at my jaw, alternating between gentle bites and soothing kisses. A moan unfurls from deep in my throat when he begins to rock himself against me.

"Better than I imagined," he murmurs against my skin. "You're perfect."

Perfect is a very high standard. The word seeps into my consciousness, kickstarting my thoughts ... and my doubts.

I wrap my hands around the back of his neck and graze my nails in the softly shaved hair. "Nobody's perfect. Especially me," I whisper against his lips before kissing him deeply. I let my tongue swipe over his, savoring his taste.

His hand slips confidently beneath the loose elastic of my pants and into my panties. His touch is criminally competent —the perfect pace and pressure—he brings his fingers to my entrance, teasing it before slowly working his way closer to my clit.

"So wet for me," he murmurs.

His touch feels incredible. I try not to think and simply enjoy the moment because I desperately want to feel good, but it's no use. I can't shut off my brain. He's doing everything right, and it feels incredible, but I know there's no point. I also know how awkward it is to let a man chase something that isn't there.

"You don't need to do that. It's okay." I angle my hips away, encouraging him to remove his hand.

Sante stills. "You don't want me touching you?"

"It's not that." I can hardly meet his eyes.

This is so fucking embarrassing.

The more I draw it out, though, the worse it'll be. I need to get it out there and be done with it.

I sigh, suddenly feeling exhausted. "I don't have orgasms, okay? It doesn't matter how long you spend at it, so it's not worth the effort. Trust me, I can't even make it happen on my own."

Not so perfect now, am I?

If my face blazes any hotter, I'll be in need of a burn unit.

"Mellie, look at me."

I do, though reluctantly. His tone tells me I have little option.

"Who did I say this body belongs to?"

"You," I breathe.

"And that's the problem. How will anyone else unlock a door when I'm the only one with the key?" It's the cockiest, most overconfident thing I've ever heard a man say, and he says it with such conviction that I somehow believe him.

Sante lifts me into his arms, my legs wrapped around his middle, and takes me back to my bedroom. He sets me on the bed, then disappears into my bathroom. When he returns, he's carrying the full-length mirror he's taken from the wall.

"What on earth are you doing?"

"You have toys?" he asks, ignoring my question.

"You mean a vibrator? Yeah, in the nightstand." I may not orgasm, but it still feels good.

"Get it."

I do as I'm told while keeping a curious eye on him as he moves the corner chair next to my bed and props the mirror against it.

He takes off his jacket and begins rolling up the sleeves of his dress shirt. "Take off your clothes."

I can't believe I'm going along with this, but he has me in his thrall. I'm desperate to go wherever he's taking me.

He crawls onto the bed and sits with his legs wide in front of the mirror. "Come here." He pats the space in front of him while his eyes devour every inch of my body.

I know I'm thin—so much so that it's a turnoff for some men. That's the nature of someone with my passion for dance. I've worked hard to achieve this level of ability, and it thrills me beyond words that his appreciation for what he sees is palpable.

I snag my finger inside the band of my pink panties and tug them off, leaving me completely bare for his ravenous gaze. I feel a tad awkward climbing into his lap, especially when I'm seated staring at my naked reflection with Sante fully clothed behind me.

His left hand presses flat against my belly, guiding me to lie back against him.

My heart bounds around in my chest like a Ping-Pong ball on meth, nearly imploding when Sante's voice rumbles a one-word command.

"Open."

I know what he means, but it feels so lewd. So vulnerable. It's hard to make myself comply.

I stare myself down in the mirror and slowly coax my legs apart, giving us both a clear view of my dripping pussy.

A primal growl of approval reverberates from his chest into mine.

"That's my girl. Already weeping for me."

I fear I might do a lot more than that to hear him call me his girl in that tone again. It makes my heart so light I might have levitated off the bed for a second. Every inch of my body begs for his touch. I know it's coming, or … I thought I knew. What he does instead surprises me.

"Show me what feels good." He picks up the vibrator and places it in my hand.

Embarrassment showers me from head to toe.

He wants me to touch myself … while he *watches*? I can't. That's too awkward. It'll never wor—

My thoughts evaporate when I catch sight of the captivated delight in his eyes. He's transfixed. The knowledge that I have that effect on him does something to me. Emboldens me. Heals me.

I spread myself slightly with one hand and use the other to tease circles with the tip of the vibrator around the sides of my clit. The intensity of the sensation startles a gasp from my lungs. I arch into the pleasure with my lips parted in ecstasy.

"You make my cock so hard it might never go soft again. *Jesus*, you're incredible." He trails a hand along my thigh. My brain glitches as it tries to focus on the two sensations at once.

"*God*, Sante. It feels so good." I dip the vibrator tip into my entrance, then go back up to my swollen bundle of nerves. When his other hand crosses in front of me and cups my breast, my eyes roll back in delirium.

"Eyes open, pet," he purrs before thick fingers twist my nipple. The zing of pure liquid pleasure is so intense that my legs twitch in unison.

"That's it. Keep those emerald eyes open and see what this beautiful body can do. Watch me watching you. I know you like it. Like seeing my hands touch you in ways no one else has. See me witness you move in ways no one else has seen you move."

The hand he was using to caress my thigh drifts upward over my hip bone and to my other breast. I work myself faster, feeling the need for more friction. My breathing now comes in haphazard pants. Sante's knuckles graze the undersides of my breasts in tandem. I arch with need, but he continues to tease by avoiding the pebbled skin so desperate for his touch.

"Please, Sante. *Please.*"

"Please what, pet? I'll give you what you need just as soon as you're ready."

"I need more." I don't know what that means. I've never felt this mind-bending sense of urgency before to be able to decipher it. All I know is that I'm filled with need—a chaotic, consuming need that threatens to annihilate me in the very best way.

His calloused fingers drift down to cup the inside of my thighs just shy of my center. He kneads and caresses before drifting back up to graze the sides of my breasts again. He kisses my neck, reminding me to keep my eyes open. I do, but I don't know where to look. I don't know what to focus on. There's so much pleasure coming at me from so many places.

I gasp and moan, my hips flexing and arching instinctively.

"Your pussy was made to be fucked, Amelie. So wet and ready and greedy for my cock to fill you."

His words light fires inside me like I've never felt. The bliss soaking my veins draws a mewling cry from deep in my throat. I feel so close. So close to something incredible that tears tumble from the corners of my eyes.

"That's it. My girl is ready. Fuck, she's so ready. Come for me, baby. Show me this body is all mine." The whole time he speaks, his hands finally twist and tug at my aching nipples. The relief to finally have his touch initiates a cascade of liquid lightning that rockets from my core out to every tiny nerve in my body. It's so unexpected and transformative that I scream, feeling as though I have no choice. The intensity needs an outlet.

As the explosion ebbs, I find myself floating on a cloud of bliss as though I was launched into the sky and now get to enjoy the peace of a weightless descent. When the vibrator's touch becomes too much, I turn it off and drop it on the bed beside me.

Holy crap, I had an orgasm. A real, honest-to-God orgasm.

I truly believed I was one of those women who physically wasn't capable, but I was wrong. I was so, *so* wrong. And it was all thanks to Sante.

I realize my eyes have drifted shut.

When I open them, Sante's gaze is there waiting. Devouring. One of his arms is curled possessively around my middle, and the other brings a finger to my entrance. I start to stiffen, knowing how sensitized I am, but he pauses, commanding me with his stare to trust him. I relax and watch in the mirror as he gently inserts a finger inside me.

It feels so fucking good that I shudder.

He makes that masculine growl again, then brings his finger up to his lips and sucks every last bit of my juices from his skin.

His hooded eyes darken. "This body is mine. I think I've proven that. When I say no other man gets to touch you, I mean it. If I'm uncomfortable with you going to a man's house alone, what I mean to say is, if he touches you in a way I don't like, I'll break his fucking legs."

It's a good thing I'm so blissed out, or I'd be totally freaking. Instead, I chide him dazedly. "Don't joke about that sort of thing."

"Have I given you the impression I'm the joking sort?"

My eyes widen, but I still can't summon the appropriate outrage. "Sante, you can't do that sort of thing. It's barbaric."

"I learned years ago that when it comes to protecting what's mine, there are no limits to what I will or won't do. That's who I am."

I'm not sure what to think about that. It makes me wonder what happened to make him so unbending about keeping me safe. This isn't the time to ask, but I will.

I twist until I'm facing him and sit back on my knees. "I've shared more with you than anyone now. I need you to return the favor and trust me where Andrey is concerned."

"It's him I don't trust. After everything you've been through." He grapples with a swell of emotion. "I met with Renzo earlier today. He told me why you left home—what your parents tried to do. If they weren't already dead, I'd have done it myself the instant I left his house. You should know better than anyone that people can be cruel, even those you think you know best."

"Exactly. I know people are unpredictable, but I'm telling you, I'll be safe with Andrey. I need you to trust my judgment." And I need my costar to have confidence in me. After the little scene I pulled, he has to wonder if I'm going to cave under the pressure. This role is too important to risk losing.

Sante's expression is inscrutable. I'm not sure if that's a good thing or not because he changes the subject.

"I also talked to Renzo about The Society, and we decided it wouldn't hurt to sniff around, make sure there's no signs of a resurgence."

All lingering effects of my first orgasm are doused in an icy shower of panic.

I'm off the bed and throwing on my clothes in two seconds flat. "Do you have any idea what you've done?" I hiss.

Sante stands and spreads his arms wide. "Clearly, I don't. Why don't you fucking enlighten me?"

"They'll know you're digging."

"*They* supposedly don't exist anymore. Care to tell me how you know otherwise?"

This is the moment I've been dreading. The falling dominos have extended beyond my control and will trigger consequences I can't begin to anticipate. No degree of desperation on my end will undo what's been done. The only thing I can do now is try to minimize the fallout, and the best way to do that is to tell Sante what I can so that he's prepared.

My limbs feel leaden with defeat as I walk to the bed and sit heavily.

"My parents tried to sell my virginity, and that's why I ran away—everyone knows that. What I didn't tell Lina or anyone else was that I saw the man. I recognized him."

I don't look at Sante, but I sense the preternatural stillness of his body. "The man who planned to rape you?"

I nod. "He's still alive, and he knows that I know. He's always kept tabs on me, and I think that's who's been following me."

The silence between us is deafening.

"His name." No two words have ever been spoken with such restrained violence.

In my head, I see a giant boulder rolling down a hill, and I know I'll never be able to stop it from gaining momentum. It's going to decimate everything in its path. The only thing I can do now is keep its trajectory pointed where it will do the least damage possible.

Biting my lip, I slowly shake my head. "I can't."

Sante closes the distance between us and cups my face. "I get it. You're scared, but I can make it all go away. This can be fixed, Mellie. I just need you to give me his name."

"It's not that simple." Tears well in my eyes. "I can't give you his name, and I need you to promise me that you won't go looking for it."

"What the *fuck*?" he roars, turning his back to me before whirling back around. "You're telling me this guy could be out there hurting other girls, and you're going to protect him?"

My body caves in on itself like a rotting apple. Tears pour down my cheeks, but I don't say a word.

"What's he holding over you?"

I shake my head. "It's not just him. The people involved in The Society are powerful, dangerous people."

In a flash, Sante is back in my face, wrath incarnate. "In case you couldn't tell, so am I. No one threatens what's mine. *No one.*"

He slams my bedroom door behind him, leaving me to succumb to a battery of fear and shame.

24
Amelie

I couldn't sleep last night. Couldn't eat. And it had little to do with The Society.

I hate that I've made Sante feel like I don't trust him. As much as his deception hurt me, I realized in the night that it doesn't change the way I feel about him. When I'm around Sante, I feel seen. I feel wanted and important—things I've rarely felt in my life.

My growing desire for him clouds my ability to know what's right. Do I open up to him and trust that no one will get hurt? Because I'm not the only one who would be affected by the potential fallout if he angers the man who haunts me. If I were the only one at risk, I'd have told someone the man's name years ago. How do I decide between my family and my heart?

It's impossible.

I'm terrified that continuing down this path will shred me to pieces. No matter what choices I make, someone gets hurt.

After hours and hours of dwelling on my predicament, I get a text from Andrey with his address. I've already made Sante so upset that I hate to make things worse, but I also desperately need a distraction. And besides, I know without a doubt that I'm safe with Andrey. I need this. I need the chance to set aside reality and hopefully keep from mangling one aspect of my life. God knows I've done a number on everything else.

Ten years my senior and a highly renowned dancer, Andrey has done well for himself financially. He lives on the twenty-sixth floor of a building bordering Central Park. The views have got to be spectacular. I love my view of the river, but something is magical about the oasis of Central Park.

I don't have to be escorted up since Andrey has given me a code for the elevator. When I knock on his door, excitement to dance gives me a boost of energy. Dancing never fails to make everything better. Therefore, the smile on my face is genuine when the door opens. Only it's not Andrey on the other side.

"*Sante?*" I blurt, my forehead crinkling with confusion. He's dressed casually and looks relaxed, but when I remember what he said he'd do if Andrey touched me, all the blood drains from my head down to my toes. The world spins.

"Jesus, Amelie." He rushes forward to steady me. "Relax, I'm just here as an escort," he says in a hushed tone. "I knew you'd come despite my objections and figured this way, no one has to get hurt."

I nod and take a few deep, even breaths, trying to regain my bearings. "Where's Andrey?"

"Here we are." The man in question rounds the corner with a toddler in his arms. "Had to change a diaper. Sorry I wasn't here to greet you."

"Oh! No problem at all," I gush with a smile. I'm acting overly friendly out of awkwardness. It only makes things more uncomfortable, but I don't know how else to act. I have no clue what Sante has told Andrey to explain his presence. "Thanks for making time to work on this."

"Happy to help. I'll just take this little one back to his mama—she should be out of the shower now—and we can get started." He crosses the living room to a hallway on the other side of the apartment and disappears.

"What did you tell him?" I whisper frantically to Sante.

"The truth. That I wasn't comfortable with you being alone in another man's house." His icy, detached tone tells me he's still upset with me. I want to fuss at him that Andrey probably thinks my boyfriend is crazy possessive rather than trying to protect me, but then I realize both are true, and Andrey's thoughts on the matter are irrelevant.

Let him have this, Mel. You owe him that much.

"Okay," I say reluctantly. "A heads-up would have been nice, but it's good you're here. You can see there's nothing to worry about—the man has an incredibly sweet wife and a baby. He'd never hurt me."

"If I had a dollar for every rapist and pedophile hiding behind the guise of a happy marriage, I'd be the richest man on this planet." The chilling certainty in his tone sends a wave of goose bumps down my arms.

How can I possibly counter that argument? He makes a good point.

I chew on the inside of my cheek instead, relieved when

DEVIL'S THIRST

Andrey returns moments later. He shows us back to his home studio, which is incredible. A miniature professional practice facility overlooking a corner of the park. Sante takes a seat in one of the two metal folding chairs and is immediately absorbed in his phone. I'm relieved to see he's not planning on watching our every move. The session goes by surprisingly quickly. By the time we leave, I'm feeling much better all around.

Sante drives us home and deposits me in my apartment with instructions to eat.

"You didn't eat enough last night, I'm sure. That's why you looked like you were going to pass out."

I get some lunch meat out of the fridge with a jar of mayo. "My stomach was upset," I quip, not pleased with his tone.

"Can't dance if you don't eat."

"I *know*. But as you're about to see, I normally eat plenty." A lifetime of remarks about my size makes it a sensitive subject.

"Good. Make one for me, too. I'll be back in a minute." He's out the door before I can respond.

"Sure, you want mayo on that? Or maybe mustard?" I say to an empty room with a roll of my eyes.

True to his word, he's back at my door a few minutes later with a loaded duffel bag and several suits on hangers.

"What's all that for?" My mouth is half full, but I'm too distracted to care.

"My things. If you won't tell me who or what's going on, I have to assume the worst. That means constant supervision. So, congrats, you've earned yourself a roommate." He sets down his things and joins me at the table, taking a large bite out of his sandwich.

"'Scuse me?" I gape at him, my cheeks still bulging with food. "You can't just—" A bit of bread tries to escape down my throat, forcing me to focus on chewing before I can finish. "You can't just move yourself into my apartment."

The excited challenge in his stare makes my chest flutter.

"Watch me." He accentuates his point with another large bite of his sandwich.

I'm stunned. I so did not see this coming.

There go those dominos falling willy-nilly all over the place.

"You know I don't have a guest room."

Sante grins wickedly. "Wouldn't be a very effective bodyguard if I left you alone at night, especially when you're known to have nighttime visitors."

"No. Nope. Not happening." I make a firm swiping motion with my hands. "I've given you a lot of latitude here, mister, but even I have my limits. You can stay on the couch, and that's final."

His warm brown eyes stare me down like they would a chess board. "Air mattress in the bedroom."

"Living room. *Couch*."

"Fine, but the door stays open."

"Good grief, this is not a negotiation."

Sante leans forward in his chair and speaks softly. "You and I both know if I want in your bed, that's where I'll be. The door stays open. That's the deal."

The epic stare down that follows is right out of a sitcom. I don't even know why I'm engaging him. We both know I'll cave, which I do with an exasperated wail. "*Fine*. You are the most infuriating man I've ever met, you know that?"

He slowly relaxes back in his chair as he takes a swig of water. "Don't remember you feeling that way last night when I was licking your cum off my fingers." The seductive caress of his words ignites a fire deep in my belly.

I take a big bite of my sandwich, recognizing that it's time to keep my mouth shut.

Once we finish eating, Sante hangs his suits in the hall closet and sets his duffel by the wall.

"I guess if you need to grab anything else, it's not like you have far to go," I muse absently.

"No need. This is everything."

"What do you mean?"

"This is all I have."

"You have an entire apartment of stuff next door."

He saunters closer, hands in his pockets. "No, I don't. I paid Sorrell to use his place for a few months. I never actually bought the place."

"You ... *what*?" I stare at him wide-eyed.

How is it that this man can continue to pull the rug out from under me? It's like his superpower.

"I arranged a convenient way to enable us to reunite." His casual tone is mystifying, as though he has no concept of how insane he sounds.

"Why not just ask me out?" It seems crazy to go through all that trouble merely to keep his identity a secret. Talk about taking the scenic route.

"I wasn't sure what I wanted, including whether I wanted to tell my family that I was back from Sicily."

I'm surprised to hear him say he was unsure when his intentions have seemed so unwavering since he walked back into my life. I start to wonder what changed when the word Sicily rings in my head.

"You were in Italy."

"I was."

The man stalking me spoke something that could have been Italian.

Or it could have been a number of other languages.

True, but how strange that—

Do you not remember Sante attacking the man? I know you're paranoid, but try to keep it reasonable.

God, I'm losing it.

I rub my eyes. "You know what? I'm exhausted. I'm going to rest before I need to get to the theater. You have everything you need?"

The intensity in his prolonged stare winds me.

"Yeah, Mel. I think I do."

Too overwhelmed to respond, I slip away to my bedroom and hope things make more sense with some sleep.

25

Sante

AMELIE TAKES A QUICK SHOWER AFTER PRACTICE. SHE'S WEARING baggy sweats when she comes out to eat the food we picked up on the way home. Maybe that's simply what she's most comfortable in, though I doubt it because I know what she wears to bed, and that's not it. Unfortunately for her, if she's trying to be unappealing, she's going to have to work a hell of a lot harder than that.

"What's your schedule for tomorrow?" I dive into my food, having waited to eat with her.

"Why, you going to shadow my every movement?"

"Maybe," I say in a clipped tone, still frustrated over our argument.

She sighs, making me want to turn her over my knee. "We

have rehearsal from one to four, then a dinner break before meeting back up for a six to eight session."

"That works. I can drop you off at the theater before meeting with my cousin."

She fiddles with a napkin. "What are you meeting with him for?"

"We're going to talk about transitioning me back into the family business."

"That's good." Her tone lightens.

"Hoping I'll stick around?" I raise a brow.

"I just meant it's good there's no bad blood between you. That's all."

"Mmm." The noncommittal sound is full of doubt.

She chooses not to challenge me and instead takes a quick bite of her parmesan chicken. I like watching her eat. I'm not even sure why except she goes at her food with genuine pleasure. And she wasn't lying when she said she eats plenty. The waif of a girl can put away some food, and I'm here for it. Maybe even more than I should be. I'm starting to worry I've unlocked some kind of new kink.

When she licks the butter from her fingertips after a bite of garlic bread, I literally moan.

Amelie stills, her eyes rounding when she sees the ravenous desire in mine. "I thought you were pissed at me." As if being pissed has anything to do with my dick.

"Doesn't mean I don't want to fuck you."

"Oh," she breathes. And fuck if she doesn't swipe her tongue over her lips. I bet she doesn't even know she's doing it.

She must realize she's walking a fine line because she eats in record time and disappears to her room. I have to restrain myself from following her, which is even harder now that I've tasted her.

I set up camp on the sofa, but only after I've taken a shower that rivals a polar plunge. I'm not too worried, however, because I know Amelie won't be able to resist me for long. She was already grappling with temptation. A couple more nights, and the sofa will be a thing of the past.

Six days. Six damn days, and we're still locked in a contest of wills. The tension between us has built a little more each day, both of us holding our ground—she won't give me a name, but I refuse to give up asking for it.

By the time Sunday rolls around, we're both dangerously on edge. It's not ideal, considering we have our first family function to attend together. Conner and Noemi's twins are being baptized at evening Mass. I'm not looking forward to the attention, but at least it's a distraction. And speaking of distractions, Amelie's presence on my arm will help keep people from swooping in with questions about my time away and why I've returned. Overall, it's a win.

When we arrive at the church, Noemi and Conner talk with family near the front of the church, each holding a swaddled infant.

"Sante!" Noemi's face beams with happiness when she sees me. She excuses herself and comes over to greet us, Conner following her lead.

"I'm so glad you're here." She gives us both one-armed hugs. "Hey, Amelie. How are you?"

"Really well, thanks."

I'm shaking Conner's hand when he lets out a muttered expletive and then shoves his baby into my arms. "Hold this for a second."

I feel like I've been handed a live grenade. When my

bewildered stare follows his retreating form, hoping to understand what the hell just happened, I see a little girl scaling the confessional wall like a squirrel. My sister and her husband have a daredevil on their hands.

And identical twin boys.

Guess it's a good thing she's got the patience of Job. She's going to need it.

I smirk and look down at the sleeping baby in my arms. I've never held a baby before. I adjust him a bit so that he feels more secure, and I'll be goddamned if I don't instinctively start to sway back and forth.

When I look back at Noemi, her eyes are full of tears.

"What?" Why the hell is she crying? Did I do something wrong?

"I'm just so glad my family is back together again."

Suddenly feeling on display, my eyes cut to Amelie. Yup, she's eating up every second of this. Great. I don't know how to respond to Noemi's emotional display. I don't understand it. Conner and the kids are her family. I'm just her kid brother, right?

When I look at the sincerity in her face, I wonder if she sees things differently.

"What are their names again?" I decide to stick to safer waters and focus on the kids.

"Roman and Ryder," Noemi says, overflowing with motherly pride.

Amelie sidles closer and smiles at the baby in my arms. "How do you tell them apart?"

"I have anklets on them. Maybe it doesn't matter if I end up mixing them up—no one would ever know, and I'm sure it wouldn't be the first time it's happened—but I feel better knowing definitively which is which. I've been assured that one of these days, I'll be able to tell on my own. Until then, they get to wear jewelry."

"You know they're going to give you hell one day," I tease.

Noemi's smile wavers. "It makes me tired just thinking about it, especially when River is already such a handful. I don't know how it happened, but I swear she's Shae's clone. I thought firstborn girls were supposed to be sweet, mild-mannered parent pleasers. Not her. She's hell on wheels. That girl isn't afraid of anything."

I can't help but laugh. "Good for her."

My sister glares playfully. "Watch out, buddy. Karma's a bitch."

Conner rejoins us with a grinning toddler in his arms and an older couple in tow.

Noemi steps forward to welcome them. "Mia, Edoardo, we're so glad you could make it." She gives them each a side hug before the woman scoops Noemi's twin from her arms while gushing praise.

I recall that Conner was adopted into his Irish family. Mia Genovese is his birth mother. The Genoveses run the Lucciano family, the same as the Donatis run the Moretti organization. These are no ordinary grandparents.

I stand a little taller.

"Sante, you may remember Mia and Edoardo Genovese," Conner says by way of introduction, releasing a squirming River back to the ground. "Noemi's brother was in Italy for a few years and has recently come home, hopefully to stay."

I shake Edoardo's hand and nod at Mia, who has her hands full. "It's good to see you both." I place my free arm around Amelie's back. "I'm not sure if you've already met, but this is Amelie, my future wife." Girlfriend sounded too trite in my head—too transient. I want everyone to know this woman is mine, and anyone who fucks with her will answer to me. The sooner word gets around, the better.

The older couple gush with congratulations while Conner and Noemi stare at me through wide, incredulous eyes. I give Amelie a small squeeze to help draw her out of her shocked state. She recovers quickly, thanking everyone for their kind words and doing her best to avoid Noemi's stare.

Before any more can be said, two things happen at once. Oran, Lina, and Violet sweep into the back of the church, stirring up a commotion, which little River uses as a distraction to climb on top of the huge wooden altar. Like highly trained commandos moving into action, Noemi instinctively grabs the infant in my arms while Conner races away to snag his daughter.

The organ music intensifies, signaling the start of the service. Lina and her family beeline for us, giving me a better understanding of the uproar. Her dress is soaked with dirty water up to her waist.

"What on earth happened?" Amelie hisses to her sister.

I'm listening, but my gaze is trained on Oran, whose glare is nothing short of murderous.

"It was so crazy," Lina says as we take our seats. "I was nearly hit by a car walking over here. I thought about going home to change, but I hate to miss the baptism. Just incredible. If I didn't know better, I'd swear the damn thing swerved to hit me. I happened to notice Oran stopped to fix Violet's shoe, so I stepped back onto the curb. If I hadn't ..." A tremble wracks her from head to toe. "Well, I hate to think what would have happened."

Before my eyes, Amelie turns a sickly shade of white.

26

Amelie

THE HOUR-LONG BAPTISM SERVICE COULD HAVE INCLUDED A human sacrifice, and I wouldn't have noticed. The only thing I was vaguely aware of beyond my frenzied thoughts were the periodic glances from Sante beside me. Even as we walk back to his car, I can sense him wanting to know what I'm thinking.

I hope he blames my near catatonic state on his outlandish proclamation that I'm his future wife. How absurd is my life that such a bold, presumptive move on his part isn't the most perplexing thing to happen to me today? I wish that was the only thing on my mind.

I'm utterly terrified that Lina's near miss with a passing car was less of an accident and more of a failed attempt at murder. I can't discount the likelihood that it was a message for me. And I think Sante suspects my fears. He saw my reaction to her recounting of the events.

I feel like I've been running on a treadmill, but the speed continues to increase until I can feel my legs failing to keep pace. I've done everything I can to prevent a fall, yet I can see it playing out in slow motion before my eyes. What if there's no stopping it? What if nothing I do is enough?

Protecting my family feels more critical than ever, but I don't know how. I can't turn back the clock and undo the past two weeks. I have no way to prove I'm not guilty of whatever they think I've done.

The fear is paralyzing.

Time skips forward without my notice until the car stops, and I realize I don't know where we are.

"What's going on?"

Sante turns off the engine, engulfing us in silence. "What's going on is we're gonna go in here and eat, then you're going to tell me what the hell is going on. My patience is at an end. You have the next hour to come to terms with whatever conflict is holding you back."

Proclamation made, he exits the car.

This isn't unexpected. He's not the sort of man who accepts defeat.

The thing is, unless he literally tortures me, I don't *have* to tell him anything. I already feel myself caving, so it probably won't come to that, but I like to think I still have options.

We eat in relative silence. Even my thoughts are uncharacteristically quiet.

I imagine this feels along the lines of a death row inmate eating his last meal. Maybe that sounds overly dramatic. I'm not so sure. My choice today could have life-and-death consequences. Therefore, I take each minute I'm given. I sit with my emotions. I appreciate the present moment for its serenity and try to assure myself that somehow, everything will work out for the best.

My grip on that coveted sense of calm falters as we leave the restaurant. The car is only a short block away, but it might as well be in Jersey when a catcall whistle slices through the air, followed by the lewd cackling of two men seated on a set of entry steps down the sidewalk from us. We have to pass them to get to the car.

Instinctively, I clasp Sante's arm. What I really want to do is turn around, but his pace remains perfectly fixed in the same direction. He has to be aware of them. They're making more and more noise as we approach, and their obnoxious tone is unapologetically belligerent. Not that I can understand what they're saying. It seems to be Russian, I think. It's hard to tell if the slurring is part of the accent or more from intoxication because the two are clearly drunk.

Ten feet.

Five feet.

I ready myself to rush past when Sante does something unthinkable. Instead of getting out of there as fast as we can, he comes to a stop.

My stomach threatens to return every bite I took at dinner.

"Must have some seriously tiny dicks to enjoy scaring a woman," Sante muses, hand in his pocket. Every word is spoken with such casual indifference that I have to wonder if he's lost his mind. Is he trying to pick a fight with them?

The man with a bald head spits at Sante's feet, then stands, grinning to reveal two silver teeth. "This little cunt seems to think he has balls, eh, Pyotr?"

The other man doesn't move. He stares us down and murmurs something to his friend in Russian. He's quieter, but that's what scares me the most. I'm reminded of a coiled snake ready to strike. And the wicked scar ravaging one cheek doesn't help.

Sante plows ahead as though totally unfazed. "Think you two owe her an apology."

Why is he doing this?

I don't want an apology. I want to live to see another day.

"Let's just go, please," I whisper pleadingly into the fabric of his suited arm.

"Listen to the cunt while you can still walk out of here on your own two legs."

Sante squeezes my hand, then shifts my body away from his. His intent is clear—you need to get back.

I don't argue.

"Biba know you've strayed this far from home?" Sante asks, still perfectly calm.

At the mention of the name Biba, the other man rises to his feet. Both glare menacingly at Sante as the atmosphere takes a decidedly dark turn.

I'm so terrified that my entire body shakes.

I fumble to get my phone out of my purse and debate whether I should call the police. Sante put this in motion—he seems to know these men—but that doesn't make me feel any better. The two-to-one odds alone are terrible, not to mention these guys look like they could take a two-by-four to the face like it was a pool noodle.

My concerns about Sante's sanity are validated when he lets out a chuckle.

"Not to worry," he says to them. "I won't say anything. I owe you two anyway. It's not often a kid gets to take a joyride in a yellow Lamborghini. I couldn't believe my luck to find that thing running."

The Russians exchange a shocked look, which Sante uses as a perfect distraction to launch his attack. His hand flies out of his pocket and pulverizes the bald man in the face with one sweeping motion. He doesn't stop there. He uses the momentum to continue turning, then kicks out behind him, landing a vicious kick to the other man's middle. Still, he's not done. Returning to his first victim, Sante gives him one more blow to the head, then does the same to the other man. Both drop unconscious to the ground.

The whole thing doesn't last thirty seconds.

I see why when he finally stills. Silver glints off his fisted hand.

"Are those ... *brass knuckles*?" I ask in astonishment.

He drops the weapon back into his pocket. "Yeah. I have this guy to thank for that." He pokes a foot at the motionless bald guy. "Taught me years ago to always be prepared. Fucker broke two of my ribs."

If my jaw hangs open any longer, I'll end up with a bird's nest in there. I don't know how to process the calculated violence of what I witnessed. Sure, he'd punched the stalker, but this was next level.

I'm still reeling when he gently takes my face between his hands and kisses my forehead. "You okay?"

I nod.

"Good. Let's get the fuck outta here." He curves an arm around my back and leads us to the car.

Once we're both buckled in, he pulls onto the road when I blurt out, "Stop!"

We lurch forward when he hits the brakes. He peers over at me, then eases the car back against the curb. I could wait until we get back to the apartment, but I'm done waiting. It's time to take that leap of faith. It's time to ask for help.

"I got a note the day after I went to the police station warning me to stay quiet. That incident with Lina today—I don't think it was an accident."

Sante nods. "Oran said as much but had no idea where the threat was from. Said he saw it all, and there was no way it wasn't intentional."

My chin quivers. "I know it was meant as a message, and I'm so freaking scared." I close my eyes and force a slow breath in through my nose and out my lips. "If I tell you the name of the man who tried to buy my virginity, I need you to promise me you won't take action without my express permission."

He opens his mouth to protest, but I stop him with a raised hand.

"If you know what my mother tried to do to me, then you probably know she did the same to Lina, except…" I struggle to fight back a cresting wave of emotion. "Lina wasn't as fortunate as I was. Sante, this guy has a video of her. He wasn't the one who raped her, but somehow he got ahold of a video. He's threatened to hurt her if I step a hair out of line, and he's using the video as leverage if anything ever happens to him—he says it'll be released all over the internet. I can't let that happen, Sante." My words are a strained whisper, no voice left to squeeze past the lump in my throat.

I have to pause and swallow hard to keep going.

"I've done everything I can to protect her because she's done the same for me, but I'm scared it's not enough. I'm so damn scared. If I tell you his name, you have to swear to me that you won't touch him—not you or anyone else. Not unless we find a way that ensures Lina isn't harmed in the process."

Sante gives a somber nod. "We can do that."

I take one more deep breath. "His name is John Talbot." A part of me half expects the man himself to appear like a Harry Potter Deatheater summoned with a touch of a dark mark.

"I've been away a while. The name is familiar, but I'm not sure from where."

"He's the attorney general for the state of New York, and he's incredibly connected."

His chin lifts in understanding. "And that's why you're terrified of cops."

I nod. "They keep him informed of everything that happens in this city, including everything I do."

"Maybe some of them, but he doesn't own the entire force."

"No, but I have no idea who's loyal to whom. Better to avoid them all."

"And you never told any of this to Lina or Oran?" He studies me intently. I can practically see the gears turning in his head, assessing what I've told him for inconsistencies or missing pieces. I'm scared he's questioning whether I've told him everything. I have to do my best to convince him.

"No. At first, I didn't tell Lina because I was scared and didn't want her to worry. She'd already gone through so much for me. I thought if I stayed quiet, it would all go away. And it more or less did until recently when that man started to follow me. I don't even know why—that's the most frustrating part. I didn't do anything. Then my call to the cops upped the ante. Now, I'm afraid there's no de-escalating the situation."

Sante's hand reaches across to cup the back of my neck while his stare locks with mine. "I will not let this man touch you or your family. You understand me?"

"But..."

"No. No buts. I understand what's at stake. It. Will. Not. Happen."

I nod, emotions clogging my throat. I'm so freaking

scared, but maybe between his family and the Byrnes, this whole mess might finally end.

"I need to hear you say it, Mellie. Tell me you trust me not to endanger you."

"I trust you."

He leans in and kisses my forehead with such excruciating tenderness that my chest constricts. All at once, I realize that I've been focused on my own concerns and haven't considered the danger he'll now be in.

God, please tell me I haven't made a huge mistake.

My entire body sags with relief when we finally make it back to my apartment. I'm emotionally exhausted from the day and ready to pass out, but as I look toward my bedroom, I find myself wishing Sante was coming with me. To have that comfort—his smell and strength and warmth to reassure me that everything will be okay.

If only my life were simple enough that I could invite him in.

He's been so understanding—going so far as to call me his future wife—but a part of me still waits for the other shoe to drop. For him to realize what a mess I am and bail. All I've done is bring him drama and chaos, and after a lifetime of conditioning to see myself as a burden, I struggle to believe this could possibly be real. That Sante would voluntarily want to bind himself to me.

He's seen plenty of your crazy already and hasn't left.

Exactly. I've given him more of myself than I ever have to anyone. If he leaves now, I'll be incredibly hurt. If I let myself love him, only for him to walk away, I won't recover from that sort of devastation.

True, but then you'll never know love.

I realize I've been standing, staring vacantly at my bedroom door. I turn to see that Sante's been watching me the whole time. "Thank you." I nervously bite my lip, feeling more vulnerable than I have in years.

"For what?" he asks softly.

"For everything."

This time, his kiss isn't remotely tender. He sweeps forward and presses his lips to mine with such demanding need that my knees go weak. The kiss is intense but short-lived. When he pulls away, his brown eyes blaze with unspoken words I can't identify.

"You don't taste like mint and menthol anymore," I say dazedly, making me realize he's lived with me for a week, and I haven't seen him smoke once.

"Someone wise told me it was a filthy habit, so I quit." The rasp in his voice brings goose bumps to every inch of exposed skin.

"Oh," I breathe. He quit ... for *me*? "You didn't have to—"

"Wouldn't have done it if I didn't want to. Now, time for you to get to bed before I do something else I've been dying to do."

My mouth goes dry.

The scalding heat in his stare tells me in no uncertain terms that *I* am what he's been dying to do. When I don't immediately retreat, he inches forward.

"Not warnin' you again." His voice is now shredded and raw. He's on the verge of losing control.

No matter how much I want to experience his brand of worship, I'm not ready. This thing between us is too big to take lightly. I'm already halfway to a panic attack merely thinking about it. So I do the only thing I can and scurry away to the safety of my bedroom, hating that I feel like a coward.

27
Sante

"I THINK IT WOULD BE SMART TO BRING ORAN INTO THIS, BUT you're the Don. My loyalty is to you and this family. If you want us to handle it internally, I'll honor your decision." The Byrne and Moretti organizations are still separate entities despite the marital ties of recent years. I don't want to make any assumptions about working with the Byrnes, whether the matter is business or personal. There's only one person who can make that decision on our end.

Renzo listened intently as I explained the situation with Amelie and the AG. Even after I've finished, his calculating stare continues to analyze and assess. When he finally responds, his observation surprises me.

"I knew they were strict over there, but Sicily changed you even more than I expected," he says in a contemplative tone.

"It's called the old country for a reason. Traditions hold value."

"True, but times evolve."

"People don't. Survival of the fittest still governs our motives and decisions. We can pretend to be civilized, but the primal instincts are still alive underneath it all. Anyone who thinks differently is simply lower on the food chain. They're prey, whether they know it or not."

Something shifts in his eyes—a flash of intrigue. "You ever gone camping?"

My brows draw together as I try to figure out where he's going with this line of questioning. "Not traditional camping with tents and s'mores. I've slept under the night sky and depended on a garden for food."

He nods. "We go camping in the summers. You ought to come with us this year. I think you'd enjoy it. And before you question my ability to pay attention, this is all related. I agree with your assessment of the world more than most probably would. The three weeks I spent with Shae in the Canadian wilderness showed me a whole new side of myself that I had never known existed. When we came back, I saw the world differently. I saw life in terms of survival rather than a business—what I can live with and what I can't live without."

This man and I were at each other's throats from the minute he became my guardian until the day I left for Italy. And now, I hear him voicing my own beliefs as though he has a front-row seat in my head. It's unnerving.

I have to clear my throat before I can respond. "Amelie is my future. I refuse to live without her or let her be hurt in any way if I can prevent it."

It's his turn to nod. "If that means working with the Byrnes, I can live with that."

"I'd like to think so since you *literally* live with a Byrne." I lighten the jab with a subtle smirk.

Renzo huffs out a laugh. "Careful, you end up with Lina's sister, and you might as well be part of the Byrne family, too. It's getting hard to tell where their family ends and ours begins."

He's not wrong. Between Noemi's marriage to Conner, Renzo's marriage to Shae, and Amelie's sister being married to Oran, the Irish are everywhere I turn.

Lazaro would have a coronary.

That's the only thing about honoring the old ways—sometimes it's important to incorporate the new. You have to figure out what's worth keeping and what's best left in the past.

"If it means having Amelie, I'll drink Guiness and eat potatoes until I die."

A smile creeps wide on Renzo's face. "I appreciate a man who knows his priorities." He's teasing me, but at the same time, the compliment is genuine. I'm surprised at how it affects me. I feel confident enough that I didn't think I needed or wanted his approval, but hell if I don't like having it all the same.

Now that I'm feeling better about where I stand with my cousin, I decide to take an undesirable yet necessary step back onto shaky ground. It's not my place to insert myself into Renzo's relationship with his brother, but I need to know Tommy has been received back into the family with the same goodwill as I have. The two talked after we did on Mother's Day. I asked Tommy how it went, and he didn't bring up any issues, but he's not exactly the sharing type.

"Tommy didn't say much about his visit with you." I

infuse as much respect and deference into my voice as possible to hopefully avoid inciting his anger. "I'd like to think you'd be as receptive to his return as you have been for me."

Hell, that sounded like a threat.

I can't help it. I'm protective where Tommy's concerned, though it's not entirely necessary. The man is probably more deadly than I am, especially when weapons are involved. Of course, that's not the sort of protection I'm worried about. Tom's dealt with enough criticism and rejection to last a lifetime. He doesn't need to feel that shit from his family, too.

Renzo doesn't even blink as he spears me through with his stare. "Maybe he didn't say much because it's none of your business."

"If it were anyone else, I'd agree. At this point, Tommy's business will probably always be my business."

His inscrutable stare holds steady. "You're lucky I want that for him, or I'd be handing you your balls in a ziplock baggie right now."

I give a single nod, acknowledging his right to do so and in appreciation for refraining.

"Tom's my brother. I'd never alienate him from the family. I don't understand him sometimes, but we're still blood. That enough reassurance for you?"

He's not that hard to understand if you'd make the effort.

I keep my desired response to myself, knowing I've already pushed my luck. "Yeah, that works. I've already looped him into the situation with Talbot, and he's doing a deep dive into the guy's digital footprint. I figure it's best to know that there's no grudges between us if we're all going to be working together."

"He always was good with computers," Renzo says,

amusement and a touch of pride teasing a tiny smirk from him.

"He's moved way past good these days. Guy's a fucking genius."

That earns me a sliver of a smile. "Let's set up a meet with Oran. He needs to know what's going on before something bad happens. With the four of us working together, Talbot doesn't have a chance."

"THE FUCKING thing didn't just swerve—it sped up. I *knew* that car was trying to hit her. Thing didn't even have plates." To say Oran is livid would be an understatement. He's so pissed he can't stop pacing. "I've been trying to think of who could have come after us ever since and come up empty. Sure, we have our enemies, but nothing out of the ordinary. Certainly nothing major going on right now."

"I can't guarantee he's responsible, but Amelie seemed pretty convinced," I tell him. "That bastard has kept her terrified for the past four fucking years."

"I can't believe she didn't say anything. She should know we'd help her, especially when Lina's involved."

"That's the tricky part. There's a catch." My eyes cut to Renzo in anticipation of the bomb I'm about to drop. "Amelie made me promise not to take action against him because he claims he has a video of Lina. Back from when she ... when The Society ..."

Shit. I knew this would be hard, but I can't even say the words. How do I bring up the time a man's wife was raped as a teenager? I feel like punching myself for him, but it has to be said. He needs to know what we're up against.

I'm about to force myself to continue when I hear the

familiar click of a gun clip releasing. Oran checks that his clip is fully loaded before holstering his gun and grabbing his keys.

"I'll cut him into so many pieces the fish won't even want the scraps."

Renzo and I both lurch to our feet and block his path.

"You can't do that," Renzo says in a firm tone.

"*The fuck I can't,*" Oran roars. "That's my *wife* he's threatening."

"I get it, man. And we'll take care of him, but we have to do it carefully, so she's not hurt all over again."

Oran stills, his eyes narrowing to furious blue daggers. "What are you saying?"

Renzo nods in my direction. Both men turn their attention to me.

"Talbot told Amelie that if anything happens to him, he's arranged for the video to be released on the internet." I pause to let the implications sink in. "I swear to you, we will make this guy beg for death, but we can't go in with guns blazing without having assessed the situation first." I promised Amelie I wouldn't touch the guy, and I won't. Not until we're ready. At that point, nothing will stop me. My responsibility to protect her trumps any promise I might make about gaining her approval.

Oran's nostrils flare with each strained inhale as he struggles to control himself. Jaw clenched tight, he finally nods and backs away. "You have a plan?"

I take a relieved breath now that the hard part is over. "First, we need to know whatever there is to know about The Society and where this guy fits in."

"He doesn't," Oran snaps. "Never heard or saw his name during the entire takedown of their operation. This is all coming out of fucking left field."

Renzo crosses his arms over his chest, his head angling pensively to the side. "He never came up at all?"

"Not once, and believe me, I made sure every one of those bastards squealed like pigs before they took their last breaths."

"Maybe he was the friend of a member?" I ask, thinking out loud.

"Or," Renzo says in an eerily calm voice, "he's the AG, and The Society offered Amelie up as a bribe. Maybe for them, it was a business transaction."

"It would explain why he might demand leverage over her as part of the exchange—a fail-safe to ensure the arrangement didn't come back to haunt him." It makes sense when I look at it in that light.

Renzo nods. "He had to be shitting bricks when The Society was getting picked off one by one."

"And I can only imagine the tactics he used to instill fear in Amelie to keep her quiet." Now I'm the one itching to kill the guy.

Oran cracks his knuckles and returns to his desk chair. "Gentlemen, have a seat. We have planning to do."

I SHOULDN'T BE HERE. We made Oran swear he wouldn't go anywhere near Talbot until we're fully prepared. The same should apply to me, but I have to see him—not some video clip from a press conference. I want to see him in his natural surroundings to get a true sense of the man. Any halfway decent hunter has to know his prey. How it thinks. Where it likes to hide. What it does when it thinks no one's watching.

I plan to learn everything I can about the piece of shit.

After our meeting, I wait outside the AG's Manhattan

office until he leaves work, then follow him home. While state government offices are technically headquartered in Albany, most departments have branches here in the city. Learning Talbot works almost exclusively at the Manhattan office was easy enough.

I could have waited for him outside his apartment building, but I wanted to see him going about his daily life. I had no guarantee he was there today or that I'd manage to spot him, but luck was on my side. It helps that I can be very persistent when I need to be. Persistent enough that I'm still outside his building an hour later when Talbot takes his wife to dinner.

That's right. *His wife.*

The fucker is married. Poor woman probably has no clue her husband is a rapist piece of shit. I reconsider my assumption after watching the pair through the restaurant window. She might turn a blind eye, but she knows on some level. The asshole has been so patronizing to their server that his wife's embarrassment had her staring at her hands in her lap. I have no clue what he said, but the young server looked ready to burst into tears.

I get in a good hour of reconnaissance before they pay the check and stand to leave. Meanwhile, I've paid the valet enough money to convince him to take a ten-minute break while I fill in for him. When Talbot sees a man covered in tattoos standing at the valet station, he doesn't stop to question the fact that I'm not even wearing a uniform.

I grab his car keys and head for the lot around the corner. Douche drives a Porsche. So fucking cliché. I bring the car around, making sure to wear gloves, and before I get out, I drop a single bullet in the cup holder with his initials carved into it.

He won't know who it's from or what it's about—he

certainly won't have any reason to tie the threat to Amelie—but he'll know someone's coming for him.

Talbot's going to know what it's like to live in fear for a change. A little karmic retribution 101.

Let the lessons begin.

28
Amelie

"It's not like it's the first time we've ever left her with someone, and all the other Byrne ladies swear this sitter is the best—they've done all kinds of background checks on her—but you know how anxious I get," Lina says as we both watch the live stream feed from her hidden nanny cam on her phone.

"Rightfully so. She's irreplaceable." I lift my eyes and smile at my sweet sister. "You're such an incredible mother."

"Thanks, Mellie." Her smile is full of gratitude. "We were lucky to have Gloria to teach us what love is. I can't imagine where we'd be without her."

"No kidding. And speaking of, is she okay? She said she

couldn't make it because of a doctor's appointment, and I forgot to make sure nothing was wrong."

"She's fine. It's her annual mammogram."

"Oh, good. I'm so glad she's taking care of herself and that we could help with that." Some of Mom and Dad's estate was put into a trust for me, but I made sure a chunk was set aside for Gloria as well. She deserved it as much as I did. Lina did too, but she refused to touch a penny of it.

Our server briefly interrupts to take our lunch order, and I use her departure to segue into a new topic. Sante told me that he talked to Renzo and Oran. He assured me that none of the information was shared with Lina, per my request. Now that I've had a few days to process, however, I decided to tell her myself. I'll be surprised if Oran hasn't already since those two tell each other everything. But even so, she and I need to have the discussion regardless. Girls' lunch ended up being the perfect opportunity with Gloria absent.

"There's something I wanted to talk to you about." I have trouble meeting her eyes and instead study the way my fingers are systematically folding the corners of my napkin.

"What's up? Is everything okay?"

"I think so. I mean, yeah." I try to offer her a reassuring smile. "I wasn't sure if Oran already talked to you, but maybe not. Anyway, it's kind of weird to bring up now after all these years ... and I don't want you to be upset with me. I know I should have said something from the beginning, but I was scared." I stop my rambling when Lina's hand covers mine.

"Mellie Bellie, whatever it is, you can tell me," she reassures me with an ocean of love in her eyes.

I take a deep breath. "I saw the man I was supposed to be with that night, back when I ran away. Not just that—I recognized him. It was an election year, and my government teacher did a unit on the local offices up for grabs."

Her face goes ghostly white. "You told me you ran before he got there."

"I know," I whisper. "And I'm so sorry I lied. I didn't want to worry you and figured it would all go away if I kept my mouth shut. The problem is, he knows that I recognized him. I was in so much shock that I said his name. That's when we argued. He threatened me, and I ran. And every so often, he still sends reminders to make sure I know that he hasn't forgotten."

"*Reminders?*" Lina hisses, her outrage flaring like a grease fire doused in water. "That man is still threatening you?"

"Not just me, Lina. He threatened you, too. He says he has a video of you … when you were raped, and that he'd post it online if I came after him. I was too scared to test him." I can't bring myself to explain everything, so I tell her what I can. "Sante convinced me to tell him the man's name. He and Renzo and Oran have promised to handle the matter discreetly. I wanted you to hear about it from me, though. I'm so sorry I didn't tell you when it happened. I hated to worry you when you'd already been through so much."

"Oh, Mellie. You can always tell me anything." She yanks me halfway out of my chair to give me a crushing hug. "I'm so sorry you've had to live with that worry. And to know a man capable of what he planned to do was out there. I know better than anyone how awful that feels."

Tears sting my eyes. "I just wanted to protect you the way you've always watched out for me."

She pulls back, her hands on my arms and eyes glassy with fierce determination. "One thing I know for certain is that Oran will keep me safe. You don't have to carry that burden anymore. Okay?"

I nod, but I know in my heart that's not how it works. I will always do whatever I can for my Lina Bean.

"And the second thing I know is I'd rather a video of me circle the world over than men like him have the freedom to keep hurting people. If that needs to come out, let it. I did nothing wrong."

God, she's so freaking strong. I am in constant awe of my big sister. "Okay," I say softly.

"Good, now let's wipe our eyes and order mimosas. We deserve them."

I laugh and use my mutilated napkin to dab at my eyes. "You aren't going to ask me his name?"

"Nope. That human cesspit is nothing to me. He's not worth the energy it takes to voice his name."

I don't know how she does it. My sister is the toughest, most badass woman I've ever known. I don't want to think where I'd be without her.

She signals the server back to our table and orders us each a mimosa. "Now that we got that out of the way, it's time for girls' lunch. I've been looking forward to this all week."

"It's only Wednesday," I tease, relieved that she's lightened the mood.

"When you have a toddler, that's a long-ass time."

We have a truly delightful lunch together. Maybe it's the alcohol. Perhaps it was our initial conversation. Either way, when the meal is over, I find myself in a particularly sentimental mood. Rather than going to the theater early for extra warm-up time, I detour to a neighborhood I usually avoid.

The skies are appropriately overcast when I approach the outside of my childhood home. Someone new lives there now with no knowledge of the horrible dysfunction and tragedy that took place within those walls.

I used to wish the place would burn to the ground.

As I take it in now with fresh eyes, I'm glad it's still around. Despite the austere facade, there are signs of joy within. A second-story window has a garden of children's peel-and-stick flowers adorning the window, and the front door wreath cheerfully announces the arrival of summer with a rainbow of ribbons and tulle. I suspected that evil had tainted the very foundation of this building, but my eyes tell me otherwise. And if love can give this place a second chance, then I'd say love can wipe clean any slate.

I'm not sure what's happening to me. I should be anxious as hell with everything going on, yet I'm smiling like a loon at a house I used to hate.

It's been three days since I told Sante Talbot's name, and so far, the sky hasn't fallen. I haven't felt my stalker's watchful eyes on me nor received any new cryptic warning messages. I'm not naive enough to think that a storm isn't brewing just beyond the horizon. I know something's coming, but I also feel an unfamiliar wellspring of hope that we can weather whatever the storm brings. I've been to hell and back in my life but never let it steal my joy. This bump in the road will be no different.

My smile stays firmly planted on my lips as I head to the theater.

Hope can be such a crucial tool in surviving life. It can also be a double-edged sword. I'm reminded of that when my hopeful thoughts of the future distract me from my usual vigilance, and I'm yanked violently into an alley and out of sight. A man holds me from behind, his gloved hand clamped tightly over my mouth and nose. We're hidden behind a dumpster that probably stinks, but I can't smell or scream or breathe past his suffocating hold on me.

Panic engulfs me, eyes bulging wide as I struggle to break free.

"*You think he doesn't know when you open your mouth?*" the man hisses by my ear. He's holding me from behind, so I can't see him, but I can tell he's incredibly strong. "Boss had me leave you a note 'cause he's generous like that, but you didn't listen. You seem to think this is some fucking game."

My struggle weakens as I grow dizzy and lightheaded. His hand lowers from my nostrils enough that I can suck in a lungful of air. The relief is overwhelming, triggering a wave of emotions that burn in my eyes and throat.

"You paying attention, *bitch*?" His hand squeezes my jaw painfully. "We have a problem again, and there won't be any more warnings."

Just when I think I can't get any more terrified, the arm holding me against him drops until he's cupping my sex in the most demeaning, aggressive sort of violation. "Maybe I'll take some of this, too, before I silence you. I hear you're into that sort of thing." His voice is laced with giddy anticipation.

I wrench myself away from him with a surge of adrenaline that has my heart racing catastrophically fast.

"Stay the fuck away from me," I growl at him savagely. I should run, but I want to see this man who's been haunting me. I want to know the face that lurks in the shadows.

He's vile in the most mundane, mediocre way I can imagine. An average man with an all too typical sense of entitlement and superiority. I want to jump at him and claw at his eyes, but I force myself to do the safe thing. I run.

He doesn't follow me. I know because I look back every few seconds. It's a miracle I don't run into anything because I don't stop. I keep running even after I've rounded a corner and am on a sidewalk filled with other people.

My body burns through every last bit of the adrenaline before I finally slow and realize where I've taken myself. I'm a block away from Gloria's apartment. Of course, I would run to the one person who was my greatest source of comfort in childhood. She was more of a mother to me than my own flesh and blood, and now that she's within reach, I feel desperate to see her. So desperate that I do something I've never done before. Something unimaginable, considering there are only four days left until opening night.

I text my director that I'm sick, and I skip practice.

I can hardly believe what I'm doing, but at the same time, I'm beyond caring. I've slipped into self-preservation mode and am dangerously close to shutting down. A person can only take so much, and I've nearly reached my limit.

29 Amelie

I'M PREPARED TO WAIT FOR GLORIA TO RETURN FROM HER appointment, but she answers the door when I knock. Her bubbly grin is quickly doused with worry the second she takes in my disheveled state.

"Mija, what's happened? Are you okay?" She ushers me inside her tiny place. The money she was given could easily buy her something bigger, but she insists on staying where she is. I don't necessarily blame her. She's spent years making a cozy home for herself with personal touches in every nook and cranny. The place is so … *Gloria* that I'm instantly blanketed in comfort when I step inside.

"Hey, Mama G. I'm okay—I've just been going through a

bit of a rough patch." My attempt at a reassuring smile is watery and weak at best.

"My sweet girl. Come sit with me and tell me all about it." She takes my hand and pulls us both onto her small sofa like we used to do when I was younger—she sits, and I lay with my head on her lap. Her gentle fingers smooth my frazzled hair and rub comforting circles on my back.

"You know I'm not big on taking risks, especially if it could hurt someone I care about," I begin vaguely.

"Of course, mija. You always think of others first. Sometimes more than you should."

"That's the thing. I think it might be time to take a big risk. To open up to someone in a way that scares me. I think it might be the right thing to do, but there's a chance it could go horribly wrong."

"Life is full of risk, Mellie. Doing nothing is a risk. We can never know what the future holds—all we *can* do is make choices that we can be proud of with the information we have. And if things don't go our way, we have to give ourselves grace because we made our choice with the best of intentions."

"But do intentions really matter if someone ends up hurt?"

"Let's see," she muses softly. "When your mother tricked me into thinking you'd come home, back when you were missing, I called Lina to the house and lured her into a trap. I had no idea your mother had used me to get to Lina. Should your sister be angry with me for what I did?"

"Absolutely not," I respond adamantly. "You had no way of knowing what they had planned."

"Exactly. My intentions were good. I thought I was sharing wonderful news. Would it be hard for me to bear if

Lina had been hurt? Of course it would, but that's life. Sometimes bad things happen. That's why we do our best to celebrate the good."

I nod and sit up so I can look into the warm brown eyes that assure me everything will be okay. "I don't like when bad things happen."

"I know, mija," she says with a sad smile. "That's what happens when your heart is full of the purest kind of love—a love that will see you through those hard times. Trust yourself, sweet girl. Listen to your heart, and don't let fear change your mind."

She's right. I have to find a way to have faith in my choices. I've already decided to open up to Sante, but I've let fear hold me back. It's time to cut away those bindings.

"Thank you, Mama G." I wrap my arms around her and take one more inhale of her lilac-scented perfume. "You always know the right things to say."

"There has to be *some* advantage to getting old." She chuckles. "Otherwise, it's just aching joints and peeing when you sneeze."

My laughter is a much-needed bandage around my battered heart.

I give her another hug, clean myself up in the bathroom, then head out. When I look at my phone, I see two missed messages and a missed call from Sante.

Sante: You okay? Why are you at Gloria's and not the theater?

Sante: Mel???

Rather than type out a long explanation, I give him a call.

"I was two minutes from getting in my car," he snaps in a huff.

I bite back a smile. "I'm not used to having to report my

movements to anyone. My parents never cared. I've sort of always been on my own in that regard."

His overprotectiveness fills me with a joy that it probably shouldn't, but I don't care. I like knowing that I matter to someone. Gloria was there for emotional support, but she didn't monitor me the way a parent or a partner would.

"I'm okay, but I need to talk to you. Can you meet me at the apartment?"

"I'll come get you."

"No, it's okay. I'm enjoying the walk, but thank you for offering."

"Wasn't really a question," he grumbles, making me smile even more.

"I'll see you in a few minutes," I say firmly but gently before ending the call.

Am I stalling? Yes. I need the next few minutes to collect myself. My paranoia isn't thrilled about walking home after being attacked, but it's still daylight, and if that jerk had wanted to hurt me, he already had a perfect opportunity. I want to make sure I'm ready for the conversation I'm about to have. It would be difficult enough even without the tinge of a bruise blossoming on my jawline. Sante won't be pleased. Hopefully, what I have to say will offset his reaction.

One way or another, I'm about to find out.

Sante is waiting for me in the apartment when I arrive. He's seated at the dining table, phone out but forgotten the second I walk through the door. I set down my things but don't join him, leaning on the kitchen counter instead.

I take in the statuesque man across from me—rigidly

unflappable on the outside while an electric storm of intensity brews on the inside. The air around us is charged with his uncompromising energy. He is an endless reservoir of purpose and passion, all focused on a singular objective. Me.

I can't tell if the army of butterflies taking flight in my chest is owed more to nerves or excitement.

"Why didn't you go to rehearsals?" Sante asks in his signature calm.

"I'll explain, but first, I need to ask you something. I need to know why, Sante. Why did you come back for me when we hardly knew one another?"

Seconds pass before he answers.

"At first, I came back to prove myself wrong so I could finally quit thinking about you."

"But then you stayed," I note, wanting more.

He shrugs. "Turned out I was right."

"About what?"

"That you were meant for me."

He slowly rises and crosses to the kitchen where I'm standing. The closer he gets, the more his face pinches with undiluted fury. His hand gently angles my face up toward the lights.

"Why the fuck is your face bruised?" His voice morphs into something no longer human—the savage awakening of a creature thought to be extinct and long forgotten.

It might have frightened me if I wasn't still swaddled in a blanket of happiness from his assertion that I was made for him. I'm starting to believe he might be right.

I place my hand on his chest and smile softly. "That's what I wanted to tell you. Talbot sent someone to threaten me, but I'm done hiding. I'm done living in fear. You know the stakes, and I trust you to handle it as you see fit."

The black daggers in Sante's eyes warm to melted pools of obsidian. "Say it again."

"I trust you," I say with quiet certainty.

"You trust me to keep you safe, but what about this?" His right hand collars my throat and guides me closer to him. "Do you trust me with your body, too?"

I can hear the hidden longing and anticipation feathering his words. Sensing the intensity of his desire for me helps calm my fears, though my heart continues its frantic pace.

"I do." The breathy admission is a relief. A release of sorts.

Sante's thumb ghosts across the bruise on my jaw. "I will handle this," he murmurs almost to himself. "I swear to you, I will do everything in my power to make sure no one ever hurts you again."

Each word is forged with an ardent commitment so fierce that emotion seizes tight around my throat and chokes off my words. All I can do is nod.

"I want all of you, Amelie. Every inch of you inside and out."

"I'll give what I can."

"What does that mean?" His eyes drift to my lips.

"It means I'm messed up," I admit, swallowing down my insecurities that try to rise to the surface.

"Aren't we all." His growled response is a statement spoken with certainty and an end to the conversation. He brings my lips within a breath of his, his hand still at my throat. "I need to taste you, pet."

I need to taste him, too.

I lean forward to finally bring our lips together, but his hand tightens a fraction in warning.

He slowly shakes his head, wicked mischief teasing the corners of his lips. "I had something even ... *sweeter* in mind."

In a flash, he lifts me in his arms and deposits me on the

kitchen island. I'm only seated for a second when he whisks my shirt off, leaving me in a sports bra and leggings.

"Lie back." His seductive command licks across my skin.

I do as he says. The granite countertop is just big enough to fit my upper body. I have to plant my heels by my butt with my knees bent in the air. The stone is cool, but the heat of Sante's stare keeps me plenty warm.

He hooks his fingers in my leggings and panties, coaxing me to lift my hips so he can slide them both off. Once I'm bare, the nerves amp up a notch.

I've never been a fan of oral because it's work for my partner, which puts even more pressure on me. Whenever I've encouraged a guy to keep going or a partner insisted he could get me to orgasm, it's always ended in frustration and disappointment. So far, Sante has proven himself different from the others, but I'm still hesitant. I desperately want to please him.

My thoughts scatter when I see Sante lift my panties to his nose and take a languid sniff.

"*Mmm* ... smells so fucking good." He drops them on the floor but keeps my leggings in his hand as he prowls around to the other side of the island. Once he's standing by my head, he stretches one leg of the leggings to its full length, then brings it down over my eyes like a blindfold.

I suck in a breath, unsure if I'm comfortable with the loss of control.

Sante must sense my reluctance. "Shhh, pet. It's going to help you feel good. Help you lose yourself in the sensations." After tying the legs at the side of my head and placing the extra fabric under my head as a sort of pillow, he trails a steady hand down the center of my chest. "No other thoughts, just pleasure."

My brain is so wired, I'm pretty sure a lobotomy is the only thing that would quiet my thoughts right now, especially when Sante's hand disappears and he walks away from the island. I strain to figure out what he's doing. My ears focus on every tiny noise as he opens drawers and moves about. The anticipation pricks at my skin from all directions. I desperately want to look, but I told him I trust him. It's time to prove it.

30
Sante

IF YOU ASK ME, WOMEN ARE INCREDIBLE STRATEGISTS AND ARE totally underutilized in our society. We make jokes about how their brains are always on, thinking of a million things at once, then we limit their access to leadership roles. It's the fucking dumbest thing in the world. Totally counterintuitive.

Those active brains help them see five steps ahead.

When tragedy strikes, they've already planned for three contingency scenarios. They see problems before they're problems. That sort of intuition is an excellent advantage in life, but every now and then, it can also get in the way—especially where sex is concerned.

Sex is physiological. The brain has to step aside and let the body take over. For some women, like Amelie, that's problematic. They need help turning off their thoughts and letting the body take over. Things like blindfolds or restraints can be helpful. Instead of dwelling on the objective of reaching an orgasm, the mind can focus on wondering what's coming next and the sensations themselves. Things that aid rather than sabotage their own pleasure.

If there's one thing I can say about my time in Italy, it's that it was educational.

Italians know sex.

As I stand over Amelie and think of how I gave her her first orgasm—how I was able to do that because of what I've learned while I was away—I'm wondering more than ever if things happen for a reason. I've never been one to buy into the whole things-work-out-for-the-best. My father killing my mother was *not* for the best or any good at all. I don't like the idea that it happened for a reason, and certainly not if I'm that reason.

However, I'm willing to accept that some good has come from her loss. At least from that perspective, the tragedy serves a purpose. Amelie is that purpose. She's been through so goddamn much and stayed so incredibly strong that nothing makes me prouder than knowing I can help keep that vibrant spirit alive in her eyes. I can keep her safe and bring her pleasure like she's never known.

I am meant for this woman, and she is meant for me.

"You are the most beautiful thing I have ever seen." The second I say the words, a succulent flush blossoms on her cheeks, spreading down her neck and chest. She's truly breathtaking.

I take the wooden spoon I found in a drawer and trail it along one of her thighs up to her delicate hip bone, then on toward her breasts. No doubt she's consumed with trying to figure out what I'm holding and what I'll do next. Thoughts that spark anticipation. Excitement.

While I circle each breast with the spoon, staying clear of her pebbled nipples, I reach down and cup her sex with my palm. I'm so satisfied with what I find that I fucking purr.

"My girl is already dripping for me." I slide two fingers on either side of her clit, slow and purposeful, then glide one of those fingers into her warm pussy.

Amelie's back arches off the counter with her gasp. I've never heard of a man's dick bursting from too much blood flow, but mine sure as hell is trying. I'm so hard that my balls ache.

I work my fingers inside her for several strokes, then use the flat side of the spoon to give a light pop to one nipple, then the other. She lets loose a throaty moan that is doing nothing for my hard-on.

"A little touch of pain feels good, doesn't it, pet?"

She nods, her pretty pink tongue swiping her bottom lip. It makes me want a taste. I move from where I stand until I'm at her head, above her, looking down. I bend and kiss along her jaw until I'm at her lips. We're upside down from one another, giving the kiss a whole different feel. While our tongues explore, I slide the bottom of her sports bra up above her breasts. I don't take it off; I just move it enough to free them.

Her hands spread wide, flattening her palms against the granite as though she's having to force herself to hold still.

"Good girl, keep those hands where they are," I encourage, knowing a task like that keeps her active mind occupied.

When I graze my teeth over her nipples, then lick and suck them, her body truly begins to writhe with need. The pressure is building, and I'm so goddamn here for it.

I shower her breasts with attention until her moans fade to pleading whimpers.

"Please, Sante. I need you to touch me."

"I am touching you," I say wickedly, giving her nipple one more twist with my fingers.

The sound she makes in answer isn't entirely human. It's pure animalistic need—the resurgence of her primal side. Her mind has surrendered to her body, and that's exactly what I want.

I finally move back to the far end of the island, taking in the beautiful sight of her arousal coating her and dripping down over her tightly puckered ass.

"Time to eat." My voice has taken its own walk on the wild side, sounding half savage.

I coax Amelie's legs over my shoulders, and she hooks her feet around my upper back. That first taste is sublime. I do one slow circle of my flattened tongue over her clit, then a languid lick along her full length.

The guttural groan of relief that resonates from her chest makes me feel like I've climbed fucking Everest. I dive in, working her folds, one side, then the other. When I add a finger to rub at that hidden bundle of nerves inside her, her hips begin to flex and roll. I make sure to let up every now and then, giving her body time to miss my touch and crave more. Only when the need has snowballed into an avalanche that can't be controlled do I hold my course and drive her over that heavenly cliff.

I don't allow the squeeze of her thighs to keep me from milking every last ounce of pleasure from her core. Her body jerks and vibrates, dancing to the music of her mindless cries.

She is unbridled beauty.

A fucking goddess.

"*Absolute perfection*," I whisper against her tender flesh before finally pulling away.

I help her place her heels back on the counter and circle around to lift her into my arms. She removes her blindfold, then hugs my shoulders, resting her forehead against the side of my neck. I take her back to the bathroom and start the shower water for her. As much as I'd love to fuck her six ways to Sunday, she's not ready.

"You get cleaned up, and I'll order us some food, okay?"

Amelie smiles shyly, then reaches up on her toes to bring her lips to mine for one last kiss.

"Fuck, my girl is sweet when she comes," I tease, patting her ass before I head back to the kitchen.

Before I do anything else, I grab a few paper towels and unbuckle my pants. If I don't do something about this monster erection, it may do permanent damage. I look over at the island, reliving what just played out, and with an embarrassingly few strokes, I'm jetting into my own hand.

Jesus, I needed that.

I clean up myself and the island, which still has evidence of our earlier activities smudged on its glossy surface. Once it's sanitized, I order Chinese, then answer a few emails until Amelie returns from her shower. She sits on the sofa beside me, though not close enough for my taste. I take it upon myself to remedy the situation. With one hand behind her back and the other around her thigh, I hoist her closer.

"Better," I grunt before picking up the TV remote. I scroll through the apps to find a handful of streaming services, but that's it. "No Hulu or local channels?"

"No, the news sort of gives me panic attacks," she admits warily. "That man does a surprising number of press conferences. I began to feel like turning on the TV was a game of Russian roulette, so I quit watching."

"News is always depressing anyway," I concede. I need to stay informed on local events, but checking a news app on my phone is easy enough. No reason to upset her if it's not necessary.

Glancing in her direction, I realize she's grinning like a kid with candy. "What?"

"I've felt like a freak for years because of my aversion to the news. Do you know how many restaurants have TVs playing on the walls? Lina and Oran know I hate the news but never knew why. It's yet another one of the things that's felt like this huge obstacle for me ... until you came along. It's like, with you around, everything is easier."

Fuck if my chest doesn't physically swell with pride.

"That's the way it should be," I mutter, not entirely comfortable with compliments. "Any man can stick his dick in a woman. There's no real value to that. A man's worth is in his ability to provide and protect—to make his family's lives better."

Again, I sneak a glance her way, and this time, that grin is practically splitting her face in two.

"What now?"

She giggles. "You callin' me your family, Sante Mancini?" She's teasing me, but it doesn't feel like a joke. I wasn't kidding when I called her my future wife.

"So long as I'm breathing," I say without a trace of humor.

Amelie sobers. I wonder if I've made her uncomfortable by being so transparent, but she surprises me by snuggling closer and laying her head on my shoulder. "What are we going to watch?"

Hell, I could watch paint dry if it means being with her a little longer.

To keep from looking like a psycho, I put on a sitcom rerun and hold my girl close. I half watch while mostly thinking about how Talbot made a huge fucking mistake by sending someone to threaten Amelie. No one puts their hands on my woman.

Dumbass doesn't know he's only making things worse for himself. He'll figure it out soon enough. We've circled him and are closing in, taking our time to make sure it's done right. And when that time comes, he'll never see us coming.

The thought has me in a relatively good mood when a text comes through from my sister.

Noemi: Any chance we can get together soon? I'd like to talk with you.

Tension ratchets into my neck and shoulders.

"Something wrong?" Amelie asks, making me realize I've audibly sighed.

"No, just Noemi."

Me: I'm pretty busy. I'll reach out when things settle.

It's not a lie. Keeping eyes on Amelie is a full-time job. The bigger problem is I still feel like shit when I see my sister. She's a constant reminder of how painfully I fucked up in my past. It's getting better now that our official reunion is over, but I'm not jumping at the chance to feel like shit. Besides, it's only been a few days since I saw her. She can wait a few more.

Noemi: It's kind of important

Fuck. What the hell is that supposed to mean?

Another sigh.

Me: I can come by Saturday

I don't want to, but I can.

Noemi: How about 3? Boys should be napping then.

Me: That works. See you then

Noemi: Thank you! I really appreciate it.

I heart her reply and toss my phone aside, not wanting to

think about the upcoming visit. She probably wants to ask me to be a godfather to the boys or something like that. Something that may be important but isn't urgent. Right now, my focus is Amelie. She needs me, and I'm not losing sight of that until this shit with Talbot is done.

31
Amelie

IF THE *GUINNESS BOOK OF WORLD RECORDS* KEEPS TABS ON THE most extreme mood swings in a single day, I'd have that title locked down. I've baffled myself at how swiftly I bounced back from utter despair and terror in that alley to floating on puffy clouds of hope and belonging. And it's all because of Sante.

Well, I'll give Gloria some props, too. She is my Mama G, after all.

Secure in Sante's arms, I feel untouchable. I have this newfound confidence that everything will work out, though I have no idea how. That's not like me. I'm not the sort to relax until a problem is six feet under, and John Talbot is still very much in the here and now.

If Sante has his way, he won't be for long.

I feel a thrill when I think about the life fading from that monster's eyes. I want him gone. The only problem with that is if he's killed, he never truly has to pay for his crimes. That's been bugging me lately. It's so unfair that I should have to suffer for years, and death would be an easy way out for him. Granted, Sante would probably draw it out to some extent—not something I want to think about too hard—but it still doesn't sit right.

Talbot should have to know what it's like to live day after day after day shrouded in shame and fear.

That would be justice.

For years, I simply wanted him gone. Now that plans are in motion to make that happen, I'm starting to reconsider.

I give it some thought here and there during the evening as we eat, then watch a little more TV. The hours pass with surprising ease, as though we've been a couple for ages. I find such comfort in his presence, that is, until we decide to call it a night. That's when my heart takes its cue to down an adrenaline cocktail and start shadowboxing in my chest.

I stand awkwardly, unsure what to do or say. I've scurried to my room like a frightened rabbit each night he's been here, but that doesn't feel right tonight. I don't want to go back there alone. I also can't find the words to invite him to join me. As it turns out, I don't have to.

"Comin' with you tonight." Sante places his hand on my lower back, guiding me to lead the way.

"Okay," I say quietly, my eyes seeking his in a brief plea for reassurance.

It's okay. Everything's going to be okay.

I take one step forward when his hand grasps me by the back of the neck. He halts my momentum, turning me around to face him. The intensity now carved in his stone features takes me by surprise. I suddenly feel like a child about to be chastened, and I have no idea why.

"I'd like to think you'd know by now that I'm not gonna make you do anything you're not comfortable doing." He's been off ever since that text from his sister, and my moment of uncertainty seems to have struck a chord.

"I'm sorry." I gnaw on my bottom lip. "I didn't mean to imply I was worried. I'm just not very good at all this." *Because hardly any of my past relationships have ever made it this far.*

Sante and I have progressed in a matter of weeks what's usually taken me months in the past. I should be upfront and explain, but I can't make myself do it. Explaining means showing him the weakest most pathetic parts of myself. Why go there if it's not necessary? Let him make his own judgments about me. It's better that way.

"You said you've been with other men, right?" he pushes, eyes narrowing.

"Yeah, I've had several boyfriends." *A couple.*

"And you've had sex before?"

"Yes." *Once.*

That's enough with question time. I let a sheepish grin crook the corners of my lips. "You really shouldn't doubt me when I tell you I'm an awkward mess. I'll keep proving it, though, if you need reminders."

He stares for three seemingly endless heartbeats before shaking his head. "Go on. You need rest before practice tomorrow."

I do as I'm told, relieved he let it go. I go to the bathroom while Sante locks up. When I open the door, he joins me inside and starts the water for a shower. The second his clothes start coming off, I chicken out and abandon brushing my teeth for the safety of my bed.

I want to scream at myself for being such a coward.

Why? Why, when I desperately want to see the gorgeous body beneath his clothes, do I feel the need to run? He's not going to hurt me. He's not going to pressure me. I hate that I have to be this way, but I don't know how to stop it.

I'm so fucking frustrated with myself that by the time he's done, I'm curled up in a ball facing away from him, a tear dangerously close to wetting my pillow.

Sante slips beneath the covers and turns out the light. He doesn't say a word. He simply curves his body protectively around mine and places a tender kiss behind my ear.

Simple as that, everything is right with the world again.

I don't know how he does it. I'd say he could read my mind if I thought that sort of thing was possible. I'm glad it's not because there's plenty I'm not ready to share—like the fact that I'm falling for this complicated, beautiful man.

He's not at all what I thought I wanted, yet he's everything I need. He pushes me out of my comfort zone without risking harm and accepts me exactly as I am.

He's also domineering, possessive, and a tiny bit unhinged.

Yeah, but I have my own fun little quirks as well. It's hardly my place to judge, right? I mean, he's sexy as hell and makes me feel like a queen. That's all that should matter.

My inner debate partner goes eerily silent, and I don't like it. She always has something to say.

Deciding not to borrow troubles, I allow the security of Sante's presence to lull me into a deep and dreamless sleep.

32

Amelie

"Look who's joined us again." Kennedy flashes a seductive grin at Sante from the stage as he selects a chair to occupy during practice. I'm walking up the stage steps to go back to the dressing room when her flirtatious words bring me to a stop.

Is she seriously hitting on him right in front of me?

The awkwardness intensifies as she continues. "Little Amelie here never told us she has a brother. Are you military? I could see you serving with big guns. If that's the case, I hope you've had a *proper* welcome home." She begins her warm-up as she talks, stretching in the most seductive ways possible.

I've never been in a catfight in my life, but there's always a first time for everything. My vision bleeds red, and all the venomous words I want to say tangle into a useless knot on my tongue.

Fortunately, I don't have to say a thing. Sante handles her in the most blasé, crude manner possible—and it thrills me from head to toe.

"That's because Amelie doesn't have a brother, and I don't fuck my sister."

Kennedy scoffs, rallying to save face. "I don't see how that's possible. She spends every waking minute practicing. If I had a man like you waiting for me, I'd make plenty of time for him." She shoots me a spiteful glare.

Sante gets out his phone, not even looking at Kennedy when he responds. "No leading role *and* no man. Sounds like you should focus on yourself and less on Amelie."

I honest-to-God snort out loud, then scurry backstage before I devolve into a fit of giggles. I don't need to see what happens next. Sante executed a perfect KO, though I'm the one in the ring with my arms held high.

I dance my heart out at practice. Only one more rehearsal before opening night, but that's not the sole source of my inspiration. I feel like I'm dancing with a sign on my back that reads *he's mine*. I'm so fucking proud of that sign. I want everyone's eyes drawn to me so they can see what it says.

I think Sante may have been right. I couldn't see it before, but I did choose him, and I'm growing more confident with that decision every day.

By the end of evening practice, I'm exhausted. Sante suggests we pick up food on the way home.

"That sounds like perfection." I rest my head back and melt into the seat. My muscles feel like a mound of Jell-O, jiggling with the slightest pressure.

"Good, because I've already called it in." He drives us to a steakhouse, which is a bit more upscale than where we've gone before.

"I thought you said takeout?" I ask in confusion.

"It is. You need the protein. Don't want you fueling up on junk before the big night."

"Okay, but I'm not dressed to go in there." And I'm not entirely sure the concealer I used to cover the hint of bruising on my jaw is still intact.

"You stay put. I'll grab it."

"Thank you." I smile appreciatively.

He's so freaking incredible that I can hardly believe how lucky I am.

Sante leaves the car running when he gets out, locking the doors behind him. I watch him walk down the sidewalk toward the restaurant until a car pulls up behind us and the reflection of their lights in the side mirror forces me to look away. I'm lost in a stare at the dashboard lights when a knock on the window startles me half to death.

A uniformed police officer is bent at the waist, looking inside the car. He motions for me to roll down the window.

Suffocating unease fills the car like water from a flash flood.

I don't like cops. I don't trust them, and I have no idea why this guy would possibly need to talk to me, but I don't feel like I can ignore him. With my luck, I'll end up arrested for belligerence over nothing.

He knocks again, spurring me into action. I roll down the window halfway. A compromise.

"Yes, sir?" I say innocently.

"I need to ask you a few questions. Please step out of the car." His tone is severe, and his piercing stare spears right through me.

The only thing keeping me from vomiting is knowing I'd

never forgive myself for ruining Sante's beautiful new car.

"Um ... can you ask me from here?" I manage to hold my ground but in the meekest most uncertain voice possible. "I'm a dancer, and I've twisted my ankle."

"Ma'am, are you refusing to cooperate?" he asks aggressively.

"No! I just..." I just what? I don't know what to tell him, but every instinct in my body urges me not to step outside the car.

Tears pool in my eyes.

"Please, my ankle really hurts," I say, not having to act when my chin quivers.

He leans forward like he's going to reach into the car when a wall of black slides between us. Sante. He's inserted himself between the cop and the car, slowly walking the officer away from me. His position prevents me from seeing what's happening. I can hear the low murmur of his baritone voice, but I can't make out what he's saying.

My eyes squeeze tightly shut.

Please, don't end up in a fistfight with a cop.

That would put a serious damper on our evening. I'm debating whether I should step in to de-escalate the situation when Sante abruptly walks away from the man and gets back in the car, setting the bag of food on the floorboard behind me. He raises the passenger window, prompting me to look back at the cop. The man's staring right at me, a vein bulging from his forehead with such force that steam might shoot from his ears any second.

"What did you say to him?" I ask as we pull into traffic.

"Nothing you need to worry about." His unconcerned tone is reassuring, but I'm still anxious.

"Do you think he's working for Talbot?"

"I think he targeted you for a reason that had nothing to

do with the law. He followed us, saw me leave the car, and took his opportunity. I don't give a fuck about his why."

I guess he has a point. I hadn't thought about the fact that if I'm with Sante, he brings a whole new set of dangers to the table because of his line of work. I'd only considered Sante's dangerous side in regard to how he could help me. The flip side of that coin is important, too.

I spend the rest of the car ride home thinking about whether the risks associated with him change my feelings about our relationship. Oran has been in Lina's life for years now and never endangered either of us. I wonder if Oran's role in his Irish family business is at all similar to Sante's part in the Moretti organization. I've never seen Oran fight anyone ever, and I've already seen Sante draw blood twice. It's something to consider.

We eat once we're home. I'm quiet and somewhat contemplative but mostly just tired. Sante seems to understand and doesn't push for conversation. I appreciate that we're able to share a companionable silence without feeling awkward. When we're done, I toss my Styrofoam in the trash and stretch.

"I'm going to hop in the shower."

He stands and tosses his trash as well. "I'll join you."

I'm suddenly very, *very* awake. He wants to shower with me. Is that a segue to shower sex? I think of the intense chemistry that lives in the air around us and can't imagine sex not happening if we're both naked and wet and oh my God so close together.

My nonchalant walk to the bathroom deserves an Academy Award, considering I'm freaking the fuck out on the inside. I start the water and get fresh towels from the cabinet. Sante follows me into the small space, making him seem that much larger.

Breathe, Mellie. You got this.

I decide now is actually a stellar time to brush my teeth. Anything to stall. Toothpaste on the brush, I freeze mid-motion when Sante tosses his shirt to the floor, finally giving me a first peek at his tattooed body. He's sheer perfection, as I knew he would be. Whoever designs his artwork is incredibly gifted. The all-black designs flow together seamlessly, covering his chest, arms, and back, leaving only his abs unmarked. Abs sculpted in stone, sleek and smooth in a way that makes me want to trace my tongue along each dip and curve.

When his pants come off, he's in nothing but boxer briefs, and he's got a hard-on. The biggest, most terrifying hard-on I've ever seen in my life.

My wide eyes stare back at me in the mirror, making me realize I still haven't brushed my teeth, and the toothpaste has fallen from my brush into the sink.

Mel, pull yourself together. Do not *act like a total freak.*

I start to wash the toothpaste down the drain, dropping my toothbrush in the process.

"You want to know what I told that cop?"

I jump, not realizing Sante has joined me at the vanity and is now leaning his backside against the counter with his hands curved around the edge on either side of him.

"Um, sure."

He looks over at me, holding my gaze captive with the intensity in his own. "I told him he was harassing my wife, and he'd better find another favorite pastime if he wanted to keep his kneecaps intact." He twists his torso to face me and guides a wayward strand of hair behind my ear. "I wasn't joking when I said I'm going to marry you. You're mine. That means I'll protect you at all costs. It also means I have the rest of my life to fuck you in every position imaginable, and I plan for us both to live very long, healthy lives. There is absolutely. No. Rush. Understand?"

How is it he can say the most outlandish thing possible and somehow make me feel better for it? He's threatening cops and telling me we're going to get married when we've only known one another for a couple of weeks. Every bit of that should petrify me. Instead, his words calm me like a cool breeze on a summer day.

"Okay," I respond to show him I got it.

What I hear is that he saw my panic and knew exactly what had me worried. I understand that, above all, he wants me to feel safe and comfortable.

Emotions swell in the back of my throat until I catch sight of one of his tattoos that distracts me. I reach forward and trail my fingers across the evil eye inked over his heart. It's not overly obvious in the mix of his other busy designs, but it jumps out to me.

"It was easier than keeping up with the ring," he offers casually. He's making light of his actions, but I can't ignore the implications of him tattooing himself with the symbol I gave him.

"Why did you leave?" I ask, suddenly inundated with a plethora of questions.

"They didn't tell you?"

"No." I shake my head. "Not really. I heard you'd gotten into trouble and went to live with other family."

He pushes off the counter. "Let's get in the shower, and I'll tell you about it." He hooks his thumbs into my leggings and helps slide them down my legs. I remove my leotard while he takes off his boxers, leaving us both naked. Embarrassment never has a chance to descend. Sante leads the way to the shower, then makes room for me to wet down first.

"You know my father killed my mother, right?"

I open my eyes, water dripping from my lashes, and nod. I don't know all the details, but I learned the basics from the other ladies mostly because of Noemi. I think she wanted me to know Lina and I weren't the only ones with a shitty home life growing up.

"Mom was incredible. One of those people who always saw the bright side—like Noemi." He motions for us to switch places. Once I'm out of the spray, he puts shampoo in his hands and gently lathers it into my hair. "I had no idea Dad was beating her on the regular—making sure not to leave bruises where people could see. He manipulated and threatened her. And when she finally took action to stand up against him, he had her killed."

"That's awful, Sante." My heart physically aches for him.

"The worst part is that it happened right under my nose."

"You were a kid," I try to interject quickly.

"I was sixteen when she died. That's old enough. And to top it off, Dad was going to do the same to Noemi, and I nearly let him." He speaks without emotion and not in a way that alludes to in-depth counseling and years of healing. His factual retelling is laced with arsenic and frigid to the touch.

Whatever happened back then continues to eat him alive inside.

"I can't even imagine what that was like."

He finishes scrubbing and guides me back to the shower spray. "It wasn't easy, but I also didn't handle it well. Drinking, stealing cars, all kinds of shit. My cousin Renzo decided it would be best if I started fresh in Sicily. I'm glad he did. It was exactly what I needed."

Once my hair is rinsed, he swaps places with me again. This time, his cock accidentally grazes my thigh. I quit breathing, my eyes dropping to his rock-hard length. A cloying need swirls deep in my belly despite my fears. He's so huge, I can't imagine having that inside me wouldn't hurt.

I suddenly realize he's been silent for a while. My stare jumps back to his. He's watching me, eyes brimming with curiosity and desire.

"You sure you've had sex before?"

I cock my head to the side and glare. "Not to inflate your already well-rounded ego, but you're ... bigger than anyone I've been with." I swallow, giving his throbbing cock one more glance. "By a lot."

He smirks, then turns me around and drowns my hair in conditioner. "Told you I won't hurt you, Mellie, and I meant it." His honeyed voice drips down my skin as tangible as the shower water.

"Easy for you to say," I mutter.

Sante gives my ass a playful smack. I yip and shoot him another glare. While I rinse the conditioner out, he washes his hair and body all in one. I'm transfixed by the sight of the bubbles drifting down every masculine inch of his body—the way they funnel into his Adonis V and the curling hairs on his legs that cause the bubbles to clump, then pop. I could watch the man shower for the rest of my life and never grow bored.

"I won't force you into anything, but I'm no angel. You keep looking at me like that, and I may not be able to keep my hands to myself." Strain shreds his voice to a ragged rumble.

I'm so intensely captivated by his body that cautionary thoughts escape me. I'm moving on pure instinct when I reach out and wrap my fingers around his soapy cock.

Sante hisses, his body going rigid.

I peek up at him, intoxicated by my effect on him. It's hard to decide where to look, but in the end, the velvety goodness pulsing in my palm owns my curiosity. My fingers don't reach all the way around him. I give a little squeeze, noting they still don't connect, then slowly glide my fist down to the base and back up. The soap is a perfect lubricant. I feel every vein and supple ridge against my palm.

At this moment, I want to see this man come more than anything in the world.

Thank God, my hand-job game is golden. It's been the saving grace for a couple of my prior relationships. When you don't orgasm and aren't normally drawn to sex, a good handy is essential.

I peer up at Sante through my wet lashes and run my tongue along my bottom lip, then add a second hand to the mix. Sante's eyes widen.

"*Fuck*, you're full of surprises." His eyes drift shut, head drifting back as I begin to twist and tug on his hardening cock. So long as I don't think about putting that thing inside me, I relish the feel of him—the soft stretch of his skin gliding over the tempered steel within.

Penises always seemed awkward to me before, yet there's nothing awkward about his. This masterpiece of nature should be pictured in the dictionary next to the word virility.

"I'm gonna paint you with my cum, pet. You ... good with that?" he says through clenched teeth.

I grin up at him, doubling down on my efforts.

He presses his fists against the walls on either side of him, his abs flexing tightly. "*Jesus, piccola.* Take it, let me see my cum all over you." A growl starts low in his chest, then rises up to release past his parted lips as jets of semen spurt onto my belly and chest.

I let my hand slip away as soon as I see him start to flinch at my touch, overly sensitized from his orgasm. I love that I now know how that feels. I understand.

Sante flattens one hand over the sticky cum on my stomach and drags it up to cup my breast while his other hand collars the back of my neck and brings us together in a kiss. His touch is reverent. He holds nothing back, and I feel each devoted swipe of his tongue for the promise that it is.

He rests his forehead against mine as we catch our breath.

"You have more to do in here?"

I nod. "I need to shave." No one likes a hairy ballerina.

"Take your time. I'll keep the bed warm." He rinses himself, then cleans the cum from my body before exiting the shower.

Despite his instructions, I hurry through a quick shave, ready to get back to him. It's a foreign feeling to me. I'm usually not a fan of bedtime for multiple reasons. None of that seems to matter where Sante is concerned.

I even decide to wear my tank top and panties that I used to wear before I started having an overnight guest. Judging by the appreciation in his eyes when I join him in bed, Sante approves. He tucks me into his side with my head resting on his chest. It feels good, but there's no way I can sleep like that, so I eventually roll onto my side, facing away from him. He grunts at my departure, but I keep at least one point of contact between us, which seems to satisfy him.

The next thing I know, I'm staring into the arctic eyes of a man I never want to see again.

He's hovering over me, calling my name.

Horror threatens to consume me. Ears ringing. Heart pounding.

I have to get away. I have to run.

But I can't. He's too strong. He's holding me down.

"Mellie, baby. Please, wake up. Mellie, you're having a nightmare. You need to wake up."

Ice blue warms to dark brown as the words start to penetrate. Confusion sets in, and my brain scrambles to catch up.

What the hell is happening?

"That's it, baby. Jesus, you scared the shit outta me." Sante wraps me in his arms.

It was a dream. A nightmare.

I close my eyes, trying to erase all vestiges of that horrific blue stare. I haven't had a nightmare in ages. It doesn't make sense to me. Yes, Talbot is more in the forefront of my mind lately, but that's because his reign of terror is ending. I feel safer now than I have in years. It's like my subconscious can't stand to let me find peace.

"I'm sorry. I don't know what happened." I dab at my forehead, finding it sticky with sweat.

"Nightmare had you in its hooks. You have those often?"

"No, not at all. Probably opening night jitters—I don't even remember what it was about." I slink away from him and head for the bathroom. I need a moment to regroup.

When I return, Sante is still awake.

"You were awfully upset for it to be about dancing." His voice has gone quiet. Calculating.

I get under the covers, grateful for the darkness. "Who knows? The brain is a strange place."

"Mel, you were crying *don't touch me*," he argues, not wanting to let the subject go.

He's in for disappointment.

"Maybe it was about my parents. I told you, I don't remember," I say more forcefully. He may want an explanation, but some things are better forgotten. He can push all he'd like. This is one hill I'll die on.

He drops the questions, but he hasn't let it go. I know because an hour later, when I'm finally drifting back to sleep, he's still wide-awake.

33
Sante

I'M UP HALF THE NIGHT THINKING ABOUT AMELIE'S NIGHTMARE. My gut tells me she knows what the dream was about, but why hide it? If it was about Talbot, why not say so? And if it was about her mother, what other horrors could the woman have forced on her?

I don't like not knowing, and I *hate* feeling powerless. I can't help her if she won't tell me what's bothering her. All of it pisses me off. Between that and a lack of sleep, I start my Friday in a shit mood. The one silver lining is that we will make significant progress on our plans for Talbot. Today is Amelie's last rehearsal before opening night on Sunday. She'll be at the theater all day. I considered staying with her, but she should be safe surrounded by the entire cast, and the timing ended up perfect.

We've been monitoring Talbot's work and cell phones, along with his admin's. He'll be in Philly all weekend. His wife primarily stays at their home in Albany, so she won't be an issue. His Manhattan apartment will be empty. We've gathered everything we can via electronic means. It's time for a hands-on search.

Once Amelie is squared away at the theater, I pick up Tommy and head to Oran's place.

"Gentlemen," he greets us each with a handshake once we arrive, then leads us back to his home office. "Have a seat. Let's make sure we're all on the same page before we do this."

"Tommy's assured me he can handle the security system," I offer.

"You have quite an impressive skill set," Oran tells my cousin. "My guys tell me your hacking abilities are top-notch."

Tommy nods stoically. "I'm glad I can help, though I wish we'd been able to come up with more."

Oran's lips thin. "We've traced his web of contacts and collected a stash of evidence against him, not to mention all the shit he's got on other people. Your efforts haven't been wasted."

No, but we haven't found anything on Lina, or Amelie for that matter. It could be that there's nothing to find. His threats could be complete bullshit. But we'd all hate to have overlooked something, so we're trying to leave no stone unturned.

"I think we'll all feel better once we've gone through his place," I say what we're all thinking.

Oran nods. "And if need be, we'll hit the Albany house, too. Though, I suspect he keeps the family home clean."

"Agreed." I look at Tommy. "Before we get moving, do you mind if I have a private word with Oran?" I don't keep secrets from Tommy, but I want to ask Oran about his wife, and he might prefer more discretion.

Tommy's chin dips. "I'll take one more look through the duffel and make sure we haven't forgotten anything."

"Thanks, man."

Oran studies me curiously while Tommy exits. "What's up?"

"I hope you don't mind me asking, but does Lina ever have nightmares?"

"Not that I'm aware of, but I take it Amelie does?"

I grimace, leaning my elbows on my knees. "First one I've seen was last night. She's never said anything, but I get the sense it's not the first."

He leans back in his chair with a sigh. "Girl's been through a lot. I can only imagine the emotional scars she'd have after her mother's betrayal, then being kidnapped on top of it and ending up with amnesia? It's no wonder her past doesn't haunt her more. I'd be a paranoid mess. Poor thing probably never feels safe."

"Fuck, I didn't even think about her being kidnapped." I stiffen, a new horrifying realization hitting me. "Someone fucking touch her when she was kidnapped?" I hadn't heard about anything, but that doesn't mean it didn't happen.

Oran shakes his head. "She was taken to the hospital after being drugged, and they did a full screening. She didn't show signs of assault. Lina made sure to ask the doctors so we'd know what we were dealing with."

The vise around my rib cage eases. "Well, that's something," I say under my breath.

"Look, she's been through more than her fair share of shit. Be patient with her."

Fuck, he's right.

I've been a dick pushing her to unload all that trauma so quickly. I merely wanted to keep her safe. I might have lost track of the fact that keeping her safe and making her *feel* safe are two different things.

An idea hits me. "You think you can drive? I have a few calls I need to make."

"Not a problem. Let's get this show on the road."

34
Amelie

Sante's mood did a one-eighty by the time he picked me up from practice yesterday. He hardly spoke more than a few words in the morning but was buzzing with energy by evening. I asked him the reason, and he said it was a surprise. We had such a nice evening that I decided to make breakfast when I got up this morning. With him in the apartment, I actually had enough fixings to make eggs and pancakes. I'm bad about groceries, but he's kept the place stocked.

"That smells delicious." Sante emerges from the bedroom, his voice still heavy with sleep. He's put on joggers, but that's it. His divinely sculpted arms and chest are on full display.

I stare at the sinewy movements of his muscles as he runs

a hand through his unruly hair. "Mmm ... delicious," I agree in a daze.

He prowls closer. His lopsided grin does incredible things to my girl bits. And when his body aligns with mine, his lips trailing kisses from my ear down to my collarbone, I forget to breathe.

"I was talking about the pancakes," he murmurs against my skin.

The reminder jars me back to reality. "Oh! Crap, let me flip them." I spin around and save the batch just in time.

Sante stays at my back, his hands resting possessively on my hips. "Glad you're up and going. We've got somewhere to be this morning, and it'll take an hour and a half to get there."

"Oh yeah?" I ask, intrigued. "This my surprise?"

"Yup." He pats my ass, then gets himself a plate. "Should be a good distraction from nerves about tomorrow."

"That works. I'm glad we get a day to rest before the big night, but man, that anticipation is a killer." I glance at him while he scoops a helping of scrambled eggs onto his plate. "You gonna give me a hint about where we're going?"

"Sure, we're going to Poughkeepsie."

"Okayyy, how about a hint as to why?" I deposit the two pancakes from the skillet onto his plate.

"Not a chance." The man flashes a grin and winks, and I can't even be mad because it's the sexiest, most adorable thing I've ever seen.

"You're lucky I'm in a good mood," I tease, pouring a couple of pancakes for myself.

"Or what? You gonna use that spatula to torture answers from me?"

I shoot a glare at him. "Never underestimate what a woman can do with a good spatula."

Sante's eyes lock with mine, and without a word, I know

we're both thinking back to the wooden spoon. A lupine grin spreads across his face while heat blazes across mine. I whirl back around to check my pancakes. Can't burn the pancakes.

Pancakes, Mel. Focus on pancakes.

I manage to finish breakfast without humping Sante's leg —a win for everyone involved. And an hour later, we're on the road to Poughkeepsie. We talk about our limited travels. He tells me a bit about Sicily, making me want to visit. His uncle's estate sounds incredible. An hour and a half flies by, and before I know it, we're in the middle of nowhere, pulling onto a dirt driveway off a rural highway.

"What on earth are we doing here?" I ask, spotting a house nestled in a clutch of trees about half a mile away.

"You'll see," he says.

As we approach, I see a large barn building behind the house. The gorgeous property has rolling hills and bright green grass. It looks incredibly peaceful, except for the chorus of dogs barking the moment we exit the car.

An older man steps onto the front porch, coffee cup in hand. "Mr. Mancini?" he calls warmly.

"Mr. Cartwright," Sante replies. "It's good to meet you."

We approach and shake hands. Sante introduces me as his fiancée, which only strikes me as odd in that … it doesn't strike me. I'm not surprised. I actually sort of … like it. I like knowing I'm his, and he wants the world to know we're together.

"Glad you could make it out here. Let's go get our girl." Mr. Cartwright leads us down the porch steps and around the side of the house.

"Our girl?" I ask Sante, trying to be discreet. Apparently, I suck at discretion.

Cartwright grins back at me. "Your girl. Though, we've had her around longer than most. Usually, dogs are homed at two to three years, but she's been with us four, waiting on the right match. From what you've told me, Sante, I think you'll find she's a perfect fit."

"A dog?" I blurt, my eyes bulging. "Are you getting a dog?"

"No," Sante says, grinning. "I'm getting *you* a dog." He looks at Mr. Carwright to explain. "I kept it a surprise."

"Well, then. You'll need to know, missy. This isn't any old dog. Freya is a personal protection shepherd with two years of intensive training. She's exceptional in every way."

Sante chimes in, "Mr. Cartwright's dogs come highly recommended—the best trained on the entire East Coast."

I hear what they're saying but can hardly comprehend what's happening. Never in a million years would I have guessed that I'd be getting a dog today. I'm so stunned that I can't even tell how I feel about it. My mother would have never agreed on having a pet, so I never entertained the idea as a kid. Once I was on my own, it never seemed practical. Plenty of people in the city have dogs. I know it's possible, but I've never felt confident I could juggle the responsibility with my practice schedule.

With Sante's help, however...

I'm getting a dog.

Oh my God. *I'm getting a dog of my very own!*

Euphoria bubbles up from deep inside me like a freshly uncorked bottle of sparkling champagne. I practically float the rest of the way to the barn.

Cartwright opens the large front door, unveiling that this building is far more than a simple barn. The kennel facility is fully finished on the interior, with a huge open area in the middle and a series of large enclosures lining the sides where the dogs are housed.

"We let them have a bit more freedom unless we know

someone's on their way out." He walks over to the third kennel on the left wall and opens the wire door. "Freya here is especially family-friendly. That's what makes her a good match. She did most of her training with my daughter, who has two little ones."

A gorgeous German shepherd walks out, her ears tall and an honest-to-God smile on her face. Her black and honey coat is long and softer-looking than some shepherds, who often have coarse hair. She's the most beautiful, magical thing I've ever seen—aside from Violet. My niece always comes first, but Freya is a very close second.

My nose burns as tears well in my eyes. "She's perfect," I whisper. I'm probably supposed to assert my dominance or some bologna like that, but I don't care. I just want to make friends with her, so I lower to the ground, sitting on my knees, and wait for her to approach.

She sits at Cartwright's heel, not even a little tempted to come over. He murmurs a command, smiling. Freya is instantly up and ready to say hello. I grin as she sniffs a circle around me.

"Here, this always helps with introductions." He hands me three strips of bacon wrapped in a paper towel. "Lay a piece flat on your palm, and she'll lick it off. They're trained not to snap at food, but it's always best not to tempt fate."

Freya prances as the savory aroma fills the air. I break one piece in half and lay it flat on my hand. She licks it off and immediately sits for more. I slowly reach out and pet her head.

"Good girl. It's yummy, isn't it? Want more?" I'm not sure I've ever been so happy in my entire life. I dole out all the bacon, along with a wealth of praise. When I tell her it's all gone, she licks my hand clean, then lies down at my side.

I look up at the two men chatting above me as if to say, *can you believe how perfect she is?*

The two chuckle, and Cartwright gets out his phone.

"Eddie, come on out with the suit. It's time to do a little show-and-tell."

We go outside and spend the next hour learning all about Freya's training. It will take me some time to learn the commands, but they gave us a packet of information as a refresher. Watching her in action is awe-inspiring. She's magnificent. A fearless warrior. A loyal companion.

I've never received a more thoughtful, incredible gift in my life.

Before we walk back toward the house, I leap into Sante's arms. "Thank you, *thank you*. I love her so much. I can't even tell you how happy this makes me."

A heady cocktail of emotions swirls in his eyes. "I thought you might like her, and I *know* I'll feel better having her around." He gives me a brief but ardent kiss, then eases my feet back to the ground.

"I adore her." *And I adore you.*

I don't say the words, but I get the sense he reads them in my eyes because his chest expands on a sudden breath. I'm glad. I want him to know how happy he's made me. How he's turned my world upside down in the very best ways.

Every day I spend with him, another one of my barriers drops. I'm in danger of falling hopelessly in love with Sante Mancini. But if this is what danger feels like, I'm ready for the front lines. I don't want to go back to being alone. I want to seize this feeling with both hands and never let it go.

35
Amelie

I'M LEGIT TORN ABOUT WHETHER TO SIT IN THE FRONT SEAT BY Sante or in the back with Freya. For a hot minute, I even consider having her sit on my lap in the front. After two hours of bonding and learning all about our new fur baby, I'm completely smitten, and I don't want her to be nervous leaving the only family she's ever known.

When she hops in the back seat and immediately lies down with a doggy smile, I realize I may have been projecting. She doesn't seem nearly as anxious as I do on her behalf.

We take the long drive back into the city, and I sneak regular peeks at Freya every few minutes. Neither of us had pets growing up, but Sante tells me about the animals on his uncle's farm. We discuss how to manage walks and exercising her. I debate whether she'd allow me to put cute outfits on her. Sante stares at me like I've sprouted a second head. I concede that an array of festively themed collars might suffice.

On our way back to the apartment, we stop at a pet supply superstore. My gorgeous girl gets compliments right off the bat. I wear such an obnoxious grin as we browse the store that I'm lucky someone doesn't suggest I be committed.

I give one more go at suggesting an adorable pink doggy shirt that says *girl boss* in sequins on the back.

"Probably best not to make the killing machine look inviting," Sante says dryly.

I gape at him and cover Freya's ears. "Don't you dare call my princess a killing machine."

He cocks a brow at me. "Babe, I didn't pay fifty thousand for her to play fetch."

My ears begin to ring.

"Fifty thousand *dollars*?" I breathe. "Tell me you're joking."

He flashes a satisfied smirk. "*Now* she gets it."

I stand awestruck as he continues toward the leashes and collars. My trust fund is plenty sizable, but having money doesn't mean I'm used to throwing it around. I've always thought of my savings as a backup plan. For the most part, I live on what I make. Fifty grand is a crap ton of money for a dog.

"What about this one?" Sante holds up a bright red collar when I catch up to him. The red would be pretty against her fur, but it's so … boring. We were given her current collar and leash, but they're black, which is even more boring than red. An exquisite dog deserves an exquisite collar.

I gasp when I spot a teal collar with bright pink flamingos, and it even has a flower made of the same fabric decorating the side. "*This* one." I beam. "It's perfect for summer."

"I suppose that works," he concedes in a teasing grumble.

We grab the matching leash, then head to the dog bed section. I insist on letting her pick out her bed. We place the options on the floor, then let her walk around them to see if she's drawn to one. She walks right past the first two, then steps on the third and sniffs it with interest.

"We have a winner," I say excitedly. "That leaves food, bowls, treats, bones, toys, and poop bags—anything else?"

"Should we think of something else, we can manage to find our way back here."

"Definitely. We'll need to get a Fourth of July collar at the very least."

He shakes his head with a wry smirk. "I've created a monster."

I hug his middle and snuggle my head under his chin. "Nah, you keep the monsters away."

His lips press a kiss to my forehead. "Always. Now, let's get this shit done. I got a text from my cousin Tommy that he's waiting for me at my place—well, Mr. Sorrell's place. He needs a hand, and it's a good chance to introduce you."

"Are you two close?"

"He's my best friend. He even went to Sicily with me so I didn't have to go alone." He pauses before continuing. "Keep in mind, he can be a little quirky. That's just Tommy—it's nothing personal."

I'm intrigued and excited that he wants to introduce me to more of his family, especially someone he considers his best friend. I'm surprised this is the first I've heard of Tommy, but we've been pretty absorbed in other matters. It's nice to do something normal like meeting his friends. Getting to know them helps me know more about him.

Inspired not to dally, we check off the last items from our shopping list and head back to the apartment. We stop at my place first to unload as much of the new dog gear as our arms can carry. I show Freya around her new home.

"She's had a big day. I say we put out some food and water and let her settle in while we head next door."

I'm reluctant to leave her, but he's right. She could use some downtime, and I'm ready to meet Tommy. We get her things laid out. I kneel to give her kisses and explain that I'll be right back so she shouldn't worry, promising to brush her when we return.

We pop next door, which feels incredibly odd now that I know it's not technically Sante's apartment. He has use of the place for another month. I suppose he's planning to take full advantage.

"Tom, I'd like to introduce you to Amelie. Amelie, this is my cousin Tommy. He's Renzo's baby brother."

I shake Tommy's hand, noting his glower at Sante over the baby brother comment. "It's so great to meet you."

"You, too." He nods, almost mechanically, then turns to Sante as if dismissing me. "I found a place that works. I thought I'd pay cash, but the bank in Sicily is giving me shit. You already transferred some money here, right?"

"Yeah, but I doubt it's enough. I don't keep that kind of money liquid."

"I only need an escrow deposit while I get this bank crap figured out."

The two guys stand by the kitchen island while I migrate toward the living room and lean on the back of the sofa. I see what Sante meant by Tommy being quirky. He comes off as aloof, but I know Sante wouldn't be best friends with someone genuinely full of himself.

In a way, I'm glad they're ignoring me. It gives me a

chance to observe their interaction. Their comfort level with one another is unquestionable. They act like brothers. And they bear a passing resemblance. From behind, I might even confuse their similar builds, but their overall looks are very distinct. Most obviously, Tommy's vibrant blue eyes and Sante's tattoos stand out in stark contrast when compared to the other.

They continue with their conversation until Tommy takes a phone call. That's when my entire world screeches to a halt.

He launches into a conversation in what I assume is Italian since he's apparently lived there with Sante for the past four years. I look at the two men, so similar in size, and images flash through my head.

The man in the hoodie smoking in the theater.

That man terrifying me in the dressing room, speaking another language.

Sante coming back from Italy for me.

Sante smoking outside our building, somehow intuiting I had a stalker.

He knew where I lived before he moved in next door and had been keeping tabs on me.

He orchestrated everything about our reunion.

The stalker was the only reason I reached out to Sante.

A stalker who never laid a hand on me except to protect me.

It can't be.

He wouldn't have…

I creep slowly forward, eyes glued to Tommy. I feel Sante, still as a statue, stare boring into me, but I ignore him. I have one thing on my mind.

When I reach Tommy, I press my nose close to his chest and inhale. I do it again a bit farther up. He holds his hands away as if expecting me to bite at any moment.

"No smoke," I say in a heartbroken hush.

"I don't smoke." His brows knit together in bafflement as he looks at his cousin for an explanation.

My eyes scrunch tightly shut as realization plows into me like a wrecking ball, shattering the perfect world I'd started to construct in my head.

"*It was you.*" I open burning eyes and level Sante with a world of accusation. "It was you the whole time."

His resolute stare is all the confirmation I need.

When my mother betrayed me, it hurt but wasn't all that unexpected. She'd never pretended to love me. While I haven't known Sante for long, he'd made me believe he actually cared.

His betrayal carves a gaping wound in my already mottled heart.

"How *could* you?" Fury rises inside me like a wrathful Valkyrie. He made me think The Society was after me—maybe not intentionally, but he terrified me regardless.

I shove Sante as hard as I can.

"Amelie, calm down. Let's talk about it." He takes my wrists in his hands as I loose a savage scream.

"How *dare* you tell me to calm down?" Righteous tears blur my vision. I'm only vaguely aware of Tommy slinking from the apartment. All my rage is focused on the man who has been making a fool of me since the day we met. "You manipulated me. Terrified me by acting like a stalker—you were in my bedroom watching me sleep! And that wasn't the first time, was it? The things that appeared out of nowhere, making me think I was going nuts. It was *you*. I called the cops because of you, and that put me in *actual* danger. Talbot might have never bothered me again if it wasn't for you." I yank my hands from his grasp, my chest heaving.

"I had no way of knowing that, and I never meant to manipulate you."

"Oh, so having Tommy pretend to be the stalker so you could scare him off—that wasn't meant as a show for my benefit?" How stupid does he think I am?

"No, ahhh, *fuck*." He slams his fist into a kitchen cabinet, shattering the wood panel. Freya barks next door, but we both ignore her. "I was trying to figure out why you wouldn't call the cops."

"So Tommy had to get his jaw broken so you'd know why I wasn't reporting my stalker?"

"*Isaac* technically didn't know about the stalker," he tries to explain, only digging himself deeper.

"Oh, the fake neighbor you created needed information about the fake stalker you also created—all of it an intricate web of lies—for *what*?" I raise my hands out to my sides, at a loss to understand. "So you could *date* me? The only way that makes any sense is in terms of manipulation. You wanted me to act and feel certain ways rather than get to know the real you."

"You have everything backward. The point is, I wanted you to see *exactly* who I am," he growls, his anger getting the better of him. "I'm the man who sees what he wants and goes after it. I'm the man who will break a man's jaw before I let him disrespect you. You think I couldn't walk past those Russians? I did that because I wanted you to *see*."

"Why? So I'd be scared of you?"

"*No*, so you'd love me in spite of it all," he roars. "Because this is who I am." He slaps a palm against his chest. "I will track you and mark my body with your name and annihilate every one of your enemies. I won't hide that from you and trick you into thinking you've married some motherfucking

Prince Charming because I'm *not*. I'm the villain, and I want you to love me anyway."

Heartbreak wraps its vicious claws around my chest and squeezes the air from my lungs.

"This isn't healthy, Sante." Tears leave salty trails down my cheeks as the weight of the world settles on my shoulders. "This isn't how trust is formed."

He steps closer, eyes gone dark as midnight. "Do not decide how to view us based on someone else's standards. Fuck healthy. Fuck normal. Have I ever hurt you?"

I rake my teeth over my bottom lip, knowing that aside from this moment, I can't honestly say yes.

"No, but—"

He doesn't let me continue. "How do I make you feel when you're around me? *That's* what you should be asking yourself—not whether this is *healthy*. You and I, we aren't healthy. We're both fucked up in a way that we're perfect for one another. You know it's true if you're honest with yourself. So what's it going to be, Amelie? Are you going to let yourself be happy, or will you run?"

36

Amelie

I'VE NEVER FELT MORE CONFUSED IN MY LIFE. I CAN HEAR HOW his argument makes sense, but I've seen dysfunction, and I don't ever want to go back to that. I've dreamed my entire life of one day having a supportive and loving family like I see in the people around me.

What you want is to be happy, and if he gives you that, does the rest matter?

Isn't that how every abusive relationship starts? I've seen all the true crime shows. I've heard about the pattern of sweeping a woman off her feet only to grow more controlling as time goes on. Like Sante said, however, he's never pretended to be charming. And he's not controlling so much as he's overprotective. How do I know that won't intensify to an unacceptable degree down the road?

No one ever knows how a relationship will evolve. That's the risk you take.

I don't like risks.

Maybe this one's worth it.

Sante wants to know whether I'm willing to take that chance. He's watching me, his turbulent stare pleading with me to try. What do I tell him?

"I ... I don't know." The words sound as fragile as I feel. I'm standing on a frozen lake, the ice at my feet cracking and groaning no matter which direction I go.

"I want to show you something." Sante comes closer and gingerly takes my hand as though he's worried his touch might scare me.

I don't pull away. Even knowing everything he's done, the warm certainty of his hand in mine brings me the comfort I desperately crave. One step at a time, he leads me back to the safety of my apartment, where Freya is anxiously waiting for me.

I reassure her that everything is okay. Her joy at seeing me helps to fortify me. When I return my attention to Sante, he takes my hand and places a small tarnished ring on my palm.

"*You* kept the monsters away for me," he tells me, voice raw with vulnerability. "When I was sleeping in a barn on dirt floors, thoughts of you gave me hope. At that wedding, I could see my own demons reflected in your eyes, yet you fought them back with such strength. I knew that if whatever had brought you that sort of pain was possible to overcome, then there was hope that I could do the same."

I stare in disbelief at the evil eye ring I gave him that night. Despite what he implied when he told me about his tattoo, he kept the ring. He still has it with him to this day.

"I wasn't winning against the demons. I was drowning," I admit, a sob clawing its way up my throat as I curl my hand into a tight fist around the ring. "You were the one who gave *me* hope. Any light in my eyes that night was there because of you. Because for the first time, I didn't feel alone."

It's the truth. I'd be foolish not to admit it.

Sante reaches for me, but I step back to keep space between us.

"I need some time to think."

His phone buzzes in his pocket, but he ignores it. Every ounce of his blistering intensity is a laser boring into me. "Nothing has changed, Mellie. I'm the same man I was this morning."

"I know, but I still need to think this through."

He runs a frustrated hand through his hair and turns toward the window. "An hour. Is an hour enough?" He looks back, and I'm almost tempted to smile because his gaze is so full of ardent pleading. He's almost commanding me to forgive him.

"I don't know, Sante. There's no instruction manual for this sort of thing."

His jaw flexes, and his phone buzzes again.

"See who it is. There could be a problem," I urge him.

He sighs and pulls the phone out, his forehead creasing with concern. "It's Conner. Shit, I forgot."

"What?"

"I was supposed to go see Noemi today."

He answers the phone, and Conner's voice on the other end is so harsh that I can hear him several feet away.

"Yeah, okay. I hear you," he clips back, his voice straining against his own anger. "I'll be over in a minute."

Sante grimaces. "Guess you get your time alone."

"I have Freya with me, and we're not going anywhere," I

try to assure him, knowing he worries about me. "I just need some time to process."

He peers down at my new shadow sitting patiently by my side and nods. "I'll be back soon."

Then he's gone, taking my strength with him. My legs feel like they might buckle.

"Come on, girl. Let's watch a movie." I curl up on the couch with a blanket and encourage Freya to join me. She's a little reluctant at first—Cartwright must not have allowed her on the furniture. But once she's settled, she happily lays her head on my legs.

When the pitter-patter of rain sounds on the window, I abandon the movie plan and let the cleansing spring shower wash over my tormented thoughts.

I have to find a way to decide what to do about Sante. He stalked me, hid his identity, manipulated me in numerous ways, and still managed to make me fall in love with him. I realize now that it's true.

I've fallen in love with my stalker.

The boy with torment in his eyes and ferocity in his heart.

I fell for him, but now I question whether it was all manipulation like some offshoot of Stockholm syndrome. How do I know my own true feelings versus what he manufactured? Can I ever trust him to be transparent with me?

That question isn't a mystery. The answer is no. If he feels like something will upset me and he can fix it without causing me worry, he'll take that option every time. What I *can* trust is that he'll keep me safe and devote himself to my happiness every day of his life.

Is that so terrible?

After all that I've been through, Sante's brand of love sounds like the sense of belonging I've always prayed for. If our quirks align such that we naturally give one another what we need, shouldn't that be enough? Maybe that's all anyone is looking for.

Maybe normal is a myth, and healthy is relative.

I open my hand, realizing Sante's ring is still balled in my fist, and study the aging piece of metal. The ring itself is worthless, but what it represents is priceless beyond measure. It's the evidence of what can happen when two broken souls find refuge in one another.

Am I willing to throw that away?

Hell, no.

The answer echoes in my mind with resounding certainty. I flinch at the mere thought of living my life without Sante. He's nonnegotiable because Sante *is* my happiness. If I deny myself him and all he entails, I'll be the only one to blame.

I couldn't choose my parents.

I had no control over being trafficked or my kidnapping.

But this is *my* choice, and I choose happiness.

37
Sante

My sister is the last thing I want to deal with right now. If Conner hadn't been so pissed and Amelie so insistent on space, I never would have left that apartment. We were turning a corner. I could feel it. Instead of resolving our issues, I'm out in the rain about to get my ass handed to me for a second time today. The only two women in this world that I love, and I've hurt both of them.

The only thing darker than my mood is the sky overhead. Damn clouds came out of nowhere, just like my problems. Everything was gravy one minute, then shit the next.

The downward spiral continues when I get to Noemi's place. There's a severity to the atmosphere that charges the air. A quiet stillness that makes me feel like one wrong step will end in my beheading.

"The kids still napping?" I ask Conner as we step into the living room.

"My mom ended up taking them for the day." He walks me to where Noemi sits on the sofa, a steaming mug in her hands.

Her face is blotchy, eyes puffy from crying. I knew as much. Conner had said so on the phone. He also said if I didn't come over and "get my head out of my ass"—his words, not mine—he would do the job himself. The way he's shooting daggers at me confirms that he's yet to cool down. What I don't understand is why. I'm not as present as I could be, but there are worse crimes. Why do they both seem so worked up?

"Hey, Em. I'm sorry I forgot to come by earlier. I've had a lot going on." I sit next to her, my body angled toward hers. It makes me think of all the times we watched movies together as kids.

A twinge of regret twists painfully in my chest.

Noemi smiles through her tears. "I'm sorry to be a pain, but I really needed to talk to you."

"What's up? The kids okay?"

"The kids are fine. And despite how it looks, I'm good, too." She gives her husband a look that must signal him to leave us alone, though he only removes himself as far as the kitchen table. I wouldn't leave either if I were him.

"You don't look fine. I'm sorry if I'm the reason. I know I haven't stayed in contact like I should have," I admit quietly.

"It's not that, either. Well, that's part of it, but I've understood. I promise."

The silence presses in on my eardrums, pressure building all around me. "Then what's got you so upset?"

She inhales deeply, then blows the breath past her nose as though preparing herself.

For what? What the fuck is going on here?

"You saw my email that I put all your stuff in storage?"

"Yeah, I actually stopped by not long after I came back."

She nods almost to herself. "I considered having an estate agent get rid of everything when we sold the house. It wasn't long after you'd left for Sicily, and you said you didn't want any of it, and I wasn't sure I wanted to wade through all the memories. But I eventually decided I didn't want to risk losing something of Mom's that I would have wanted to keep. It took me a couple of months. I went through her bedroom and closet, then boxed up your room. At the last minute, I decided to look in Dad's office in case there was anything of Mom's in there." Noemi stares at the mug in her hands, her chin starting to quiver. "I found a stash of old letters with pictures. They were from Umberto's mother, giving Dad updates about him from the time he was little." The sympathy and remorse in her eyes when she lifts them to mine clamps a fist around my throat.

Umberto was Dad's lieutenant, essentially. His right hand. He was close to Noemi's age, brought on to work for Dad when he was maybe sixteen and became a semi-permanent fixture in our home. Loyal to Dad until the very end.

"Why would his mother send Dad updates about him?" Had Dad *bought* Umberto in some kind of strange trafficking arrangement to breed loyal soldiers? It's far-fetched, but my father was capable of anything.

Noemi is fighting back sobs, unable to meet my eyes any longer. "I didn't want to tell you over the phone. I kept thinking surely you'd come back, but then years passed. I considered not saying anything at all, but … but I couldn't bear carrying that. You know I'm not the secretive type."

"Bear what, Em? What are you trying to tell me?" My tone is harsher than it should be, and I hear the scrape of a kitchen chair as Conner rises to his feet.

"Umberto was our half brother," she whispers, her eyes pleading with me to understand. To forgive.

I hear her words, but they don't make any sense in my head.

"He couldn't have been. We'd have known."

I would have known if I killed my own brother.

Her head shakes slowly side to side. "I'm not sure he even knew. We looked into it, though, and it's true. Umberto was born six months before me. I wanted to know who this woman was that Dad had been with. When we found her, she was practically destitute. Dad had been helping her get by, but not with much, and without him, she was facing eviction. She's kind. I could see why he'd been with her. She wasn't all that different from Mom."

I want to slap my hand across my sister's mouth to keep her quiet. To stop her words from ripping apart my world as thoroughly as if the rain outside was made of pure acid. But I don't. I can't. My entire body is frozen solid with shock while Noemi continues.

"She's a victim of his as much as the rest of us. I decided I wanted to help her, which is why I felt like you needed to know the truth. I didn't want you to find out some other way and hate me for hiding it from you." She pauses, her voice lowering. "I'm so sorry, Sante. I hate to make things worse. You've been so hard on yourself about everything that happened, but you were just a kid."

"I was sixteen when he killed her," I say tonelessly. "That's old enough to read the writing on the wall."

"I didn't know either. They both hid the destructive nature of the relationship better than I could have imagined."

"You caught on and tried to stop him."

"Only because Mom told me right before she died."

I rocket to my feet, my rage boiling over. "He did the same fucking thing to you as he'd done to her right in front of my *fucking* face, and I *still* didn't see it." The manipulation. The nuanced threats sprinkled into everyday conversation. There were clues, but I simply ignored them.

Conner storms over, but Noemi tries to call him off with a swipe of her hand.

"We don't see what we don't want to see. That's *natural*. Umberto practically lived with us, and I never noticed how much he looked like Dad until they were both gone. That's how our minds protect us."

I recall the pride in my father's voice when he spoke about Umberto. I think back to when Umberto first started coming by the house and how upset Mom was. I told myself she didn't want work brought home. I convinced myself the reason Dad brought Umberto into the fold rather than me was because I was too young. I told myself everything but the truth.

"It's a tempting excuse, but it doesn't change the fact that I killed our brother."

"No," Conner interjects. "But I would have if you hadn't. Maybe you forget that I'm the one who killed your father. Your relation to them doesn't change the fact that they were both rotten."

He's right, but it doesn't nullify the geyser of molten anger rising inside me.

I'm so fucking sick of living with this guilt. My innate weaknesses caused me to lose so much when none of it was necessary. If I'd been less naive. If I'd been strong enough to see the world for what it is.

"I have to go," I say tonelessly.

If I don't get out of here, I'm going to lose my shit.

They must sense the bleak nature of my mood because neither of them tries to stop me. The rain has let up, though the sky is every bit as ominous as before. I have no business going back to Amelie's place while my head is such a mess, but I need to check on her. I drive home in silence. No music. Only me and my seething anger at my father.

I hate that he's not here for me to punish.

I'd thought I was over that emotional hiccup and had moved on to learning from the experience, but this has sent me reeling back to the past. I feel like that teenager who got shipped off to Sicily all over again, and that makes me angrier than anything. That my father, yet again, has made me feel powerless, even from the grave.

When I let myself into the apartment, Freya begins to growl. I assure her it's okay, but the noise is enough to wake up Amelie where she's fallen asleep on the sofa.

"Sorry to wake you," I say in a hollow voice. I feel so shitty I can't even look at her, afraid she'll see the shame in my eyes.

"It's okay. I hadn't even meant to fall asleep." She stands.

"You can stay there. I can't stick around. I just wanted to check in."

"What's wrong?" she asks warily, her voice etched in concern. I don't want her concern or her pity. I don't deserve any of it, and I know if I tell her what I've learned, she'll say the same things as my sister.

"Nothing you need to worry about."

"If it's got you this upset, I think I should know."

"*No*," I snap, finally meeting her wide eyes. "Nothing you can say or do will change any of it. The problem is that no one fucking tells the truth. Families keep secrets from one another, which leads to people making bad choices because they don't have all the facts. If people would just be fucking honest about who and what they are, we could all go about our fucking lives."

I've taken out my anger on Amelie and regret every word of it the second it's out. Even more so when I see the wounded crease in her brows. She looks close to tears, and I'm disgusted with myself.

"Shit, I'm sorry. I shouldn't have said that. I'm just upset, okay? I need to clear my head, and I'll be good once I'm back."

I don't risk staying a second longer. She's safer with Freya right now than she is with me. I'll have to make things up to her in a big way once I get my head on straight.

Once I'm in my car, I text Noemi.

Me: What's his mother's address?

Noemi: Why? You're making me nervous. She's a good woman.

Again, my anger surges. I'm not going to fucking hurt the woman, but Em doesn't know that. She only knows that I'm upset, so I rein it in and try to explain.

Me: I just want to see her, I swear. Not even going to talk to her.

The conversation dots come and go twice before a text with the address lights the screen. I put it into my GPS and start to drive. On my way, I pick up a bottle of whiskey because fuck if I don't deserve a drink.

Evening sets in early because of the heavy clouds overhead, making it hard to see by the time I arrive at the building. I don't know what I'm doing here. It's not like I even know who to look for—I just feel like I need to be here. To process. Maybe to grieve. Fuck if I know.

I watch people come and go on the sidewalk as I sip my whiskey straight from the bottle. The next thing I know, two kids knock on my window and light streams in all around me. It's morning, and I need to piss like a motherfucker.

"I told you he wasn't dead," one of the kids says to the other when I open the door.

"Jesus, I feel like I might be." Did I drink that whole damn bottle? Not even close, but what I did consume was enough to give me a wicked headache.

The kids snicker at me, then run off. I look up and down the sidewalk, trying to figure out where I can piss, when a woman rounds the corner, several reusable grocery sacks hanging from her arms.

I physically flinch, feeling like someone's put a fist into my gut.

She looks so much like him. I don't doubt for a second that it's her—Umberto's mother.

She locks eyes with me and slows. The world around us disappears while time stands still. In our momentary bubble outside of time and space, I sense she's just as unsettled as I am. Just as wounded.

A car whizzes past us, kick-starting the world back into motion.

I take a small step backward. The woman takes my movement as her cue to pass. She walks forward, her eyes fixed on the sidewalk at her feet. We don't speak to one another. I think we both prefer it that way, or maybe it's just me. It's hard to trust my own judgment at this point. What I do know is she's merely a normal woman taken in by a conman like all the rest of us.

The truth is somewhat deflating, but not in a bad way, per se. It's simply sad to know what could have been without the poisonous influence of a selfish, evil man.

And if you let him drive a wedge further between you and Noemi, you've let him win.

Shit, it's the truth.

I've been letting my father steal that relationship from me for years now. That has been my choice, as much as I hate to admit it. I let shame keep me away from my sister. The one person in the world willing to risk her life to protect me. What a terrible way to show my gratitude.

Fuuuuck.

I have a lot of apologizing to do—to both women in my life.

It's time to go home.

38
Amelie

I'VE NEVER WITNESSED A DRIVE-BY SHOOTING, BUT I IMAGINE I got a glimpse of how it might feel. Sante's whirlwind visit leaves me stunned. I can't imagine what would have him so upset that he'd lash out like that. I play his words over and over in my head.

…families keep secrets from one another, which leads to people making bad choices…

What secret did Conner reveal to Sante? He must have learned something that upset him—something that affected his decisions. It wasn't exactly his decision to move to Sicily, so I doubt it's related to that. Something about his father's death? Could be. Aside from that, the only thing I know he's been involved with lately is me … and Talbot.

I lower myself back onto the couch, a chill setting in.

Sante has been working with Oran and the other Byrnes to take down John Talbot. They know he has video of Lina. They'll be hunting for that video.

Stupid, *stupid* Amelie.

I never considered what else they might find in that search.

My stomach seizes painfully tight, and I can't hold back the vomit that rises in my throat. I run to the bathroom and make it just in time. I heave until my abs are sore, and nothing but acidic saliva is coming out. After I rinse my mouth in the sink, I sit on the cold tile floor with my back against the wall. Freya lies next to me with a gentle whine. I absently stroke shaking fingers through her soft black fur to comfort her.

...families keep secrets from one another, which leads to people making bad choices...

He knows.

That's why he couldn't look me in the eye.

That's why he couldn't stand to stay here for more than a minute.

He knows that I've been keeping a secret from my family, and learning the truth has made him regret coming back for me. It all fits too perfectly.

He knows the truth and wants nothing to do with me.

Pain unlike any I've ever known cleaves my chest wide open. I thought I'd known every form of pain before. As it turns out, there's always a new and more devastating variation lurking in the shadows.

I hold my hand flat over my chest, where I'm sure a gaping hole must be because only a physical injury could hurt this bad. Surely, his rejection can't be the sole cause of such agony.

Yes and no.

His rejection confirms my greatest fear—I am too damaged to ever be loved.

I am too damaged.

To ever.

Be loved.

I crawl to my bed and summon enough strength to climb up and under the covers.

I get Freya to join me. If my suspicions are right, Sante won't be back.

Sorrow holds me in her suffocating embrace for hours before I finally succumb to sleep. I think I fought against the reprieve of oblivion because of a foolish refusal to cling to one last spark of hope that Sante would come back, but it never happens.

I wake at sunrise to find Freya and I are still alone.

Being right has never felt so devastatingly awful.

"At least I have you, girl," I whisper to my sweet puppy.

She licks my face, and somehow, it makes me feel the tiniest bit better. I know she needs to potty. I'd probably stay in bed all day if it weren't for her. Instead, I force myself to take her for a short walk. It's enough to get my blood flowing and my thoughts focused.

Today is my big opening night. My debut in a principal role with the National Ballet Theater. I have spent my life dreaming of this sort of accomplishment and refuse to let him or anyone else steal it from me. My heart may be broken, but that does not have to prevent me from dancing.

By the time we get back upstairs, I've embraced a newfound determination to quit being a victim. I may be hurting inside—I may feel like crumbling—but I have the strength to persevere. I've done it before, and I can do it again.

I am a survivor.

Me: You up?
Lina: Unfortunately, why?
Me: I'm coming up.

"Come on, girl. Let's pack our things. I think it's time for a change of scenery." Time for a number of changes.

I gather Freya's bowls and food since she'll need to stay with Lina while I'm at the theater. It'll be a long day, and I hate to leave her alone. Plus, it's a good chance for her to make friends with Violet. I also pack an overnight bag for me. I won't be done until late, and I'd prefer not to come back here. Too many painful reminders.

"Lina's going to think we're moving in," I mutter as I grapple with a rolling suitcase, the dog, and her giant bed. I want Freya to be as comfortable as possible after uprooting her yet again.

When Lina opens her front door, her eyes widen as she takes in the chaotic mess in front of her. I was feeling so inspired that I'm still in the clothes I slept in from yesterday and haven't even brushed my hair. I may even have vomit on my shirt. Anything's possible at this point.

"You have a dog," she finally manages.

I give her a small smile. "This is Freya, and a lot's gone on in the last twenty-four hours. Mind if we come in?"

"Puppy!" Violet comes running around the corner, startling Lina into action. She swoops up her daughter and gives Freya a wary glance.

"Sorry. Come on in. You just surprised me." She relieves me of the dog bed and deposits it by the door. "Are you staying with us?"

"I thought I might tonight. I kind of need Freya to hang out here today and thought it'd be easier to crash here after the performance."

"Of course, yeah. That works." She stands, hands on her hips, still taking everything in. "So this is … Freya?" she asks. Violet strains toward the floor, wanting to get closer to Freya.

"Yeah, she's a personal protection dog, but she's super sweet. We got her yesterday. Picked her out especially because she was raised with little kids around unlike most of the other dogs."

Lina looks even more guarded as she studies the large shepherd. I dig around in the suitcase and pull out the muzzle Cartwright gave us. The dogs are trained to wear them, so the apparatus doesn't bother her.

"We'll definitely use this until everyone is comfortable with one another. Or indefinitely, if that's best." I totally understand her concerns. A mother should absolutely want to protect her child.

My sister takes a relieved breath. "Thank you. She's a gorgeous dog." She puts her hand forward and lets Freya sniff her, then lets a still-straining Violet get her hand sniffed.

"She's so well behaved, and I feel safe having her with me. I wish I'd thought of it before."

"Where'd you get her?"

"Sante found some highly recommended breeder up in Poughkeepsie. You wouldn't believe how much she cost." An ache radiates through my chest at the reminder of how generous it was of Sante to get her for me.

"I was just having coffee—come sit with me and tell me how that's all going." She leads us to the kitchen, where she gets me a steaming mug with plenty of creamer, the way I like it. I keep Freya leashed at my side. Lina has a moment of indecision about Violet, but eventually decides to let her down. The toddler goes straight for the dog, of course, but I encourage her to be gentle, and Freya shows no signs of distress. After a minute, the opening credits start to run on the cartoon Vi has on TV, snagging her attention. She runs back to the living room, sees her breakfast on her big girl table and chairs, and completely forgets about the dog.

I look at my sister while she's smiling proudly at her little girl. Lina's such a great mother. She's an awesome sister, too, and an all-around incredible woman.

I should have trusted her with the truth.

She could have handled it. I could have handled telling her. It would have been hard, but we could have gotten through it together.

There's no time like the present.

Yeah, I know. Cut me some slack.

"Lina, I have something to tell you," I say softly. "I should have told you from the beginning, but I didn't want to cause you more pain when you'd already been through so much. And then the years went by ... and there didn't seem to be a reason to dredge up the past." My gaze struggles to meet hers, finding solace in the swirling circles of creamer on the surface of my coffee. "I told you that I knew the name of the man waiting for me in that hotel room, and I did, but that wasn't ... the whole truth."

When I steal a glance at my sister, her entire body has gone rigid, and ferocity intensifies her stare. She seems frozen in her unblinking state. A captive in a building she knows is about to come crashing down around her.

My chin begins to quiver, but not entirely because of the memories. My heart is aching most because of the pain I know I'm about to bring her.

"I told you I ran before he could touch me. *I lied.*" The last two words are hardly a whisper, barely more than a poorly formed breath. But it's enough. The full impact of the truth barrels into her.

Her eyes slowly close, and her lips part on a broken exhale.

"Mellie Bellie, I'm so, *so* sorry," she says before meeting my gaze with watery eyes.

"You did everything you could to protect me. You warned me Mom might try something awful."

"I should have told you exactly what she'd done to me so you'd be prepared. I was too vague."

I shake my head. "No, you can't try to take the blame like that. That's a big part of why I didn't want to tell you. I knew as soon as it happened that *that* was what you'd warned me about and if you knew, you'd blame yourself."

She reaches over and takes my hand in hers, a tear running down her cheek. "She promised me you were never to be touched. She promised me."

Lina allowed herself to be raped when she was only seventeen when our mother threatened to substitute my six-year-old self if Lina refused. She sacrificed herself for me. I only found out the truth after I ran away to my sister—after I'd been raped, too. Knowing what she'd done secured in my mind that lying to her had been the right thing to do. How awful to know you voluntarily suffered something so horrendous ... all for nothing.

"You paid the ultimate price for me—a piece of your soul—and I have no words to express the depth of my gratitude. You have been more of a mother to me than she ever was." I have to swallow back the emotions threatening to steal my voice in order to continue. "I told you I fought back and ran because that was what I wished I'd done. That would have been worthy of you and the incredible example of strength you've shown. But, I didn't fight. I let it happen, Lina, and I've been so ashamed of that."

A sob breaks free, though I keep it as quiet as I can, not wanting to traumatize little Violet. Lina is up in a heartbeat, and then we're locked in an embrace of shared pain and solidarity. We bleed tears of sorrow for one another, cathartic tears that seep into that years-old festering wound in my heart and finally starts the healing.

"Huggies!" Violet cries out before throwing her arms around our legs to join in.

The joy of innocence turns our tears to laughter. We pull away and wipe our faces. Vi takes her cue to run back to the living room for another bite of banana.

We sit back down at the table and collect ourselves, taking sips from our mugs.

"I'm glad you told me," Lina says softly, "but why now? Has something happened in they guys' hunt for Talbot?"

My blossoming relief withers back to solemnity. "I think so. Last night, Sante came home really upset. He said something about families lying to one another leading to people making bad choices. He couldn't even look at me. I realized that in searching for tapes of you, they could have found a tape of me, too. I never even considered it might exist, but why not? That way, Talbot could relive the experience over and over," I say with disgust.

"He couldn't look at you?" Lina balks, her face contorted in disgust.

I shake my head. "He was there for a few minutes, lashed out, then left. He never came back," I whisper. "I think it made him reconsider our relationship. I've struggled with … intimacy. I haven't ever actually had sex since the rape." The admission is embarrassing. I know it shouldn't be, but it is what it is. "I've done other stuff, but when it comes to that part, I panic. I think he put it together and realized I'm more of a mess than he's prepared to take on."

She rises from her chair like a vengeful goddess, the kitchen lights even casting a glowing halo around her golden-blond hair.

"*Fuck. Him,*" she decrees with a pointed finger and a lifetime of wrath.

Violet jumps up and down in the living room. "Fuck 'im. Fuck 'im," she calls gleefully.

Oran chooses that precise moment to saunter out from the bedroom. He looks at his daughter, then at us. "I miss something?"

Lina waltzed over to my suitcase. "Yes, lots. This is Freya. She and Mellie are going to stay with us for a bit."

Oran looks at my dog, his wife, me, then back to his daughter. "Sounds good. What's for breakfast?"

39

Sante

SHE'S NOT HERE. I LOOK AROUND HER APARTMENT IN A STUPEFIED haze.

Fucking whiskey. I should have known better.

I do my best to block out my pulsing headache and think. GPS on her phone and the bracelet are registering in this building. The dog's stuff is gone. I look in the bathroom. Her toothbrush is gone.

She's got to be upstairs with her sister.

She fucking better be, or I will never forgive myself.

I take the elevator up to Oran and Lina's place. Oran opens the door after I knock. He looks me up and down, taking in the full effect of my disrepair.

"Don't know what the fuck you did, but you better be ready to grovel." He steps back to let me in.

"I know," I mutter under my breath.

"Is that him?" Comes Lina's voice bounding round the corner. "You've got some nerve, you piece of *shit*. How fucking *dare* you even show your face here?" The woman comes at me, prepared to claw my eyes out. Her husband has to grab her arms to restrain her.

I'm a little dumbfounded. I know I shouldn't have snapped at Amelie, but Lina's acting like I beat her little sister to a pulp.

"What the hell is going on here?" Oran demands.

"Fuck 'im," sings a toddler as she runs through the living room leading Freya by her leash.

That's when I spot Amelie stepping around the corner from where her sister first appeared.

"Why are you up here?" I ask her, frustrated that whatever is happening is going down in front of a crowd. "Something happen?"

"Oh, I'll tell you what happened," Lina starts in again. "This asshole decided he's too good for my sister, like his shit don't stink as much as everyone else's. Well, I have news for you, bud. It's *you* who's not worthy of *her*. She's a thousand times the person you'll *ever* be."

Fuck, she knows how to kick a guy when he's down.

I feel her words like a steel-toed boot to the balls, making it hard to breathe. "You don't have to fuckin' convince me how incredible she is. I feel the same," I ground out, losing patience. "What I don't understand is why you two think I've decided I'm too good for her. I'm anything but."

"Then why'd you walk out?" Lina asks, but my attention is focused on Amelie, who slinks closer.

"What about what you said about families keeping secrets

and leading to bad decisions?" she asks softly. "If that wasn't about us, what was it?"

I haven't had a chance to wrap my head around what I learned about Umberto, let alone think about whether I want to tell anyone. But there's been some kind of huge misunderstanding. Judging by the looks on all their faces, I have to own up to what I did, whether I want to or not.

"I found out last night that my father's right-hand man—the one I killed when Conner killed my father—he was ... he was actually my half brother." Each word peels back a layer of my skin until I am raw and exposed. "Noemi learned the truth while I was away. You can understand why I was upset, but it had nothing to do with you, Mellie. I was upset with myself. If my father hadn't been keeping that secret—if I'd known Umberto was my brother—I never would have killed him."

All three wear matching looks of horror laced with pity as they stare at me.

"Jesus, man. I'm so sorry." Oran's the first to speak. He releases his wife, who exchanges a look with Amelie.

"Yeah, I'm very sorry, too," Lina says softly. "We misunderstood..."

Clearly.

I look at Amelie and beg her to get us out of here. I hate feeling like a circus act on display.

She nods and looks at her sister. "You mind hanging onto Freya for a few minutes while Sante and I go talk?"

"Of course, not. You go."

Seconds later, it's over, and we're finally alone in the hallway. I breathe a heavy sigh.

"What just happened in there, Mel? What did you think I meant that had you so upset?"

She chews her bottom lip anxiously. "Let's go back downstairs, and I'll tell you everything."

Her choice of words has me bracing for impact. What the hell is there to explain that we have to go downstairs for privacy? I don't like it. At all. I can't imagine what this is about, but I'm about to find out.

40
Amelie

I DON'T KNOW HOW I COULD HAVE BEEN SO WRONG WHEN WHAT Sante had said fit so well, like when a puzzle piece is the perfect fit, but the image doesn't line up at all. Once he revealed the full picture, it was obvious I'd made a huge mistake.

I'm glad it happened, though, because it was the one last push I needed to finally end the secrecy. After I tell Sante, everyone will know the truth. I'll have nothing more to hide. I can sense the weightlessness of relief waiting for me, just out of my reach. To get there, I'll have to strip myself bare one more time and pray the outcome is worth it.

I lead us into the living room and sit on the sofa. It's been a rough twelve hours for us both, and if we have to go through one more traumatic unveiling, the least we can do is be comfortable. Sante sits with his body angled toward mine, one arm resting on the back cushions.

"Tell me what's going on, Mel. Why did you think I'd broken things off with you?"

"When you got upset about people keeping secrets and it leading to bad decisions, I thought you'd uncovered the one last secret I'd been keeping. I thought you'd found out, and it made you realize coming back for me was a mistake."

His face twists as though he's taken a bite of something bitter. "What kind of secret could possibly create that sort of fear?"

"It's not a secret anymore. I've told Lina, and before I tell you, I understand if it changes things for you. Really."

"You're kinda pissing me off, Mellie. Tell me what this is about, so I can tell you how wrong you are."

I nod and take a deep breath of confidence. "When I saw Talbot and ran, it wasn't before. It was … after."

God, I don't want to say it.

I don't want him to look at me differently, even if it's pity in his eyes rather than disgust.

"After…" His piercing stare roots me to the spot while he processes my words. "After he raped you," Sante finally says, his voice clinical and cold.

I slowly nod.

He gives a single nod in return and stands from the sofa. My heart plummets to the floor thinking he's leaving, but he detours to the hall closet instead where he stashed his empty duffel bag. He roots around, then stands, now holding a black handgun.

I leap to my feet and rush over to him. "Sante, *please* don't do this. I know you're upset, but—"

"No buts. That piece of shit doesn't deserve his next

breath." He's absolutely livid.

"He doesn't, but he also doesn't deserve an easy out. Please, just listen to me."

He sets aside his fury long enough to hear me out.

"I've been doing a lot of thinking lately, and with Lina telling me she'd rather her video be out than men like Talbot go free, I've decided that I don't want him dead. I want him exposed. I think he should have to suffer the same as his victims. Have his world stripped away with him powerless to do anything about it."

Sante sets down the gun on the nearby counter and brings his hands to either side of my face. The fury in his stare has calmed to tender adoration. "Do you have any idea how incredible you are?"

A balloon of emotion swells in my chest while tears prick the backs of my eyes. I shake my head, unable to speak.

"We're going to make him pay, my piccola ballerina. I promise you. It's already in the works." He places one reverent kiss on each eyelid, then rests his forehead on mine. "Now tell me, why would you think knowing what he did would make me leave you?"

"Because I figured you'd realize that's why I'm so bad at intimacy."

He takes my hand and leads me back to the couch, pulling me onto his lap. "Having trouble achieving an orgasm isn't the same as being bad at intimacy."

"It's not just that," I say warily, embarrassed to admit what I'm about to say. "I've been too scared of how much it hurt to try again. I panic."

His brows scrunch together as he studies me. "But you said you've had sex."

"I mean, I have, technically. Once."

"*Jesus*, baby. Being raped isn't sex." He wraps his arms

around me and hugs me to his chest. "I know this is gonna sound really fucked up, but I like knowing I'll be your first."

I pull back and look up at him through my lashes. "It's not fucked up. It's a relief. I couldn't think of anything worse than you looking at me as damaged. I love when I see that desire in your eyes. I didn't want to lose that."

His brown eyes glint with mischief. "There is nothing in this world that could make me want you less." He pauses, a somberness settling over him. "I want you to know, though. It was never about sex. Even back at that wedding the first time we met, it was your spirit that sank its claws into me. The way you held on to joy despite whatever shit you were going through. You inspired me. And you've continued to inspire me every damn day since."

My soul takes flight at his praise.

I realize I had it wrong when I thought there were only two possible outcomes for that butterfly in a jar. Instead of releasing it or plucking off its wings, its captor could also find it a new home where it could thrive. Somewhere protected yet with plenty of room to soar.

"I thought about what you said—before Conner's call interrupted us—about choosing happiness. I realized you were right, and everything that's happened today only proves that point. Your issues and my issues? They're sort of perfect for one another. I can't let labels tell me this is wrong when it feels so right."

Excitement and trepidation crank up my pulse to a dizzying flutter. I shift my body to straddle Sante's lap, my hands coming to rest on his taut chest while his give my hips a squeeze.

"The thought of losing you last night gutted me. You make me feel safer, sexier, and more confident than anyone ever has." I look down as nerves hit but push myself to continue. "I love you, Sante Mancini. I love you, and I want you to be my first."

"I love you beyond reason. Always will. But are you sure about this? There's no need to rush into anything."

"It's not rushing. Every time I look at you, I feel my body craving you. The residual fear isn't going to go away until I prove to myself that sex can be good, and there's no one else I want or trust enough to give me that."

"Baby, you have your show tonight. No matter how good I make it for you, you might be a little sore."

I smirk. "I'm a ballerina. I've never *not* been sore. And besides, I can't think of anything more perfect than getting up on that stage on opening night and feeling your presence is still with me."

"Fucking, Christ. How can I say no to that?"

I grin a heartbeat before his lips claim mine. He hardens beneath me, making my hips instinctively rock forward with the need to feel him.

Sante carries me to the bedroom. The shades are still drawn, casting the room in a soft glow.

"You have second thoughts about this, all you have to do is say stop," Sante says as he sets my feet on the ground. "No judgment. No questions. That's important to me. I need absolute honesty from you on this."

"I promise."

"We also need to talk birth control. Dance is too important for you to take chances."

I appreciate that he gets that and cares enough to make it a priority. "I'm on the pill."

"Good because I'm clean, and I don't want anything between us if we don't have to."

He takes his shirt off then mine. One article at a time, we undress one another reverently then move to the bed, the whole time kissing and touching and worshipping one another.

"I'm going to make you come," he tells me once I'm on my back beneath him, "and while I do, I'm gonna work my fingers inside you, help get you ready. And I don't want you to worry about a second orgasm. That's not what this is about. It's just you and me and our connection."

"Okay." It's a relief to know what he's thinking. Otherwise, I'd end up worried about his expectations the whole time. I desperately want to please him.

Sante's tongue has my body craving more in a matter of minutes. When he puts two fingers inside me, I feel the stretch, but it's not uncomfortable.

"It's definitely snug, but we got this. Okay?" he reassures me.

I'm feeling good enough that I'm not worried, and it helps that I'm not actively looking at his enormous cock. When he sucks on my clit, the indescribable sensation distracts from the twinge of pain as he slowly adds a third finger to his efforts.

"Fuck, you're incredible. I love knowing all this is mine."

"Only yours."

"Goddamn right," he rumbles against my core.

So full. Oh my god.

He works my body for a good ten minutes—not that he'd need to for an orgasm. Now that I know how it feels, my body is like a heat-seeking missile, targets locked on that perfect moment of release. But he wants me to be fully primed, and he makes it happen. By the time my body quakes with the onset of an explosive orgasm, his fingers make squishing sounds as they glide through my arousal.

I cry out in exquisite release, my veins flooding with liquid pleasure until I must be glowing. The ecstasy flooding my system is too intense not to be generating some sort of visible electric current.

Sante kisses my body on his way up, giving me time to recover. Then he's above me, our bodies aligned. He looks deep into my eyes and, and I swear I feel him drop anchor somewhere in the depths of my soul.

"I watched you for two weeks solid like an addict on a bender after four years of going without. I can't get enough, and I don't think I ever will. You give my life meaning."

He slowly eases inside me. My body is quick to remember the delicious feel of his fingers and wants more. He advances with such painstakingly small movements, more like rubbing than thrusting, that the pain I expected never comes. I feel full and stretched but in the most magical way.

Once he's all the way seated inside me, he kisses me. I taste the obsession on his tongue, and its delicious. I love the way he loves me.

Slow and steady, he begins to pump inside me, moving a bit more with each new movement.

"Amelie Brooks?"

"Mmmm?"

"I don't ever want to know life without you." He stills, bringing our gazes back together. "Tell me you'll be my wife. Tell me you'll be mine forever."

I can't believe he's truly asking me to marry him. It's all so fast ... and utterly perfect.

"Yes," I breathe. "I'll be your wife. Yours forever."

Triumphant joy shines in his eyes as his thrusts resume, picking up pace until I moan with pleasure.

Having him inside me felt good, but speed and intensity make it all that much better. I'm stunned at the difference. I feel my inner walls clinging to him, and I know he feels it too because each time they contract, he hisses and groans.

"Too tight for me to last long," he manages between breaths, "but probably best so you're not too sore."

At the moment, I can't imagine this making me sore, but he knows better than me. I simply delight in the feeling. Incredibly, I feel his cock thicken even more. He inhales harshly then his entire body stiffens as he clings to me, pumping once, twice, and a final time before resting his face in the crook of my neck.

I wrap my body around him in a full-body hug as giddiness envelops me.

I did it.

I had sex ... with a man ... and I *loved* it.

AND I think I may have gotten engaged.

When Sante pulls back to look at me, he huffs out a laugh at the ridiculous grin plastered across my face. "Not exactly the response I expected, but I think we've established normal isn't our thing."

"Sante?"

"Yeah, baby?"

"Did you mean it?"

"Not sure what part you're referring to, but I suppose that doesn't matter since I've meant every word I've spoken today."

"You really do want to marry me?"

"I'd take you to the courthouse now if it was open."

My grin widens, if possible.

"Fuck my girl's cute when she's engaged."

I giggle then moan as he pulls out.

"Okay?" he asks with concern.

"Yeah," I assure him softly.

"Good, stay put. I'm gonna clean up my bride-to-be then get her some food. My baby's about to be a star."

41
Sante

Perspective is such an odd beast. One minute you step in a mound of horse shit and think your day is ruined, then find out you won the lottery and decide horse shit is your new lucky charm.

I'm not happy about what happened with Umberto. It's a tragedy any way I look at it, but it's in the past. Nothing can be done to change what happened. And if things with my father hadn't played out the way they did, would I still be here making lunch for my new fiancée feeling like the fucking king of the world? Maybe, but I'd hate to risk it. I've never been so goddamn happy in my life.

"Here you go. Turkey on white with the fixings and a dab of mayo, as the lady requested. Wish I was sending you off with something nicer, but this is all we have time for." I set our plates on the table, then grab chips from the cupboard.

"I can't eat much before a big night like this, anyway. I'll throw a protein bar in my bag, though, just in case." She takes a hearty bite of her sandwich.

I love seeing her eat. I don't even know why I like it so much, but I have to make myself eat my own sandwich or all I'd do is watch her, and I'm on a time crunch, same as her.

"Once I drop you at the theater, I'm going to visit with Renzo. I haven't had a chance to tell you, but we got some good stuff accomplished at the AG's apartment."

"You guys got in his place?" she asks in surprise.

I give her a smug smile. "Course we did."

Her jaw stills, a bite sitting in her cheek unchewed. "You find anything?" Her hesitant question is bathed in a mixture of hope and apprehension.

"No videos of you or Lina, if that's what you're worried about. We got what we needed and also found an email from your mother that might relate to his connection with The Society. It's vague, but it looks like they struck a deal. We can't find any evidence he was a member. We think the deal he made with your mother was part of a bribe. Not that his motives matter. The important part is justice will be served," I assure her.

Her entire body visibly softens. At this point, she's conditioned to be on high alert for potential dangers. I hope that one day, a second set of conditioning will immediately respond with assurances that everything will be okay. It may take years, but I'll prove she's safe in my care.

I scarf down the last of my sandwich and get the kitchen cleaned up while she finishes. "I'm going to run upstairs and grab Freya while you get ready."

"Thank you! I should be good to go by the time you get back."

An hour later, Freya is back home, Amelie is safely at the theater, and I'm sitting down with Renzo to talk business and futures.

"Amelie ready for her big night?" he asks as we get comfortable in his living room.

"I think I may be more nervous than she is," I mutter with a hint of humor.

He huffs. "You ought to try watching the woman you love take on a bear. I nearly shit myself."

I have to laugh. "Hopefully, that's a bridge we never have to cross."

"Things going well, then?"

"You could say that." A smile bullies its way across my face. "She agreed to marry me."

"Well, fuck me. Congratulations." Renzo reaches over to shake my hand.

"Thanks, man. Coming back was definitely the right move for me. And there's no way I could ask her to leave her sister and move back to Sicily, so I want you to know I'm here to stay. I want to pledge my loyalty and do whatever I can to prove myself to you."

His gaze takes me in with careful consideration. "You've got nothing to prove, Sante. It would be an honor to work with you."

Fuck, that hit harder than I expected.

I have to clear my throat before I respond. "I appreciate that. Though, there's something I need to tell you, just so you're aware."

He lifts a brow for me to continue.

"I found out that Umberto was our half brother. It's sort of a moot point now, but I felt like you should know, especially considering I killed him."

The master of stoicism doesn't even flinch. "This may sound cold, but your mother was my family. A traitor's bastard son means nothing to me." Renzo never did pull any punches.

I dip my chin in a respectful nod. Whether I agree or not, he's made it clear that's the end of the subject, and I'm happy to oblige. "That leaves us with the matter of John Talbot and finishing what we started yesterday."

"We need him to be caught in the act of something —*anything*. For someone in his position, it doesn't take much to get the feds involved. We could tip them off, but I don't think an anonymous tip would be sufficient to give them probable cause. Without anonymity, I'm worried it'll get traced back to us and could end up impacting Lina and Amelie."

"We could always stage something."

"We could, but I think it brings in a lot of risk that the case against him ends up problematic. The closer we stick to reality, the better."

I can't hold back a grimace. I understand where he's coming from, but I also want this asshole off the streets as soon as possible. We've confirmed he won't be in the city for Amelie's opening night, which is a relief, but we need him gone for good.

"It won't be forever," Renzo says, sensing my frustration. "Considering what we already know about the guy, I'd say it takes us a week max to line something up. He has no idea we're coming for him. Best to take our time and do it right."

"Yeah, alright. I'll get with Oran and Tommy to see if they have any ideas."

"Good, and in the meantime, your girl has her opening night. She'll be plenty distracted all week."

"True," I admit, wishing I could say the same. I won't be able to think of much else until Talbot is behind bars—or dead, whichever should come first.

"We've got tickets for tonight, so we should see you there."

I stand and reach for another handshake. "Thanks, man. That means a lot to us both. I know Mellie will be thrilled to see familiar faces."

Renzo surprises me by pulling me into a hug. "Proud of you, kid," he says, allowing a tinge of emotion to color his words. "Don't think I said it before, but welcome home."

Gratitude clamps tight around my throat, preventing me from responding. I nod, instead, and let the respect and appreciation in my eyes speak for me.

On my way back to Amelie's apartment, I have a somewhat of an epiphany.

While I was pleased with all the ways I changed during my time in Sicily, it took coming back to New York to realize a crucial element was still missing. I wasn't truly happy. How could I be when my family was thousands of miles away?

Fixings my relationship with Renzo and finally talking to my sister—those things have filled me with a lightness I haven't felt in years. Uncle Lazaro and his family were good to me, for the most part. I appreciate their role, but they aren't my real family. I belong here in the city with the people who raised me and the woman I love. They are the most important part of my life.

That thought has me stopping in my tracks and changing directions. I have one more stop to make before I head home. One more chance to set things right, and this time, I won't fuck it up.

CONNER'S GLARE hits me like a swift kick to the ass. I half smile, half grimace since I deserve the full brunt of his displeasure.

"Before you deck me, I'm here to apologize." I raise my hands in surrender.

He still doesn't look pleased, but it's enough to get me in the door. "Have a seat. She's back with the boys. I'll go get her."

He disappears, and a few minutes later, my sister joins me. I see the sadness in her smile and hate that I put that there. Someone as loving as Noemi should never have to be sad. I know that's not realistic, but I can keep myself from being the cause, at the very least.

"Hey, Em. You doin' okay?"

"Yeah, I was getting the boys down for a nap. What's up?"

I cross over to her and do something I should have done ages ago. I hug her. I wrap my arms around her and hold her in an embrace built by a lifetime of love. "I'm so sorry, Emi. I know it's been a long four—nearly five—years, and I've put you through hell and back, but that's over." I pull back and look earnestly deep into her eyes. "I'm here for you—for the kids. I'm back, and I swear I won't let you down again."

"Oh, *Sante*. You never let me down," she says in a shaky voice, eyes growing glassy. "I worried about you, that's all."

"Well, I felt like I let you down in so many ways. That's why it's been so hard for me to face you, but that was fucking selfish of me. You're my Little Big. You will *always* be my Little Big, even when we're in our eighties."

She makes a strangled sobbing noise and lunges at me, hugging me tightly.

"I wasn't done yet," I tease, holding her close. "I didn't get to tell you how much I appreciate everything you've ever done for me. I couldn't have asked for a more incredible sister."

Noemi devolves into a sniffling fit of hiccuping sobs. Conner rounds the corner like he's ready to rearrange my face but stops when he sees us hugging.

"I'm s-s-s-sorry. It's the h-h-hormones," she forces through her tears.

I smile and kiss the top of her head. "No worries, Em. You cry all you need, so long as they're happy tears."

She nods against my chest. Conner slips back out of sight, and I finally toss aside the first boulder from the mountain of guilt I've been carrying with me.

42
Amelie

Most Broadway performances run Thursday through Sunday, with rest in between. Opening nights are usually scheduled for a Thursday or a Sunday. This time around, we open on a Sunday, which I prefer because that means a few days off after all the hype of a first big performance. It also means an earlier show. The curtain draws at five thirty, and we're nearly there.

We did a light rehearsal to warm-up and address any last-minute issues—more to settle nerves than anything. Our director gave a teary pep talk slash thank-you speech with a gentle reminder about the critics and reporters in tonight's audience. As if we could possibly forget.

Lights and sound have been checked, and the orchestra is

warming up. The cast is fully costumed with Hazel and her crew on hand to deal with any wardrobe malfunctions. And most importantly, the audience has begun to enter the theater.

Our months of tireless preparation are about to be put to the test.

The air backstage is electric yet subdued as though we've all won the lottery but also have a room full of sleeping babies we don't want to disturb. Even in the dressing room, where we can't be heard on stage, everyone speaks in hushed tones.

I adore the feeling of opening night jitters. Sure, my stomach is in knots, but there's also a giddy sense of relief and anticipation. Even more so tonight since this is my first principal role. I can't wait to prove myself worthy of that honor, though only one set of eyes truly matters to me. I know exactly where he'll be sitting, so I'll dance for him tonight.

"Hey, all ready?" Hazel asks when she joins me while I stretch to keep my muscles warm.

"Definitely." I grin at her. "You get everything handled?"

"Yeah, Melody's headpiece refused to stay put, but she may have to be buried in it now. That thing's not going anywhere."

"She'd probably prefer to lose a chunk of scalp than risk the thing flapping around during a key moment. I know I would."

Hazel snorts. "Hey, is your new man going to be here tonight?"

"He is." My grin is infectious. "Haze, I didn't say anything earlier because I don't have a ring or anything, but he proposed."

Her jaw hits the floor. "*What?*" she shrieks.

"I know, it seems crazy fast, but it's just ... right."

She gapes at me for a second before shaking her head as if to snap back to reality. "Hey, when it's right, it's right. And your families are close, so that helps, but I'm still blown away. Mellie, you're *engaged*!" She pulls me into a borderline aggressive hug. "I'm so happy for you. And seriously, if I had a man that hot begging me to marry him, I'd say yes, too."

I giggle at the thought of Sante begging because it would never happen. He'd probably roofie me into marriage before he begged. I keep that little nugget to myself. Just because I've accepted the unique nature of our relationship doesn't mean everyone else will understand.

"Okay, I'll let you get back to stretching. You're hitting the after-party tonight, right?" She stares at me expectantly.

"Yeah," I assure her. "I'll be there."

"Excellent. Knock 'em dead out there!"

I blow her an exaggerated kiss on her way out, then put my AirPods in to get in the zone. I have an inspirational playlist I listen to before performances. The lyrics empower me, while the music helps me focus. By the time my alarm goes off, signaling the start of the show, I'm ready for the performance of my life.

The production opens with Andrey and other dancers on stage setting the scene with a tragic yet enticing musical number that bleeds into a riotous scene at the famed Moulin Rouge. That's my cue.

Deep breaths. You got this.

The second I step foot on stage, a spotlight locks in on me, and the entire scene draws out into slow motion as Andrey's character catches sight of mine from a distance. The change of lighting, pace, and music is exquisite. While I'm not looking at the audience, I sense their captivation. The silent stillness of hundreds of enchanted patrons.

The thrill is intoxicating.

I perform my first dance sequence as I cross the stage. Once I'm on the other side, I have a moment of stillness while Andrey's character reacts. Normally, I would never look into the audience, but I can't help myself knowing Sante is out there. I want to see him. I know exactly where he is, so it will only take a second to peek.

I allow my gaze to seek its target, only it never makes it that far. Instead, my eyes lock with a sinister pair of blue eyes that laugh at me right along with the vile smirk on his face.

John Talbot is here, taunting me from the third row.

I have to fight back the cacophony of voices that begin shouting in my head.

This is not the time. You have to focus!

Thank God for muscle memory. My body automatically flows from one step sequence to the next at certain cues. Meanwhile, my thoughts are overrun with emotions. Terror at the mere sight of him. Fury that he continues to haunt me. Uncertainty and frustration and practically every other negative emotion on the spectrum ... except one.

Shame.

I used to feel so ashamed that I hadn't stopped it from happening. But now that my secret is out, it's taken the shame with it.

I did nothing wrong.

He's the monster.

He's the one who should be ashamed.

He's the one who should be punished.

The world needs to know what he's done, and I may be the only person capable of making that happen. Sante and the others will make sure he's punished one way or another, but I want the truth to be told.

I want him to know I'm not scared anymore.

He can't control me anymore.

The chaos in my head minutes ago filters away to resounding clarity. I submerge myself back into the music, allowing all residual emotions to be expressed through the dance. When we reach intermission, I feel more confident and prouder of myself than I ever have in my life. So self-assured that I'm not even worried about my career when I step toward the front of the stage seconds before the curtain falls behind me.

Some things are more important than a career.

And now that I don't have to worry about protecting my family, I can put integrity and justice first.

The lights come up to signal intermission, but nobody moves. Everyone watches me curiously. I can hear whispers from the dancers backstage, panicking over what's going on with me. Despite the enormity of what I'm doing, I feel remarkably calm.

"Good evening, ladies and gentlemen," I call out, projecting my voice from deep in my lungs. "I apologize for the interruption, but there is a matter that must be addressed. Almost five years ago, when I was seventeen, John Talbot raped me."

The audience gasps as a whole.

"Again, I know this isn't what you came here for tonight, and I apologize. However, Mr. Talbot has made the poor choice of joining us tonight, and while he's silenced me with threats for years now, I'm done staying quiet." I look him dead in the eyes—his wide with indignation—then lift my gaze toward the back of the theater. "If security would come and escort this man out, I would appreciate it."

Talbot doesn't move. He remains seated, his icy stare locked on me.

One at a time, dozens of others stand from seats all over the theater. I scan their faces one by one and see Conner and

Noemi, Renzo and his wife Shae, Sante, Tommy, Oran and Lina, Pippa and Bishop, Stormy and Torin, and even Mama G along with so many more—all standing and glaring daggers at Talbot.

They're all here for me.

To show their love and support. Because they're family —*my* family—and that's what true family does for one another. They've been there all along. I was simply too traumatized to see it.

I'm so fucking grateful that my corseted top strains from the fullness of my heart.

Talbot finally peers around as if amused at the absurdity of our spectacle. When two uniformed security guards arrive at either end of his row, he slowly stands and buttons his jacket before shooting me a malicious grin. "You'll be hearing from my lawyer." His words are spoken casually as though he's totally unruffled, but violence shines in his eyes.

It's enough to make my legs feel unsteady. I command them to stay strong, unwilling to show this monster any weakness. When I sense my director joining me on stage in silent support, I cross my arms defiantly and watch Talbot make his exit. He gives me one last parting glare before making his walk of shame out of the theater, Sante and Oran joining his procession.

I did it.

I stood up to the demon who's haunted me for years. I fought back.

Pride wraps me in her feathered wings and assures me that I'm stronger than I ever knew.

"Thank you for your patience, everyone, and enjoy the rest of the show." I give a ballerina's bow, then gracefully follow my director backstage with my head held high and my heart soaring.

43

Sante

I've never seen anything more courageous in my entire fucking life. Amelie's grace, determination, strength, and loyalty already keep me in a perpetual state of awe, but what she did tonight—there are no words. She is incredible beyond measure, and she's *mine*.

I will strive every damn day of my life to be worthy of her.

My first task in that pursuit is to make sure John Talbot rots in hell.

Oran and I follow Talbot and the guards into the lobby. I have no idea how the asshole ended up front and center in the theater without any of us noticing. We never even detected he had tickets to the show, or I would have ensured that motherfucker didn't make it in the door.

One of the guards redirects Talbot toward the office area when he tries to go to an exit. The AG spins around to confront him but does a double take instead when he sees me. I can almost hear his thoughts as he places me as the valet from weeks ago. The thing about tattoos like mine is they're recognizable, which can be a good thing and a bad thing. Today, it's priceless.

That's right, asshole. We got you.

He sneers, turning back to the guard. "You can't keep me here just because some lunatic makes accusations on a stage."

"We can, and we will. Theater policy is that all incidents are to be reported to the authorities. If the cops get here and say you're free to leave, then you can go."

"This is harassment and false imprisonment. Do you have any idea who you're dealing with here? I'll have you both fired by morning."

I inch forward and stare down the attorney general of the state of New York with palpable violence. "You walk out of this building, and I'll detain you instead. I can promise you now, you won't enjoy that option."

Talbot holds his glare, trying to be tough, but after a glance at the mob of people joining us to stretch their legs and get concessions, he folds. *"You people are going to wish you never crossed me,"* he hisses quietly before storming toward the office.

I'm about to follow them back when an idea hits me. I place a quick call.

"Malone here," the officer answers. He'd given his number to Amelie, and out of an abundance of caution, I'd saved it in my phone.

"Sir, this is Isaac calling on behalf of Amelie Brooks. It's been a few weeks, but you came to her apartment after a man broke into her place at night. That ring any bells?"

"I know exactly who you're talking about. Is she alright?"

"She's fine, but she decided to confront the man who raped her and has been stalking her. We're at the Metropolitan Opera House. I don't have time to explain, but we need you here so this guy doesn't get away." I'm not above stroking an ego if it gets me what I want.

"I'm not far from there, but I'm not on duty. I won't be in uniform."

"Uniforms have already been called, and theater security is detaining the man, but we need someone here who knows the situation."

"I'll be there in ten." The line clicks dead.

Fuck, yeah, we got him by the balls now.

Talbot is talking to someone on the phone when I join them in the office. I give a subtle nod to Oran, telling him I have shit under control. We wait another five minutes before two uniformed officers arrive. The security detail shakes hands with them, then explains the situation. Talbot launches back into his threats with much more impact on his new audience. The two cops look anxiously at one another.

"Mr. Talbot's right. If the young lady wants to file a report, she's welcome to do so, but in the meantime, we have no reason to detain him."

I take my turn to speak up. "She stood in front of hundreds of people and confided the most painful, horrific thing that ever happened to her, and you two are dismissing it?"

Again, they exchange an uncertain glance.

"It's her word against his," one of them says, trying to sound firm. "She can't go around slinging allegations without some kind of proof."

If I could strangle the motherfucker, I would.

"Cunts like you are the reason women like her are scared to speak up." Each word is ground out past gritted teeth.

Oran coughs, warning me to keep my shit together.

"That's it," Talbot cuts in. "I'm leaving." He flings open the door to find Officer Hotshot on the other side.

"Looks like I'm the last one to the party." Malone scans the room, taking in the scene.

"Who the fuck are you?" Talbot demands.

Malone takes his time clipping his badge onto his belt. "Officer Dean Malone. I understand tonight's incident is in relation to an ongoing investigation."

"The fuck? There *is* no investigation. This is all a bunch of bullshit."

Malone moseys forward, forcing Talbot to retreat back into the room.

Time for me to clarify matters.

"Officer Malone, Amelie acknowledged on stage tonight that Mr. Talbot here raped her four years ago and has been threatening her ever since. She suspected he was the man who broke into her apartment but was scared to tell the truth. First thing in the morning, she'll be changing her statement and adding charges of sexual assault of a minor, among others."

"I never broke into her apartment," Talbot balks, not even realizing how incriminating it sounds that the rape wasn't the first thing he refuted. "You know who I am? I'm John Talbot —you work for me, Officer Malone—and these people are setting me up."

Malone locks eyes with Talbot, slowly looks him up and down, then turns back to me, completely dismissing the aging pedophile.

"I knew something wasn't right about that night. I'm glad she's taking the risk to come forward and tell the truth."

"*What?*" Talbot wails. "Are you fucking kidding me? That's it. I'm outta here." He makes a move to push past Malone, who slaps a cuff around one of his wrists and then the other in two seconds flat.

"I was going to suggest we have a seat, but if you'd rather do it at the station, by all means." He guides Talbot by the arm. The AG protests, then realizes the lobby is still full of audience members and goes quiet to keep from drawing attention to himself. The two sycophant cops are similarly silent, seemingly hopeful everyone will forget they were ever involved.

I follow Malone out to his car, pulling him aside once Talbot is secured in the back seat.

"Listen, she just finally opened up about this to me last night. She didn't have plans to make it public, but his attending the show was the last straw. You need to know that he claimed to have filmed the assault—that's what he's used as leverage all these years. That and his power. He had these two assholes by the balls before you arrived. I'm telling you now, this is big. The feds will need to be involved."

Malone slowly nods, taking in what I've said. "In other words, don't fuck it up."

"Glad to hear we understand one another," I offer respectfully.

I looked into Malone after he called Amelie to the station that day. I couldn't find a single speck of dirt on the guy. No affiliations or rumors. Clean as a fucking whistle. One of the very few who does the job for the right reasons. We may not be on the same team, but I respect that shit.

"So, Isaac with no last name, you going to tell me who the fuck you are?"

Amusement teases my lips into a smile. "Name's Sante Isaaco Mancini. I'm Renzo Donati's cousin and a member of the family." I know he'll recognize the name and get my drift.

Malone shakes his head. "Fucking Christ, she's up to her eyeballs in Mafia."

I sober, my stare locking with his. "Doesn't mean he didn't hurt her. That monster needs to be off the streets. She wants to see justice done by the books with him behind bars, which is fine by me. But one way or another, he *will* pay for his crimes."

"You're doing the right thing," he says sincerely.

I arch a brow at him and extend a handshake. "Don't make me regret it." With that, we part ways, though I suspect we'll be seeing one another again in the future. Good cops like him always pop up like a bad case of herpes.

Back inside, the lights are dim, and orchestral music drifts out from beyond the theater doors. Time to watch my girl shine.

44

Amelie

I'VE NEVER FELT SO AMAZING ON STAGE. SO INSPIRED. I PUT MY heart and soul into every movement, and at the end of the performance, we had to do two extra curtain calls. The audience couldn't get enough. It's always hard to say what an audience's reaction will be to the adaptation of a celebrated work into a new format. Our director can breathe easy after tonight. The reviews should be phenomenal.

I just hope the sensational news of the incident at intermission doesn't overshadow any talk about the performance itself. Not that it can be helped. I'm sure I made quite an impression, but I don't regret it for a second. I'm incredibly proud of how I handled the night.

I was a little worried my fellow cast members might be

upset that I wasn't more discreet until, one after another, dancers approached backstage and gave me hugs and words of encouragement. The director? Not so much. Despite his show of support, he didn't say a word to me after intermission. And I totally understand. His name is tied to the success or failure of the production.

The dancers allow the audience to clear out before we return to the main theater to see the family and friends waiting for us. More than a dozen people are clustered together just for me, though I only have eyes for one. I fling myself into Sante's arms the second I'm close enough. He bellows out a laugh and spins me around.

I'm showered in congratulations and bathed in praise. All comments revolve around my performance rather than the AG, and I'm grateful. It's time to focus on the good and let the past go. Tonight is a night of celebration.

"The theater is hosting an after-party at the Skylark. You're all welcome to join for as little or as late as you like." It's a Sunday evening, and most of them have young kids, so I don't expect many to come, but damn if there aren't nods all around.

"Awesome! Let me change real quick, and we'll meet you there." I start to turn, but a hand clamps around my wrist, spinning me back around. I gasp when Sante pulls me straight into a passionate kiss, dipping my body backward like we've stepped off a 1930s movie set.

Our family and friends tease us with whistles and catcalls. I can hardly kiss him back, thanks to the irrepressible grin that may never leave my face.

Sante rights us and whispers, "So fucking proud of you."

"Never would have happened without you." His unwavering support and strength have bolstered me in ways I never expected.

That grin is back, drawing out a matching one on his face. I pop up on my toes and give him a quick smack on the lips before rushing off. "Back in a jiff!"

The dress I brought for the party is phenomenal. I wish I didn't have my hair in a bun, but that's the nature of the beast. The concrete holding this thing smooth isn't going anywhere until I shower. Therefore, I'll rock the half-movie star, half-librarian look.

Sante studies me intently when I return. "I'm not sure I'm comfortable taking you out in public like that. I'll end up in prison." He's teasing. Mostly.

I grin. "Let them look. You're the only man I'm going home with."

He grunts in agreement, sending my grin into orbit.

Our group is well into their first drink when we arrive. They've gathered around two bar tables, clusters of animated conversations in progress. We're easily absorbed into the group and welcomed with cheers and hugs.

"Champagne?" Sante asks.

"Yes, *please*," I answer with enthusiasm, to which he smirks before fading into the crowd. When he returns, he raises his glass to gain the attention of our clutch of family and friends.

"On behalf of Amelie and myself, I want to thank all of you for coming out tonight. Having you here makes this big opening night that much more special. I know Mellie is capable of thanking you herself, but I wanted to steal the stage for a moment because there's something important I need to do, and having you all here makes it the perfect opportunity. You see, Amelie here has graciously agreed to marry me."

Everyone around us gasps and squeals—at least, the women do. The men mostly give macho grunts of approval.

I smile like an absolute loon.

Sante steps closer, setting down his drink and pulling a box from his jacket pocket.

My jaw hinges open.

"And I don't want to go a minute longer without seeing my ring on her finger." He opens the box, and I see a flash of sparkling brilliance. Then he's holding my hand, sliding the most beautiful diamond ring I've ever seen on my finger. The central diamond is round with a halo of smaller diamonds surrounding it—like Sante and I now with our closest loved ones all around.

I'm overwhelmed with joy. Radiantly happy. Incandescently in love.

"Sante—" I breathe.

"Mellie, you're mine, my piccola ballerina, forever and always."

Before I have a chance to burst into tears, he kisses me, and this time, the entire room erupts in riotous cheers.

I'm quickly swarmed with congratulations from the ladies as soon as the kiss ends. One after another, they give me hugs and beg me to show off my stunning new ring. Noemi holds off until the rush subsides, saving her congratulations for last. When she finally gets her turn at a hug, she holds me so tight I can't possibly question the sincerity of her joy.

"Oh, Amelie. I'm so incredibly happy for you two." Tears shine in her eyes when she pulls back with a warm smile. "And I'm so grateful to you for giving me my brother back."

"I didn't really do anything," I say sheepishly, feeling a bit awkward from all the praise.

"Of course you did. You gave Sante a reason to love again. Your beautiful soul helped him heal, and now he's back where he belongs. He's happier than I've ever seen him, which thrills me, but I'm also overjoyed to get such a wonderful new sister."

Now I'm tearing up, which sends us into another round of hugs.

"Thank you, Em," I whisper, hoping she can hear me over the music but unable to speak any louder past the emotion constricting my throat.

"Okay, enough of the sappy stuff!" Noemi says with a grin, wiping the moisture from her eyes. "Tonight is about celebration. I'd say it's time for a toast!"

Another round of cheers fills the air around us. The next hour is a brilliant blur of happiness—hugs, laughter, stories … more hugs—everything that makes family such a blessing.

Eventually, however, our group begins to thin as folks head home. I don't complain. I've had enough champagne to give me the courage to test something I've daydreamed about for weeks.

"I think it's time we head out as well," I suggest to Sante.

"Your wish is my command." Moments later, we get the keys from the valet and relax in the quiet of his car.

"Hey, babe?" I ask warily.

"Yeah?"

"I left something at the theater. I bet it's locked up by now. Youuu … wouldn't happen to knowww … how to sneak in, would you?" The answer is obviously yes—the man snuck in to stalk me for weeks—but I'm feeling playful.

"Yeah, I think I can make that happen."

"Good because I'd prefer not to wait."

Back at the theater, he shows me the side door he used to get in. The man has a damn key.

"How did you get that?" I gape at him. Here, I'd envisioned some sort of Spider-Man-style climb to an upstairs window. Not actually, but a key had never entered my mind.

"I stole it from security and made a copy."

"Well, that's a little alarming."

"You're telling me. That's why I didn't like you being in there alone. Who knows who else can get in," he grumbles.

"If I'd known stalkers were so considerate, I would have found one ages ago."

Sante bares his teeth, then takes a playful bite at the air. "Too late. And if anyone gets any ideas at this point, I'll pluck their eyes right out of the sockets. Hard to obsess over someone you can't see."

I look at him, knowing he's not joking in the slightest.

"You say the sweetest things," I tell him in a tender voice to make sure he knows I'm not joking either.

"Yeah, it's time to get home. I need to be inside you."

"Okay, okay. We just need to hit the dressing room real quick." I lead us back there and go to my vanity, but the problem is, there's nothing among the makeup and supplies that I need. What I wanted was something a little twisted, and I'm not sure how to ask.

As it turns out, I don't have to.

When I turn around, Sante is leaning on the wall in the same place he did that night he wore the mask. I practically start to salivate as I combine my knowledge of him with the memory. I feel like any shrink would tell me that being turned on by that night is a red flag for all sorts of mental health issues, but I'm tired of caring what other people think. I find it hot as hell.

My breathing turns shallow, and I'm pretty sure my panties are now soaked.

"Oh, pet, what have you done? You should know better than to let a man like me see you thinking thoughts like that." His voice rakes across my sensitized skin, drawing out a shiver. "Stay," he commands, then disappears back into the hallway. When he rounds the corner again seconds later, he's wearing the mask. I can hardly believe my eyes.

"Where was it?" I can't stop from asking.

"Giant lost and found bin in the hallway." He resumes his station at the wall, crossing his arms over his chest. "The dress. Take it off."

I reach back to unbutton the single-loop closure at my neck. The emerald-green dress is long-sleeved and square cut, outlining my frame without being glued to me. Elegant and almost professional if it wasn't for the length—possibly my favorite part. The dress is super short, which shows off my toned legs to their full potential. The perfect mix of sexy and sophisticated.

I lift the fabric over my head and drop it on the floor. I wasn't wearing a bra, leaving me in my panties and heels. My nipples pebble from the exposure and knowing Sante is starving for a taste.

"Panties off." His voice is ragged, worn through like the knees on an ancient pair of jeans.

I slide them down to the ground.

"Take that chair and set it facing me. Then have a seat."

I do as he says, laying one of Hazel's misplaced scraps of fabric on the wood seat before I sit.

"Spread your legs, and let me look at you. I want to see that beautiful pussy weep for me."

I have never felt sexier in my whole life.

I press out my chest, hands on my knees as I open them wide.

"*Fuck*, I can taste you already." He walks to where a robe hangs on a hook and slips the belt from its loops. He then prowls around behind me. "Hands," he demands.

I bring them together behind the back of the chair. It's easy enough as the wood chairs used in our dressing room have been around for decades and are petite café-style chairs. He uses the soft terry to loosely bind my hands.

"If any of this is too much, you say so. I want it to be enjoyable, not triggering. Understood?"

I nod readily, eating up every second of this delicious fantasy.

"Look to your left."

I do, just as his hand cups my breast. I see it all play out in the vanity mirror beside us. I arch into his touch, silently begging for more.

"Such a performer, pet. I approve, so long as this sort of show is only for me."

Again, I nod. "It only feels good because it's you." If I truly was in a room with a masked stranger, I'd be petrified. This is different. Role-play. Fantasy. This is safe.

"Keep your eyes on the mirror."

I watch him circle before me and undo his pants, letting his swollen cock fall free. I see it bobbing in the mirror and desperately want to turn my head, but I don't. I want to be his good girl, and he hasn't told me I can look yet.

He steps one leg between mine and rounds the other to the side of the chair. The side where the mirror is. I can now see the crimson head of his cock inches from my face, though I'm not looking directly at it.

"So good at following orders," he purrs. "So good at pleasing me." His hand trails along my jawline, then down to my breast, where he twists one nipple in the perfect mix of pleasure and pain. "Tell me, pet. Would you like to please me by wrapping your fuckable lips around my cock?"

"Yes, please." *God, yes.* When it comes to this enigmatic man, I want everything. All of him.

"Good girl. Keep watching that mirror while you suck my cock. Look at how well you take me." He keeps himself close enough for me to reach while still letting me remain in control. I can tell how mindful he's being about not pushing me too far, and the comfort that brings me emboldens me. I'm able to lose myself in his salty taste on my tongue and the feel of his smooth skin gliding past my lips.

Wanting to see how much of him I can take, I relax my throat as best as I can and press forward.

Sante groans. "*Jesus*, such a greedy girl." He pulls free of me and adjusts himself back into his pants before moving in front of me and scooting my butt to the very edge of the chair. "My turn."

Then he's on his knees, devouring my pussy like he hasn't eaten in a week. His hands roam my thighs and up to my breasts while his mouth teases and taunts my core. When he inserts two fingers inside me, I nearly come undone. He builds the pressure to excruciating levels, then lets it recede enough to start over. Tears slip from the corners of my eyes. I don't even know why. I'm not crying. It's like my body is so full of pleasure that it's leaking out in the form of tears.

"*Please*, Sante. Please let me come." It's a breathless cry that causes him to stop rather than keep going. I think I might actually weep until he has me stand, unties my hands, and has me rest them on the vanity. I watch him in the mirror behind me as he frees himself again and takes hold of my hips. Seeing the unfiltered desire on his face as he admires my backside has my inner muscles clenching with need.

I whimper, only to be rewarded with the fullness of his enormous cock inching inside me.

"*God, Sante. It's so good. Yesss, so good.*"

He rips off the mask, our eyes locked in the mirror. "Look at me. I want you to see the man who owns you. This body is mine—to fuck and feed and protect. You're mine, pet." He fully sheathes himself inside me and continues his movements. Possessive and dominant and oh-so delicious.

"*Yes!*" I cry, so close.

An orgasm builds just out of my reach, the wave of pleasure easily reforming after his earlier ministrations.

"Touch that pretty pink clit, pet. Make that pussy come all over my cock."

The second I reach for my center, his thrusts intensify. I don't know if it's his actions or my touch or a combination of the two, but I'm catapulted over the edge into an abyss of pleasure. I have to lock my knees to stay upright.

Sante hisses. "Fuck, you squeeze me so good, so tight." Then his release starts with a growl deep in his chest as his entire body strains and flexes. He grips my hips even tighter, curving his body around mine. "Made for me," he breathes, wrapping an arm around my middle and holding me to him while his other arm supports us, leaning on the vanity.

After a minute of recovery, he kisses the center of my spine and pulls out of me. Wetness immediately starts a slow trail from my core to the top of my thigh. I stand awkwardly and look around for a tissue when Sante appears already armed with a roll of paper towels.

"We'll do a proper cleanup at home. This should do for now." He tenderly wipes the excess cum from my body, extra careful at my most sensitive areas. Once I'm dry, he helps me get my dress back on and zips himself back in his pants.

We're about to make our exit when he pauses. "Can't forget this." He takes the mask off the floor and shoves it in his pocket.

I laugh quietly. "We could always get one of our own."

"This one's got sentimental value. Besides, no one here is going to miss it."

I can't argue with that. Nor do I want to. The way I feel right now, I may never argue with anyone ever again.

Let's not get carried away.

Touché. Maybe just until tomorrow.

That's more like it.

45
Sante

I take Amelie to the police station the following morning to file a formal complaint. She's just as surprised that I take her to Malone's desk as Malone is to see the engagement ring on her finger. He doesn't say anything, but I see it register when they shake hands. His eyes cut to mine. I give him a look that says *and don't you forget it*.

We give Malone a full rundown about The Society, what Amelie's parents did to her, and the subsequent fallout, minus the part where Oran's family kills off the entire disgusting organization. It's a ton to unpack. To his credit, Malone doesn't hesitate to take it all in. He asks good questions and reinforces my confidence that he'll handle the case properly on his end.

Talbot was allowed to leave the station in the night. I figured that was likely, but the reprieve is only temporary. And the next time he's taken into custody, it will be a whole different story.

After we leave the station, Amelie is noticeably quiet. Even a little withdrawn.

"You okay?" I ask once we're in the car, though I don't start the engine. I want her to have my full attention if she needs it. I can't imagine the past few hours were easy.

"I think so. I'm just worried it's not going to be enough. I can scream the truth at the top of my lungs, but if a jury doesn't believe me, he could get away scot-free."

"I'd say that's highly unlikely. When the feds have a look at his computer—which they'll do with your allegations that he claimed to have video evidence—the cache of child porn they find will keep him locked up for good."

Her head whips around, large green eyes staring at me in shock. "Child porn? I thought you said you guys didn't find anything substantial on his computer."

"We didn't." I let the information sink in. "We may not have found evidence of rape on his part, but the man is a pedophile and a rapist. We know that for a fact. The evidence they find on that computer ensures justice will be done."

"You'd already planned to set him up," she says quietly.

"Yes and no. We made sure the evidence was present. We weren't quite sure yet how to bring it to the attention of the feds. Your bravery took care of that for us."

"He's not going to get away?" The cautious optimism in her tiny voice makes me want to build her a castle where no one can ever harm her again.

"I swear on my mother's grave, John Talbot will spend the rest of his life in prison."

Joy and gratitude light her face. "Have I told you before

that you say the sweetest things?"

"Yeah." I wink at her. "I think you've mentioned that."

Ten minutes later, we pull into a parking garage at yet another government building.

"City clerk's office?" Amelie reads off the sign. "What are we doing here?"

"Getting our marriage license. Gotta have the license before we can do the deed." I get out of the car and go around to open her door when I notice she hasn't joined me. "Something wrong?"

"Don't people get those right before they get married?"

"Yeah, they expire after a while, so people usually get them like the week before the wedding."

Amelie stares at me. I stare back, then squat so we're at eye level.

"Baby, I stalked you, coerced my way into the apartment next door, then moved myself into your place—did you actually think I'd wait for a wedding when you agreed to marry me?" I know I should take this seriously, but I have to tease her a little.

Her glare tells me she's not impressed.

"Sorry, I couldn't help it. But honestly, I love you. You love me. We know we want to be together, and I want the world to know you're mine. I went four years without you. Now that I have you, I don't want to waste another minute."

"Well, when you put it like that ..." she says softly, her head angling to the side.

I help her out of the car and kiss her cheek. "And that's why there will never be anyone as perfect for me as you are."

"Now you're just buttering me up." She shoots a playful glare. "What else are you planning?"

"Nothing!" I raise my hands to proclaim my innocence. "No actual *plans*. I have ideas, that's all."

She shakes her head with a laugh. We walk hand in hand to the clerk's office and leave an hour later with a license to get married tucked securely in my jacket pocket. Only one thing left to do today, and it may take a while, so it's time to get my girl home. I have the perfect wedding gift in mind, and something as important as that can't be rushed.

"Furry pink handcuffs. Are you serious?" I stare at Tommy as he secures John Talbot's arms over his head, hooking the ornamental cuffs to a chain hanging from the rafters. He's not suspended, just uncomfortable.

"You said to bring something that wouldn't leave marks. If you wanted something else, you should have been more specific."

I huff and swipe the black fabric sack off Talbot's head. He looks absurd restrained in fur cuffs, and I decide it's actually a nice touch. Anything to demean him works for me.

"Let's get this show started." I yank the duct tape off Talbot's mouth.

He sneers and looks like he's about to spew some garbage threats until he spots his cohort bound in a chair, bloody and covered in bruises.

"John, I believe you know Sean." Identifying the thug that Talbot paid to do his dirty work was easy. Finally getting to punish him for threatening Amelie was the perfect appetizer before the main course. That way, I don't get carried away with Talbot. I made a promise, after all.

"What the fuck is this? You think you can hurt me and get away with it?" Panic raises the pitch of his voice, despite his effort to sound tough. "I'm a public figure. You can't make me disappear without causing a stir."

"Why would I want to do that? You're an innocent man, right?" I say without a hint of emotion.

"I don't kill people like your sort."

"I'm glad you recognize the precarious nature of your situation because I am exactly that *sort*." I grab a heavy pair of scissors from a table filled with tools. When I start toward him, Talbot's tune quickly changes.

"Shit, there's no need for this, okay? I can make your life easier—a friend on the other side of the fence."

I yank his shirt out from the waist of his pants and slice the fabric from hem to collar. As the metal glides closer to his face, his sniveling worsens.

"*Fucking Christ*, don't do this. Please, just tell me what you want from me."

"We'll get there soon enough."

Once his shirt is nothing but scraps of fabric on the concrete floor, I do the same with the rest of his clothes until he's completely exposed. I make sure to take my time. The suspense is half the fun, and judging by the bulging vein in his forehead, Talbot appreciates every tantalizing second.

"If you're good here, I'm going to head out," Tommy says after helping me secure my subject. He's not a fan of torture, but not because of the pain it involves. He hates messes—blood splatter makes him twitchy. I think that's why he's so great with a sniper rifle and throwing knives. Minimal cleanup.

"Thanks, man. I'll be in touch."

While his retreating footsteps fade, I examine the sharp edge of the shears and slowly walk toward Sean, who is awake but in rough shape and silenced with a wadded-up rag in his mouth.

"Back in Italy, my uncle has a pig farm. What they say is true—those things will eat anything," I muse as if talking to myself. "No pigs here in the city, but we have the next best thing."

I click the lock on the giant barn door and slide it aside, opening the warehouse to the river several feet below. "Feeding someone to the fish may sound cliché, but it's a classic for a reason."

When I turn my stare back to Sean, he tries to scream at me. Looks like he's not totally out of fight.

"Fuck, man. You've terrorized him enough. Look at him," Talbot pleads on behalf of his cohort, but it won't do any good.

I position the blades on either side of his pinky finger, then clench the scissors shut. Sean passes out while Talbot starts praying.

I pick up the discarded digit from the floor. Holding an inanimate body part for the first time is strange, but you get used to it.

"You're a fucking psychopath, you know that?" Talbot spits at me.

"At least I target those who deserve it and not innocent young women." I peg him with an icy stare as I toss the finger into the river.

"What do you want from me? I'm telling you that she came to that hotel voluntarily. Her own mother set it up."

I make a tsking noise and angle my head to the side. "See, that's the thing about statutory rape—even if she had consented, which we both know she didn't—it's still. Fucking. *Rape.*" Unchecked violence bleeds from my words. I can handle a lot of shit, but hearing this twisted asshole trying to paint himself as anything but a pedophile seriously pisses me off.

When I head back to the table, I swap out the scissors for a battery pack and clamps. Talbot is noticeably freaking out, but he doesn't know the half of it until I attach that shit to his shriveled dick. He tries to thrash to shake off the clamp but hisses in pain and stops.

I have news for him. It's going to get much worse.

Not as bad as I'd like since I can't leave any marks, but sometimes less pain for longer intervals can be even more effective.

I ignore his worthless pleading and flip on the battery, savoring his screams.

The big bad attorney general openly sobs when I turn off the machine. "What do you want? I can't undo the past."

"No," I agree. "But you can suffer for your actions."

His watery, hate-filled stare lifts to mine. "Doesn't that make you just as much of a monster as me?"

"Possibly." I shrug indifferently, then turn on the battery again. I give him about twenty seconds to endure—enough time that his clenched teeth look like they might give way at any moment—then turn it back off.

"Tell me about your connection to The Society," I instruct calmly.

His head hangs low, his chest heaving with panted breaths. "All I know is the shipping mogul Wellington was under investigation—a woman had been taken from his home after being trafficked. The case was a mess. Our guys fucked up all the evidence. I knew we didn't have a leg to stand on, so when the Brooks woman came to me and offered a trade, it was an easy choice. The trial never would have happened anyway."

"Wellington goes free, and you get to rape a seventeen-year-old girl. A win-win, is that right?"

Talbot starts sniveling and sobbing. "Her mother assured me … it was fine, and the girl never … seemed upset. It wasn't like she fought me or anything."

I'm so enraged I can't speak. Instead, I turn the machine back on and watch him writhe until he pisses himself. I don't turn it off until he looks on the verge of passing out. The asshole in the chair starts gagging on his own vomit. I take my gun from its holster, point it at the choking man and put a bullet between his eyes. I don't need him anyway. He was a loose end and a convenient lesson to motivate Talbot. The attorney general is the only one who matters.

His story aligns with what we suspected. I'm glad to have confirmation, but I still need one more thing.

He's panting while he weeps, his feet standing in a pool of his own urine. "Please, no more. Please."

"We're not quite done. I need one more thing from you. You told Amelie you had videos of her and her sister. Where are they?"

"I lied," he blurts without a filter. "I swear, it was a lie. Her mother told me her sister had done the same thing—that it was some sort of ritual in their family. I think she was trying to assure me that it was normal for them. That's as much as I knew, but when she died and people started disappearing, I panicked. Telling her that I had videos of her and her sister was the only thing I could think of to keep her quiet, short of killing her. I'm not a killer. I'm not a killer." He breaks down again, sobbing, snot and saliva dripping from his lips.

When I reach for the battery, he cries out. "Please, if you're going to kill me, just do it. You already marked the bullet. Just finish it."

I walk closer and slowly circle him. There's nothing like uncertainty to enhance the mindfuck of torture, and I want to make sure he leaves here with emotional scars worthy of his actions.

"Even if I were planning on killing you, I'd never let you

off so easily. I'm afraid I made a promise to my fiancée that I'd let the justice system do its job where you're concerned."

"That what you call this?" he whines before instantly retreating with a litany of apologies.

I glare at him, waiting for his stupidity to run dry. When he finally quiets, I continue. "I'll let the feds do their thing now that I've had the opportunity of a private word with you because I want you to remember this day and know that if you so much as think about Amelie or her sister, I will hunt down and erase not only you but your entire bloodline. The fact that you continue to breathe is only because she wills it. Don't ever forget that."

He opens his mouth to say something, but I'm done talking. I flip on the battery and text Renzo that I'm ready for help with cleanup. He tells me he's got someone on the way. By the time I'm done typing my reply, Talbot is unconscious. I flip off the machine and head outside to wait.

The old me would light up a cigarette and hold in that first lungful of smoke until it burned. The temptation is still there, but I won't go back to it. Besides, knowing I've done my job and kept Amelie safe is better than any nicotine high. I feel like I've proven myself worthy. I've learned from my past mistakes, and for the first time ever, I can honestly say I'm proud of the man I've become.

Now, when I take Amelie as my wife, I can tell her she no longer has anything to fear. While she and Lina were strong enough to risk videos of themselves being leaked, I know it still worried them. No one wants to risk that sort of public exposure and violation. My gift to her is the assurance that she's finally free. She can set her fears aside and know that I will always keep her safe.

ONE WEEK LATER, we meet up with Oran and Lina, Conner and Noemi, Gloria, Tommy, and Freya, of course, at a garden rooftop for an intimate ceremony.

"Mrs. Mancini, you take my breath away." I hold her hands beneath an archway built of swaying ivy and marvel at my good fortune.

"I haven't said I do yet," she teases me.

I shrug. "A technicality."

Oran cuts in. "One we're about to remedy. You two ready?" As our officiant, he stands to one side of us while the rest of our family forms a semi-circle on the other. Everyone in our families always gets married in churches, so this wedding is unorthodox, but so are we. This is our big day, and we're doing it our way.

Besides, it's not like we have parents who will fuss about the location and traditions.

"Absolutely," I say without hesitation.

Mellie grins at me. She's truly stunning, having chosen a 1950s Hollywood starlet look with an ivory sheath dress, hair styled in perfectly smooth waves, and topped with a small fastener hat with a delicate white birdcage veil. Every inch of her is perfection, including the bright red lipstick I can't wait to see circling my cock.

"I know we're all incredibly honored to be here today to share in this special occasion. At this time, the couple will exchange vows." Oran agreed to officiate under the express condition that he wouldn't have to wax poetically about love and commitment. We assured him our aim was short and sweet, heavy on the short.

We wrote our own vows and haven't shown them to one another. Our relationship is too unique to fit into a cookie-cutter script.

"Amelie, I vow to follow you to the ends of the earth and

love you throughout the journey. To live my life dedicated to your happiness and to strive each day to be worthy of your love. I will honor you, protect you, and keep you all the days of my life." I know I've done well when she has to blink away tears before she can recite her own vows.

"I choose you, Sante, to be no other than who you are. To grow with you and fall more in love with you each day. I trust in your integrity and have faith in your abiding love for me. I vow to love and cherish you so long as we both shall live." The pride and adoration in her voice shreds me. I had no idea a few simple sentences could have me so choked up.

"Do we have the rings?" Oran asks, eyes scanning our small group.

Tommy steps forward and pulls the rings from his breast pocket. I'm so out of sorts that I almost take my own ring.

Oran nods and peeks at his phone. "Sante, we'll start with you. As you place this ring on Amelie's finger, repeat after me. With this ring, I thee wed—"

"With this ring, I thee wed—"

"And pledge you my love, now and forever."

I repeat the words and slide the wedding band onto my bride's slender finger. She grins ear to ear as she holds my wedding band and repeats the same pledge to me. When that ring slides onto my finger, something ancient from deep inside me roars with satisfaction.

"By the power vested in me by the state of New York, I now pronounce you husband and wife. You may kiss the bride."

Anticipating his words, I've already pulled her close and am pressing my lips to hers when he announces the kiss. Our family cheer and holler, surrounding us in love and encouragement—the perfect way to start this next portion of our journey together.

EPILOGUE
Amelie

THE *MOULIN ROUGE* PRODUCTION HAS BEEN RUNNING FOR A month now with nothing but rave reviews. It's become a pivotal turning point in my dance career, and I'm so incredibly grateful. I'm amazed at how much has changed for me in such a short time. How much *I've* changed.

I feel like I'm finally figuring out who I am beneath all the trauma of my circumstances. I'm learning who I am when fear isn't an influencing factor and finding that this new version of myself is pretty dang awesome.

Buzz about my showstopping announcement faded relatively quickly, though Talbot wasn't so lucky where his legal problems were concerned. The feds did find damning evidence of child pornography on his computer, and once my complaint became public knowledge, a whole slew of other allegations followed, from assault to bribery to racketeering. The judge even denied bail because of the risk he posed to witnesses.

No more Fourth of July barbecues for him.

On the other hand, I'm surrounded by family and stuffed to the gills with delicious food. Conner and Noemi are hosting at their place. Most everyone here is a Byrne, and while Sante and I don't carry that name, I know they're still our family. This is the first weekend I've had off in three months, and there's no one else I'd rather spend it with.

"Watching the kids play together is adorable." I'm sitting on the sofa with the other ladies while the kids run from room to room, causing chaos. "Stormy's little girl Mae, River, and Violet are seriously already forming a girl gang. Add Pippa's twins to that in a few years, and those cousins are gonna be an epic force."

"Hopefully, this little guy can help Kellen, Roman, and Ryder keep them out of trouble," Stormy pats her round belly. She's only about three months along but has a sizable bump since it's her third.

"Eh, the girls outnumber the boys, as it stands. My money's on a Byrne Queendom down the road." I grin triumphantly.

"I'm so not ready," Lina mutters, her hand on her forehead.

"No need to get too worked up yet," I assure her. "You look like you're going to pass out."

"It's not that. I've had horrible heartburn lately, and the smell of those pickles has been bothering me since we ate."

Every one of us gapes at her with wide eyes.

"Lina?" I say gently. "Did you ever by chance make that doctor visit we talked about?"

Her eyes snap to mine, then do a sweep of the other ladies. "There was no reason. I've been fine, really. Just a little tired."

"And sensitive to smells?" notes Stormy.

"Chronic heartburn?" adds Noemi.

"When's the last time you had your period?" I ask.

Her brows knit together. "I had it last month. I mean ... it was light. The last two have been ... really light," she says slowly.

"Oh shit. Here we go again," Pippa chimes in.

I wasn't around, but I heard about the dinner party a few years back when Stormy and Noemi *both* discovered they were pregnant. The story is a family favorite.

"I have tests in the cabinet from the boys' pregnancy." Noemi jumps up and disappears down a hallway.

Lina's eyes round. "Here? Now? You guys want me to—" She looks over at where the guys are gathered around the kitchen island drinking beer. "You want me to pee on a stick right *now*?" she whisper-yells.

"Might as well, Lina Bean," I tell her. "You'll find out one way or another."

She slumps in her seat. "I know, but I'm not sure I'm ready. I suppose that's why I've ignored the signs. It could be something else, after all. Like an iron deficiency." Her gaze searches for someone willing to support her, but our group is full of empathy instead.

"Oh, honey. We've got you," Stormy says in her warm Southern drawl. "Babies are never easy, but that's why we have one another."

Noemi strides back to the group and slips Lina a box of pregnancy tests. Apparently, we're keeping this a secret from the guys. I'm not sure why, but that's fine so long as I'm in on the surprise.

Lina sighs heavily, then heads to the bathroom. When I glance at the kitchen, Sante is watching. He's always watching. His eyes shift toward the bathroom briefly as if asking *what's up with your sister?* My eyes round innocently, and I give a *whatever-do-you-mean* shrug. He gives an almost imperceptible shake of his head, his tiny smirk saying *this should be good*.

Lina's not gone a full two minutes when she returns in a zombified state. "It can't be," she murmurs.

All of us ladies gasp and squeal. It's enough to finally draw the guys' attention.

"What's all the fuss about?" Bishop asks with a wide grin. He's the most outgoing of the group and always up for a laugh.

When none of us say anything and instead, look wide-eyed at one another, the guys migrate closer.

"This can't be good," Conner deadpans. "What are you up to?"

"Surprise," Lina says, holding up the pregnancy test with a mystified half smile.

The entire room turns to Oran. He blinks twice before an enormous grin splits his face.

"Hell, yeah! We're having a baby!" His excited cheer sends the entire room into celebration mode. Hugs and congratulations and laughter fill the huge great room, even drawing the attention of the little ones who tug on legs to find out what's happening.

"We're having a baby!" Oran says to Violet, giving her a big kiss on the cheek.

"We're having a baby!" someone else cries.

"Yeah! We're having a baby," another chimes in.

"No! I mean it, we're *having a baby*," Pippa says in an increasingly panicked voice. "*Two* of them."

Everyone goes silent and looks at the very pregnant Pip, who is now holding her crotch.

"Seriously, my water just broke. Someone get me a freaking towel and take me to the hospital!" she cries.

The ladies launch into action while the guys stare, dumbfounded.

I migrate to Sante's side and watch in fascination. "I did *not* see that coming."

"Looks like none of them did. When's she due?"

"Not for three weeks, but the doctors said the twins could come at any time and should be fine. Guess they cook faster or something. I don't know much about that stuff."

"One of these days…" he muses.

"We talked about this. Not for several more years, right?" I ask pointedly.

He turns big brown puppy-dog eyes to me and smirks. "Yeah, baby. Doesn't mean I'm not excited. Seein' my baby grow inside you is gonna be the greatest feeling in the world."

I shake my head with a smile. He's incorrigible but in the very best way.

A wave of people congregate toward the door while Lina and Oran join us on the sidelines.

"They all headed to the hospital?" I ask Lina.

"Just Pippa and Bishop for now. I think the rest of us will head over shortly."

"Will it happen that soon?"

"With her water already broken and it being twins, I doubt they'll let her go long. One way or another, those babies are coming soon enough."

"Come on, babe." Oran puts his arm around her shoulders. "Let's get Violet home, and we can decide what we're doing from there."

She nods and heads off to corral little Vi.

"Tommy texted earlier asking if we could stop by his new place," Sante says, sipping from his beer. "He wants our opinion on something. Sounds like we have a little time on our hands. How about we head over there, then drop Freya at home before heading to the hospital?"

"Works for me. I still haven't seen the place since he hired that interior designer." I call Freya over. She's done amazing adapting to the new family. We still keep the muzzle on her around kids, but I'm hoping to move past that soon. She makes sure to lie where she can see me. Otherwise, she's very chill, even in a party setting. I snap on her leash, and we say our goodbyes.

Tommy's new apartment is in a surprisingly trendy area—lots of nightlife and active young people. His place is one of only two apartments on the forty-second floor. The building is relatively new. From what I understand, the changes he's been making are primarily cosmetic. I'm intrigued to see how he's chosen to decorate his new place.

"Hey, man. How's it going?" Sante says when Tommy opens the door for us. The two hug, then I give Tommy a half hug. I'm still not entirely sure if he's comfortable with that sort of thing. He's not an easy man to read.

"All good. Thanks for coming by." He shows us inside to a much more inviting space than I'd imagined.

"You bet. We've been looking forward to seeing the place."

"Tommy, it's gorgeous," I say, genuinely impressed. It reminds me of a Scandinavian feel because of the simplicity and white walls, but plenty of rich wood furniture and muted landscapes on the walls bring a touch of warmth and life. The biggest surprise, however, is the number of live plants all around—some in large pots on the ground, some in planters on shelves, and others hanging in woven baskets. While there's more than I would have expected, it's not too much.

"I love how much space you have," Sante says, then looks at me. "We've really got to upgrade to something bigger."

"Yeah, my place worked for me, but adding you and Freya makes things a bit cramped."

Sante nods. "I'll get with an agent."

I grin, excited about the prospect.

I love that he's so proactive—or maybe the word is competent. He doesn't sit around and wait for someone else to make things happen. He sees when Freya needs more water and fills the dish. He starts the laundry if I haven't gotten to it. And if we need a repairman—or in this case, a real estate agent—he does the legwork and gets the ball rolling.

My cozy thoughts swooning over my husband scatter when a sound catches my ear. I still when I hear it again, realizing it sounds like— "Is that ... a woman *yelling*?" I'm genuinely not sure, but it's definitely coming from nearby.

Sante narrows his eyes at Tommy. "Is that what you needed our opinion on? Christ, Tommy. I thought you wanted help with a fabric color or some shit."

"I do," Tommy says earnestly, turning to the dining room. "My designer suggested an accent wall to break up the white. I told her nothing too bold, and I can't decide if I like it or not."

One wall is a soft beige rather than the white coating the other walls and ceiling. All three of us stare at it. The slight variation in color is hardly an accent, but to Tommy it probably looks like a smudge on a pristine wedding cake.

"I like it," I say. "Once there's a painting up, the color difference won't be as noticeable. It gives the place a bit more warmth."

"Yeah, looks good," Sante says distractedly. "Now let's talk about what the fuck is behind door number two."

Tommy frowns. "I caught her breaking in this morning."

Oh shit!

He actually does have a woman stashed in a back bedroom. I told myself it was a television left on a little too loud, but it seems Sante knew better.

We follow the cries to the back of the apartment and a series of closed doors. I walk to the last one on the left and open it to the sight of a woman duct-taped to a rolling chair. She's young, probably close to my age, and very pretty despite her disrepair. Natural strawberry-blond hair that no dye could ever duplicate, wide, teary eyes that plead with me for help, and a perfect smattering of freckles that make her look as innocent as a peach.

"Tommaso Donati, what on earth have you done?" I fire at him angrily.

"Me? She's the one who broke into my apartment."

"So you tied her up and left her back here?" I gape at him.

He shrugs noncommittally. "I had somewhere to be."

I smack his arm, ignoring the snicker coming from my husband, then carefully remove the tape covering the poor woman's mouth. "Are you okay?"

"I'm so sorry. This is all a big mixup. I thought the apartment belonged to a friend who was out of town."

"You steal shit from your friends when they're away?" Sante prods, his voice dripping with suspicion.

"I wasn't stealing," she shoots back defensively. "I just needed a place to stay."

"Ah, so you're a squatter, not a thief."

"Sante," I say in warning. "You're not even letting her explain."

His incredulous stare balks at me for giving her story any weight.

My returning glare reminds him not to be a dick.

He grimaces, then makes a *by all means* motion, allowing her a chance to speak.

"I have a photographer friend from school who used to live here. I didn't realize he'd moved, but I knew he was on shoot in Iceland, so I was hoping to use his place while he was gone. I would have checked with him, but the shoot is remote, and he couldn't be reached."

"You don't look homeless," Tommy notes without inflection.

"I'm not." She juts her chin out a hair. "I needed to lay low for a bit."

Sante suddenly takes more interest, his eyes narrowing. "Lay low sounds an awful lot like hiding. Who are you running from?"

The woman's eyes squeeze shut with frustration before reopening. "It doesn't matter. Look, I made a mistake, and I'm really sorry, but no harm was done. Can you please just let me go?" Her genuine fear on the subject is obvious, and I know that will only make the guys more insistent.

"*Who?*" Sante demands.

"You wouldn't know him," she says in exasperation. "And trust me, you wouldn't want to if you did. He's dangerous—that's why I needed a place he would never look."

Tommy pulls a gun out of thin air and points it right in her face. "Who?"

The silence around us thickens to a suffocating tension.

"Who … who are you?" the woman says in a breathless pant, terror bleaching her already pale skin to a pasty white.

Tommy responds, seemingly unaffected. "The last person you'll ever see if you don't give me a name."

I know Tommy won't shoot her. I've started to understand the way he acts and thinks, and I'm pretty sure he simply sees the gun as an effective way to move this conversation along. But I feel for the girl because she doesn't know that, and she's clearly terrified.

She squeezes her eyes tightly shut again. This time, tears roll down her freckled cheeks, and she whispers, "His name is Biba."

The words hang in the air before a curse from Sante blasts through the air like gunfire.

"*Fuck!*"

I remember that name. He's one of the Russians.

Why would this girl be running from the Russian mob?

I stare at Sante, pleading in my eyes. *Please, help her.*

He glowers, teeth gritted as he shakes his head at me. "What am I supposed to do, Mel? We don't know what the hell she's gotten herself into. This could draw us into a full-blown war."

"We can't send her out on her own. I know what it's like to feel hunted and alone. Please help her."

"I can get her a plane ticket. I hear Venezuela is a great place to disappear," he suggests dryly.

"Is that what you would have wanted for me?" I ask, hands propped on my hips.

He grimaces, arms spreading wide. "What else do you suggest? I can't put her up in a hotel forever."

"No, but we could hide her while we figure out what's going on and see if there's a way to help." I don't know why I'm so determined to help this woman, except something tells me it's the right thing to do. She needs us.

"You and I hardly have room for ourselves, let alone a

guest. Not that I'd let you bring that sort of danger into our house anyway." He pauses, then turns to his friend. "You've got plenty of room, though, don'tcha Tommy?" Sante's voice takes on a mischievous edge.

"No fucking way. It's not happening," Tommy insists.

I walk up to him and square my shoulders, summoning every ounce of authority I can muster. "You owe me, Tommaso Donati, for pretending to be my stalker. Don't think I've forgotten about that."

His eyes widen a fraction. "*Owe* you? I took a fist to the face for that."

"That was between you and your delinquent friend over there." I nod toward my husband, then press a finger into Tommy's hard chest. "This is between you and me. It's not forever. Give her a place to stay while we figure this out, and we'll call it even."

"Un-fucking-believable," he breathes. "You going to say something, Sante?"

"Yeah, happy wife, happy life." He shrugs.

I grin.

Tommy roars.

And a new adventure begins…

BONUS EPILOGUE
Amelie

"Grab your jacket. I want to show you something."

"Now?" I ask, surprised. "The fireworks are going to start soon." And aside from that, I have a New Year's surprise for my husband that I'm giddy to show him.

Sante hands me my jacket since I've made no move to get it myself. "Just upstairs, but it might be chilly."

Upstairs? To Lina's place? We were there earlier in the day and specifically made plans to celebrate our first New Year's alone. Why would we go back up? And why would it be chilly?

"Wait, we're not going on the roof, are we? That'll be freezing."

"Just get your jacket on and trust me." He shoots me a warning look that is both annoying and ridiculously sexy.

I sigh and do as he says, though somewhat petulantly. "We'll be right back, Freya girl." She huffs about being left behind and lays her head back on her paw.

Once we're in the elevator, Sante punches the button for the forty-fourth floor. Now, I'm intrigued. Where on earth are we going?

Like Oran and Lina's apartment, only one door is across from the elevator on the forty-fourth floor since there's only one residence on the entire floor. That's when it hits me.

"Oh my God, Sante. There's no way." I gasp.

We've been hunting for months for an apartment that would suit our needs without having much luck. The chances of something going on the market that checks off our wish list *and* is in the same building as Lina was starting to look like a pipe dream.

"I was hoping to surprise you for Christmas, but the timing didn't work out, so it's a New Year's surprise instead." He punches in the code and opens the door for me.

I step inside and take in the tall ceilings and wide open space. It seems too good to be true, but he wouldn't show it to me if it wasn't a good fit.

"Sante, it's incredible." It's so much larger than our current place, and while I'm not a huge fan of the kitchen finishes, the layout is perfect. Without any furniture, it's easy to see the potential. "We could extend the island granite to create seating. I want people to be able to sit around the island."

"I was thinking the same." He takes my hand. "Let me show you the best part." He leads me down a hallway to the far side of the building, where there's an enormous gym.

"Oh, Sante. It's *perfect*," I breathe in awe.

The floors will need to be changed, but one wall is already lined with mirrors, and opposite is a wall of windows looking out over the river. We had a view on the third floor, but from this height, I feel like we can see the entire world. The skyline is spectacular.

"It doesn't overlook Central Park like Andrey's studio, but this way, you're still close to your sister."

"Absolutely—this is everything I was hoping for. Thank you *so* much." I throw my arms around his neck, and he lifts me off the ground with the force of his hug.

"Anything for you, Mellie. Always."

I pull back to meet his gaze, my feet returning to the floor. "Actually, I have a surprise for you, too."

I take a step away so we're no longer touching and drop my jacket on the floor. With my back to the wall of windows, I slowly unbutton my blouse. My eyes never leave his, watching raptly as he takes in my show. At first, his brows raise with a nod to the window, questioning what he thinks is a bit of exhibitionism on my part, but then he notices what's beneath my shirt, and his head angles with cautious curiosity.

I pull the two halves of my shirt aside to expose my chest. I'm not wearing a bra, but what I do have is a protective bandage taped below the middle of my breasts. I gently peel the sticky padding away to reveal a freshly inked tattoo. It's an exact match of the evil eye inked over his heart. I had the artist add some decorative lines above and below to give it a somewhat bohemian look, and it came out perfect. I've been beside myself with excitement to show him all day, thinking I'd wait until we chimed in the new year, but this is even better.

His face is priceless—total shock and awe.

"But you went to the doctor with your sister—I checked," he murmurs, eyes still devouring me.

I fight back a sheepish smile. "I knew you would, and I wanted to surprise you—you're not an easy person to surprise—so I had Lina wear my bracelet, and we swapped phones and purses. Before you get upset—" I raise my hand, seeing his face darkening. I knew he wouldn't like that part. "I had Freya with me, and Lina and Oran knew where I was."

His wariness melts to molten desire as he steps closer. "You're the fucking sexiest thing I've ever seen. Hope it didn't hurt too much."

"Nah. I'm tough," I tease.

He's too swept away for humor, his eyes glinting with the need to ravish me. "So goddamn tough, and all mine." His lips crash down on mine with the force of his love. A domineering, devoted force that I'm happy to absorb. I melt against him just as the first fireworks explode over the river.

I nearly jump out of my skin, making us both laugh.

Sante turns off the lights and walks us to the windows for the show. One brilliant burst of sparkling joy after another lights the sky.

"Hands on the glass," Sante rumbles in my ear. He's standing behind me, and I'm suddenly ultra aware of his body aligned with mine.

I do as he instructs, a searing desire heating my insides. The shirt is still unbuttoned, the two halves pulling apart when my palms press against the cold window. I'm not fully exposed. If I had fuller breasts, I might be, but the shirt is still just barely covering my pebbling nipples. It's the perfect tease —the chance of exposure while not actually being on display. I feel like a sexual siren.

"Take a step back and show me how badly you want my cock."

I do, arching my spine seductively. His hands grip my hips with a hiss. He pulls my leggings over my ass enough to give him access but not expose my front with the way my body is bent.

"That's it," he rasps. "There's nothing I want more than to ring in the new year buried in my wife's tight pussy." His fingers slip through my folds, teasing a moan from me. "So fucking wet. Hope you're ready, pet, because this isn't going to be gentle."

"God, yesss. Give it to me, Sante. I'm so ready." And I am. I've learned to crave sex with my husband. He knows my body better than I know it myself, and I adore turning myself over to his care because he never fails to light my world on fire.

I gasp when he thrusts inside me. He only gives me a second before he begins hammering into me, the fireworks celebrating each glorious thrust.

"Fuck, you feel so damn good, pet." His strained voice is such a turn-on that I push back against him, wanting every devastating centimeter of him inside me.

As the city's pyrotechnics burst into a chaotic finale, my body does the same, dizzying elation pulsing through me in powerful waves. Sante's arm curves around my front, holding me closer as he gives in to his release. I love the way his body curves around mine like he's a part of me. Sculpted by life to be a perfect fit for one another.

"Happy New Year, baby," I whisper, then twist to place a tender kiss on his cheek.

"The happiest. So long as you're mine, life doesn't get any better."

Thank you so much for reading *Devil's Thirst*!
The Moretti Men is a series of interconnected standalone novels in a large mafia world encompassing my *Byrne Brothers* and *Five Families* series as well.
There's two directions you can go from here:
1. *Silent Vows* (*The Byrne Brothers*, book 1)
2. *Forever Lies* (*The Five Families*, book 1)
*Read more about each option below.

Missed the first Byrne Brothers novel?
Silent Vows (The Byrne Brothers #1)
Conner chose his arranged marriage bride because she was mute, thinking he wouldn't ever have to talk to her. But when he learns Noemi was silent to protect herself from an abusive father, he becomes obsessed with his new wife and vengeance on her behalf.

Want to see where it all began?
Forever Lies (The Five Families #1)
When Alessia gets stuck in an elevator, she's trapped with

Luca, the hottest man she's ever seen. But she can tell something dark hides beneath his charming facade—especially once he decides he's not letting her go...

Keep in touch!
Make sure to join my newsletter and keep in touch!

ABOUT THE AUTHOR

Jill Ramsower is a life-long Texan—born in Houston, raised in Austin, and currently residing in West Texas. She attended Baylor University and subsequently Baylor Law School to obtain her BA and JD degrees. She spent the next fourteen years practicing law and raising her three children until one fateful day, she strayed from the well-trod path she had been walking and sat down to write a book. An addict with a pen, she set to writing like a woman possessed and discovered that telling stories is her passion in life.

Social Media & Website

Release Day Alerts, Sneak Peak, and Newsletter
To be the first to know about upcoming releases, please join Jill's Newsletter. (No spam or frequent pointless emails.)

Official Website: www.jillramsower.com
Jill's Facebook Page: www.facebook.com/jillramsowerauthor
Reader Group: Jill's Ravenous Readers
Follow Jill on Instagram: @jillramsowerauthor
Follow Jill on TikTok: @JillRamsowerauthor

Made in United States
North Haven, CT
03 May 2025

68539044R00208